I0707595

A Song of Bones

Isaac Anderson

Norland Press

Copyright © 2024 by Isaac Anderson

Cover art by Josh Anderson

Illustrations by Chloe Anderson

Additional Illustrations by Abby Anderson

That's a lot of Andersons...

All rights reserved.

No portion of this book may be reproduced in any form without written permission from the publisher or author, except as permitted by U.S. copyright law.

For Carlene Brown. You gave me stories.
This one's for you.

BEFORE

HAPPENED LIKE THIS.

On an evening near harvest's end, where the river curved south along the reeds, a day's walk from Border Town, there was a little homestead. It sat back a-ways in the trees. The place was far enough to hide from the dirt road, but not so far to lose the music of the river. A mouse family lived there. They were just two folks and their kid, but they had dreams of growing it bigger. They'd dug out a home in the hill big enough for eight.

The homestead's still there. Family isn't.

Happened like this.

The sky dipped to orange as Jed Howe, fresh from his patch of onion and squash, waded through the tall, gripping weeds and up the hill. He walked stooped, one shoulder higher than the other, but his eyes were bright and young. The basket he carried didn't show for much. The winds had been cruel that summer and his little garden suffered under harsh skies and little rain. They would have to gather what they could from the Deep Wood. Maybe hike to Border Town and trade what was left of their spoons for beets or potatoes, something to carry them through the winter. Jed could imagine Sal's face: worried eyes and a thin frown.

The woods didn't think much of them, was how Jed saw it. As he marched for home, the trees stretched overhead to cover the sky. Only a pockmarked pattern of orange and red showed through the branches. He'd even heard tell that farther into the Deep Wood, the sky vanished entirely.

A little window peeked through the weeds ahead. A simple thing cut into the hillside. One day he might afford to set it with glass, but for now, they made do with shutters. He'd often seen Vincent's face peeking through, but the window was empty today. Jed didn't think much of it. His son often vanished in the afternoons only to return with sticks in his hair and burs in his ears. He'd heard Vincent mention something about spotting a fish down by the river. He was probably chasing minnows, Jed thought.

Besides the window, the only hint the mice were there was the line of smoke rising from the squat chimney in the hillside and the mournful dirge of wind chimes his wife had made from reeds gathered along the river. He walked the subtle path to their little door, cut the mud from his boots on the porch, and ducked inside.

Jed's home was as modest inside as it was outside. Candles lit the space. The dirt walls were unpainted and smooth. He'd spent a good sum of his savings on a colored rug with rich patterns that he'd measured for the space. His wife had a little kitchen where she could chop and boil vegetables. Jed had spent last winter building furniture; chairs, tables, and benches, most of which they sold off in Border Town. They'd kept Jed's more wobbly attempts, so there was no want for a place to sit in their house. He'd promised her a sink, but that was something he wanted to buy in town rather than make himself. For now, they did all their washing by the river.

A kettle rattled over the stove and Jed's wife sat at their cock-eyed table, oblivious to the noise. She'd often lose hours this way, hands folded upon her lap, eyes drifting out the window toward the trees beyond. Even now, the Deep Wood remained alien to her.

"What if the squirrels run us out?" she'd sometimes say. "Or fill our bed with arrows while we sleep?"

"We're not in their half of the wood," Jed would say.

"And what if that monster happens by? The flying one with teeth? My aunt would tell the worst stories."

At this, Jed would smile and hug her close. "No creature in this world can fly, save for skitter-bugs. Fly'n but a fairy story, love. If it's one thing I know: it's tall tales and fairy stories can't bite ya none for worse."

Then Vincent would ask to hear *"bout the flyin' monster,"* with those wide eyes only children have. The answer was always no, of course. Nothing good could come out of filling the space between his lopping ears with blood and terrors. Jed wished on more than one occasion his wife didn't have them lurking in her noggin, but wishing was foolishness as Jed often said.

He dropped his basket on the table. Two onions and a miserable squash rolled about inside for a moment before giving up and coming to rest. Sal risked turning her eyes from the window to peek inside. She pulled out an onion and turned it idly in her hand, eyes returning to the window.

"Vincent with you?" she asked, lines of worry deep on her face.

Jed settled next to her. "I think he's on the river," he said.

"He told me he wanted to help you with the garden."

Jed smiled. "Oh?"

"Told me he'd rather plant onions than cut onions."

Sal pulled her gaze from the window and stared down at the bare table. The grain swirled about the round knot in its center like waves. When Vincent was younger, he'd trace those lines with his pudgy fingers, his brow pulled heavy over his eyes.

"Well, he never made it to the garden. I guess he got distracted," Jed said.

Sal nodded. It was common enough. She traced a line on the table, following its lazy curve. "He's too at ease in the wood," she said. "And he goes out too far. He's so small. What if something happens to him?"

"There's nothing in these woods that could harm him," Jed said, pulling her close. "Snakes are fifteen years gone. And he's smart. Smarter than me."

"Don't talk like that—"

"No, he is. I never got book learn'n like you, and Vincent already knows everything I ever did. Just think how clever he'll be when you can give him his letters. He'll know his histories and numbers. He could end up doctor'n."

"Not much call for doctor'n out here."

"But there will be. Some day. Mice aren't made to shut themselves from the land and the forest. Folk might wear green, but it ain't true green. That city's nothin' but grays. One day soon, these forests will have more folk than that smelly city, mark my words."

"I was from that smelly city, Jed."

"You deny it smelled?"

"Not all of it."

Jed Howe looked out into the dimming forest. The sky beyond was blooming to pink. You never saw a pink sky in the city. Folk there were so busy fretting over walls and armies and kings they'd forget they don't just exist; they live. His wife had spent most of her childhood not knowing grass underfoot and horizons unspoiled by walls made from cold, dead stone. Neither of them wanted that for Vincent.

"Do you wish that you'd stayed?" He asked.

Sal shook her head. "Stayed in Green Hill? No. I've had enough smog and hysterics for one lifetime." She peered out the window at the path bending out from view and toward the river. "But I do wish that boy wouldn't wander so far this close to dark."

The kettle hissed and popped behind them, and Sal jumped, her breath catching. She pushed from the table and used the hem of her apron to take it from the heat. She strained her neck away from the steam.

"Just soup tonight," she said. "I found some mushrooms this morning and mixed it with the last of the broth from yesterday."

She managed a tired smile. "And Vincent found some berries before he ran off. We'll have them for dessert."

She left to grab mugs, collecting them in her arm. "You should have seen his face. Sticky and blue. His jacket's stained beyond anything, but I think he can wear it when he goes out to…"

Her face drifted then. *An odd thing*, Jed thought. He'd known his wife to worry on occasion, but he'd never seen panic cross her face. It took a moment before he recognized it. And before he could ask what had bothered her, he heard it too: hiding beneath the sounds of evening, a small scream wavered. Shrill. Terrified.

Sal's face snapped to attention, her ears flying up. A mug slipped from her grasp, landing with a hollow *thunk* on the carpet. Jed's chair crashed to the floor, its back snapping. He stumbled past it for the door and Sal was quick behind him. The two ran into the growing dark.

There's no moon tonight. Jed strained his eyes to see the tall shapes of the trees as the sky sank into gloom. Pink had faded to blood. *The river*, he thought. His son was by the river.

"*Vincent,*" He called, his voice strong despite the cold pit worming into his stomach. His wife clung to his side, shaking. She added her own call. It carried far. Some near to Border Town claimed to have heard it that night.

Vincent answered with another scream.

No one knows what Jed saw when he reached the river. Wasn't something he'd speak of to anyone, though many tried in the following years. Mrs Howe would share some of what happened years later, but that awful night had fallen quickly, casting dark shadows on dark memories. Even today, Sal couldn't say for certain what had been real and what had been delirium.

Sal watched Jed race ahead. Though he ran crooked, he powered through the scratching bushes till he met the trail and leaped from sight. Sal did her best, but her legs had turned into shaking clumsy things. She stumbled after her husband as the autumn air stung her lungs. *He doesn't have his cap*, was the impossible thought that came to her then. Her son had left his knit cap on the kitchen floor. Why that felt important, she couldn't say.

Sal never knew what caused her to stumble. To this day, she swears the Deep Wood *moved* to stop her; to wrap its roots around her like in the old stories. She sprawled to her side, tasting blood on her lip. In that horrible quiet that comes after you fall, when everything comes to a painful stop, she heard Jed scream.

Rage and horror. Blinding horror.

She pushed her feet beneath her and ran. Her breath cut her throat, her eyes saw only shadows, and her hands trembled like leaves over her mouth. Her view of the river was blocked by thin trees with white, flaking bark. Sal tore through them. Underfoot, weeds and vines did their best to slow her. One of her toes found a stone in the undergrowth and broke. She'd only notice later after Vincent was gone.

She stumbled onto the bank of the river.

Sal saw Jed first. He was a dark shape in the fading light. Over his head, he held a branch and stood like a breaker over a stone. Before him was a shadow. A shadow with eyes. Sal couldn't see Vincent.

Jed brought the branch down on the thing's head, his arms as taut as the ropes of a ship, but the shadow was fast. Sal screamed when it struck her husband. The shadow's arm struck like a snake at Jed's chest. She saw a flash of its face: eyes as terrible as the moon. Face like a tombstone.

It was smiling.

Jed fell, the branch falling harmless to the side. Sal saw Vincent now. The shadow had him, sharp fingers leaving marks on her boy's arm. Then the thing turned its white eyes to her. It laughed, showing a dark tongue, and spread its arms. A dark cloak filled the world.

Sal leaped to grab her son, to pull him away from the horrible shadow. Vincent reached for her, fingers spread.

Then he was gone.

A thud of wind and her son was in the air, staring down with wide eyes. Then the shadow beat its wings and Vincent's face became a little dot above the trees. Sal fell and watched them go, her shaking legs at last giving up. Even from here, she could see the white shine of the monster as it flew.

It flew.

Every story returned to her. And in all the stories, if the monster took you, you never came back.

Sal stared into the stars as her son disappeared. Her mouth opened in silence. The only sounds left in the Deep Wood were the mournful song of crickets and the burble of the river among the reeds. Behind her, Jed stirred and coughed wet. He pulled himself up and looked out with empty eyes. Those eyes would never look young and bright again. At his chest, he clutched Vincent's jacket, torn and stained with berries. Together, they wept by the river as the Deep Wood droned around them.

And above, far away, Vincent shivered in the frigid Autumn sky as the trees passed beneath him. They would never see each other again.

Happened like this...

ONE

—A Creed of Mice

BRYCE FOLLOWED THE OTHERS in the dark. As the mice crept, hugging the wall of the chalky tunnel, he knew in his heart it was a bad idea.

A horrendous idea.

But Vincent had made up his mind to steal a knife. *Tonight.*

Bryce thought of all the ways the rats might kill them should they fail. *When* they failed.

Might they hold them under the mud? Or perhaps drop them from one of the walkways over the dig site? Maybe they'd get lucky and Fletcher would just bash their skulls in with a club. A painless way to go, all things considered. Bryce couldn't fathom why none of this had occurred to Vincent. But what bothered Bryce the most was he was right behind him, following along. You'd think after all these years, he'd know better.

It wasn't just Bryce, of course. Gavin and Sampson decided to tag along as well, while all the others in the burrow had decided to be wise and stay behind.

"We just need a knife," Vincent had whispered to the others, grinning at their shocked faces. "Think about it! We could climb up to the first bridge and cut the ropes. Then it'll be the rats left down here in the dark, not us. They'll be the ones digging."

Bryce had nodded along with the others. Yes. Good. A knife. Why hadn't anybody thought of that before? No one had asked how they would go about collecting this miracle knife. And now, here he was, padding along a dark and dusty tunnel, keeping the flat of his hand gliding over the rough face of the wall.

The mice of Dorgue's Tree might burn their lives away digging like worms, but they were clever worms. The team who dug this particular tunnel had left gouges every twenty paces or so, and two gouges before the tunnel met another. When Bryce's hand went *tap, tap* on the wall, he knew a new passage was about to open on his left.

Nearly there, Bryce thought. Quiet now...

Instead, Bryce's face crunched into Gavin's shoulder as the other mouse skidded to a stop. Sampson, bringing the rear, followed after. Bryce tried throwing up an arm to stop him, but it didn't do him much good. The giant very nearly ran him over. And the lummox managed to stomp on his tail.

"Would you get back!" Bryce shoved him away. He couldn't see the other mouse in the dark, but he knew Sampson's face would be bordering on a smile and threatening to break into a rumbling laugh. He pulled his foot off Bryce's tail.

"Why'd we stop?" Sampson's whisper hummed in the tunnel.

In the dark, Gavin said, "Vincent smells something."

The mice fell silent. Held their breath.

Vincent's sense of smell was worthy of silence. Silly thing to think, Bryce knew, but that's how it was. Vincent's knack for picking a scent out of the air had saved their ears more than once. Bryce could hear him, taking the smallest of sniffs lest the sharp sound carried down the tunnel.

They waited for the glow of a torch or the sound of a boot crunching in the packed earth, but—at last—Vincent came to them in the dark, throwing his arms around their shoulders.

"One of the rats ahead." Vincent choked back a chuckle. "I think we got lucky. It's Garrow."

Of all the rats in Dorgue's Tree, Garrow was the meanest. He threw stones at them from the walkway. He'd snap a whip over their ears just to see them jump. Garrow spat and kicked, and knocked water rations from your hand if you didn't pay attention. But, and Bryce found a smile growing on his face at the thought, Garrow had another quality they could count on.

"I can smell it, he's stone-cold drunk," Vincent said.

Bryce tried, but no matter how he twitched his nose, he could never quite catch the scents Vincent seemed to pull from the air. Sampson rumbled behind them. "All I smell is candle smoke."

"But is he awake?" Gavin asked. He pulled from them and padded closer to the tunnel's mouth. "I thought the point of all this was to sneak up while the guard's nap'n and snatch what we need."

"Oh, he's asleep," Vincent said. Bryce could hear the mouse's smile. "I haven't smelled a rat this soaked since we dug the new burrows."

They inched closer, Bryce feeling his way along, waiting for the flicker of light to appear. He didn't have to wait long. Soon, Bryce could see Gavin and his boxy, cauliflower ears, and Vincent's ragged vest and twitching fingers. Bryce turned to see Sampson looming behind him. His pale fur, turned gray from oil smoke, was still crusted with mud from the day's work. The taller mouse picked a bit of it away mindlessly with his good hand. The bad one he held at his side, curled like a spider.

Bryce looked down at his own hands, calloused and crisscrossed with white and gray. A fresh cut from the day stood out in an angry red line hugging his palm. He imagined he'd receive many more if Garrow caught them out after curfew.

As far as rats went Garrow wasn't particularly tall but he made up for it with his belly, which tended to precede him through doors no matter how tightly he cinched his belt. That being said, he was still taller than Bryce could jump. Even Sampson was dwarfed next to the rat. As they approached, Bryce caught a whiff. It was indeed Garrow. Ahead, he heard the rat's steady breath and his sputtery exhale.

Asleep.

Even so, the mice held their breath, edging out into view a hair at a time.

Garrow sat at his post with a candle shivering on the ground. The rat's head lulled on his shoulder like a growth, his mouth slack. An empty wineskin lay across his lap, and tied to his belt hung a knife in a leather sheath.

In the meager light, Bryce saw Vincent's face gleam. His fingers twitched. "Think he's out enough for me to just grab it?" he said.

It was Gavin who answered. His eyes blazed at the sleeping rat. "I don't care," he said. "I say we use it on him. Stick him before he has a chance to wake up."

"Then the rats will know we have a knife," Vincent shook his head. "They'd kill everyone, most like. No, we'll just take it. When Garrow sees it's missing, he'll just think he dropped it."

Bryce itched beneath his bandana with shaking fingers. He said, "What if Garrow tells someone his knife is missing?"

Sampson had to smother a chuckle. "Then it'll be him Fletcher holds under the mud."

"He wouldn't tell a soul," Vincent promised. "I doubt he'd even suspect it was one of us who snatched it. He'll think it was Lou or Randal."

Vincent moved first, staying close to the ground. Bryce and the others hurried behind, careful of their step in the faint light. Garrow loomed over them like a mountain. The rat's hands folded over his protruding belly, and he let out a rumbling snore as the mice drew alongside. They saw the rat's lip twitch as he sneered in his sleep. His gray teeth shone in the candlelight like curled fingers. Bryce pulled at his ears. Every ounce of his being screamed to run, to hide, but Vincent only had eyes for the knife. He worked his fingers and reached for the blade. It took both of his fists to wrap around the large hilt.

Bryce didn't know what to watch: the knife, Vincent, or Garrow. Worst of all was the little noise of the blade as Vincent inched it free, little by little. Garrow did little to care for his knife and the dirty blade gripped the sheath stubbornly.

Garrow rumbled in his sleep. Shifted. Vincent jumped from the knife like it had cut him, fingers splayed wide and eyes even wider as they watched the massive rat settle again into puttering snores. Each mouse shook. Breathed. The knife stared at them, peeking from the sheath and winking orange in the candlelight.

Bryce shied away in quiet agony. He couldn't watch. *This wasn't going to work! He's going to wake up!*

But Vincent rolled his shoulders and brought his hand again to the hilt of the knife. "We need this," he whispered. Again, he worked the knife, drawing it out.

Then Garrow woke up.

The rat grumbled. He snorted his blunted nose and peeled open his rimmed eyes, squinting in the candlelight. The mice froze. Vincent, not daring to even blink, kept his hand tight on the hilt of the knife.

The rat's neck creaked and popped as he rolled his head along his shoulders, eyes fluttering. Bryce felt as if he were falling. His arms and legs were numb, and his insides tremored like so many worms.

Then Vincent ripped the knife from the sheath and Gavin chucked a rock at the rat's head.

Garrow screamed and clamped his hand to his lumpish nose and the mice scrambled for the tunnels. The rat's curses came at them, heavy with wine and pain. He kicked his seat into a splintered ruin against the wall and stumbled for them, arm thrown over his bloodied face. "Gonna burn your ears off!" His scream shook the tunnel air as the mice rounded the corner. Familiar darkness enveloped them like a friend urging them to hurry.

Had he seen them? Not if they'd been lucky, and luck was a rare thing in Dorgue's Tree. Still, Bryce didn't want to chance Garrow finding out which burrow they'd come from.

"We have to lose him in the old tunnels!" he whispered.

Gavin, a little ahead, growled through his teeth. "We still need to get back before the headcount. What if we get lost?"

"We won't get lost," Vincent said.

Some things need to be said of Dorgue's Tree. While the mice were well versed in the tunnels in and around the dig site, the old tunnels and the ones nearer to the surface were all but alien to them. Other mice had dug them, and they weren't around anymore to give a map. Even the little signs left to guide and protect the diggers (like the gouges in the wall) would be invisible to them.

That said, mice did go down there on occasion. Sometimes to hide from the day's work, sometimes to plot in secret, and some mice just…broke, scuttling away into forever darkness, deeper and deeper. The Old Tunnels looped and dead-ended, rose and fell, some led to deep caverns even the rats didn't bother to explore. Their only interest was the dig site, you see.

So, when Bryce followed after Vincent and cut through an ugly split in the wall; there was some hope that Garrow might give up and return to his post in a cursing fog of migraines.

No such luck.

The waver of torchlight jumped its way on the jagged walls. The rat was coming.

"We have to cut around him," Vincent said. "Isn't there a crossway farther ahead?" This, he asked Gavin. He'd explored the farthest into these caves, vanishing after curfew and shimmering back in line just in time for the headcount.

Gavin huffed. "I've never gone this way, but if I ever did, I'd sneak a candle with me. I'm not running blindly to who knows where."

To prove the point, Bryce's foot clipped a hook of stone and the mouse crashed to the tunnel floor, scratching his arms and hands. He felt Sampson's arms force him upright again.

Behind them, they heard Garrow call out. "Dangerous, running in the dark," the rat said, slurring his words. "Hope you bit your blasted tongue off, runt."

The light of the torch shivered closer, and Bryce saw they'd stumbled upon a confused mix of passageways. He could see the others now. The Knife looked large and out of place in Vincent's hands, Sampson's wide frame was almost too large for the little space, and Gavin's gray eyes glared into the growing light, jaw set.

"We can take him," Gavin said. "These tunnels are too puny for that fat tick. We got the knife. I say we use it."

"Then he'll know us." Vincent pressed the knife into Bryce's hands. "Get this back to the burrow, we'll lead him off."

Bryce juggled the hilt like it was scalding. The blade's edge winked in the light, not terribly sharp but humming with menace in Bryce's fingers.

"Me?"

"Yes! Don't get tripped up again," Vincent pointed him away toward the deeper tunnels. "Find a switch-back, get to the burrow, and we'll figure out how to hide it. We'll keep Garrow busy."

Bryce faced the empty dark of one of the smaller passages. It angled up, but that's all Bryce could figure. It looked like a mouth. He inched a toe away. "Gavin should take it," Bryce said. "He knows his way around better."

But Vincent pushed him on, "I need him to help us lose Garrow. Now go! I can smell him, he's nearly on top of us! Move!"

Bryce ran into the dark.

Tunnels held no reason the farther down you went. The old dig teams had a rhyme, according to the stories. Anyone who knew it would never lose their way. Those mice had sometimes spent weeks outsmarting the rats. At least until the rats finally had enough and plugged up the holes. The rhyme died along with them and they brought in a fresh bunch of mice to replace them. Then the head rat, an ancient creature named Dorgue, decided to center all work in one spot: the dig site. Less opportunity for the mice to think themselves clever with exactly how they dug. Now there was just one direction: down.

Bryce had no idea if any of this was true, of course. All he knew was if you were foolish enough to dive into the Old Tunnels, you needed a good reason for it.

The small space twisted farther up, with Bryce having to keep a hand over his head to keep from clocking into any buckling rock in the ceiling. More than once he scuffed his arm or stubbed a toe as he worked his way deeper into the rough tunnel. His ears constantly batted at air, straining to hear any change in the space around him, like the opening of a tunnel or the sound of another cave-diver.

If he was lucky, this passage would circle back, and he could sneak out the way he'd come. He would hike back to the burrow, settle into his bunk, and (if he was lucky) catch an hour or so of sleep before the headcount. Bryce ran his hand over the rough wall as he went, out of habit more than anything, and felt an odd shape as he brushed past. Like a circle. Bryce frowned. What does that mean?

His next step found only empty air and the ground left him.

Bryce tumbled through the dark. He flailed his arms, clawing at the little space as he passed through. This is a passageway, some little part of him said. A shortcut between levels. There's a ladder here somewhere. Grab it. But Bryce could hardly tell which way was up. The knife tore from his grip as the blade struck the wall. A flash of angry sparks lit the pitfall. In that brief heartbeat, Bryce saw the carved walls and the dashing imprints of a ladder cut into the stone itself.

Then the darkness returned, and Bryce hit the ground.

All air whooshed from his lungs and the clangor of steel against rock shouted into the space as loud as any crack of the rats' whips.

At last, the stale air of the tunnels returned to him, and Bryce rolled, gasping and coughing. He padded his chest, his neck, his arms. *Nothing was broken.*

His knee was the problem. When the mouse collected himself enough to stand, prickly flashes of white exploded across his vision. Bryce hissed through his teeth and forced himself up anyway. Busted knee or not, he wasn't going to spend another second in these old tunnels. He'd feel his way back and get the knife to—

The knife. He'd dropped it.

Bryce gripped his ears as a freezing pit opened in his stomach. He couldn't lose the knife. *Everyone was depending on it!*

Bryce dropped to all fours, gritting against the flaring in his knee. He swept his hands over the stone floor, sending pebbles flying. Ancient dust billowed into his eyes and mouth. He searched from wall to wall. He pitched his arm over the whole of the floor. He even used his tail, swiping behind him waiting for the cold touch of steel. At last, Bryce stood in the dark, hands curled into shaking fists at his sides.

He felt sick.

What would he say when he returned to the burrow? "Sorry gang, maybe we'll get lucky in a year or so?" Bryce slumped against the wall, ignoring the grumble in his knee, and sat with his arms tucked around his legs.

It was gone. It could be farther down the tunnel or dropped into a crevasse hidden in the rock. or even might have tumbled into another pitfall, waiting nearby for Bryce as well. It could be in any of a thousand places.

He stared into the dark, eyes straining, seeking even a hint of some shape around him, but all was blackness. He sniffed, echoing. This tunnel was larger than the one he'd left so suddenly, perhaps meant as a highway to ferry the dirt out. If he followed it, he might find—

Another sniff answered his own. It echoed around him in the dark. Bryce felt his heart seize in his chest and he heard a voice farther down the passage.

"No more tricks," Garrow said, hissing his words. "I've walked these tunnels since before you lot were even thoughts."

Bryce pulled himself standing again, dragging his useless leg. Down the way, he could spy shapes forming in the dark and smelled the oily smoke of a torch. He could smell Garrow, too.

Bryce spun in the dark, fingers searching for a hold in the wall. If he could climb back up... Torchlight and smoke inked further in. Bryce heard the stomping trudge of Garrow. The rat grumbled and spat. Ghosts of shadows flickered to life around him. Then Garrow's belly lurched into view. The rat rounded the corner, waving the flame and scowling into the shadow, and saw...

More empty tunnels. No mice. No intruders.

Garrow grumbled and spat at the ground. He never once looked up. Didn't see the mouse clinging like a shaking spider in the little hole up the ceiling. Bryce held his breath as the rat passed beneath him. The smoke of Garrow's torch found his hiding place and steamed past his face, stinging his eyes.

Garrow, cursing and pawing at his own bloodied face, waddled past. Gavin's well-placed stone had puffed the rat's face to an ugly purple.

Bryce held his breath till the light died in the tunnel below, then let his legs swing down into the cool air and let his knee spark and stretch. He dangled from the handholds, gasping.

Then he climbed, pulling himself back up into the little tunnel he'd started in. Bryce clawed his way back to solid ground. He could trace his steps. Get back to the burrow. Run. He knew he should run. He just needed a moment to catch his breath. A moment to be still.

Just a moment.

TWO

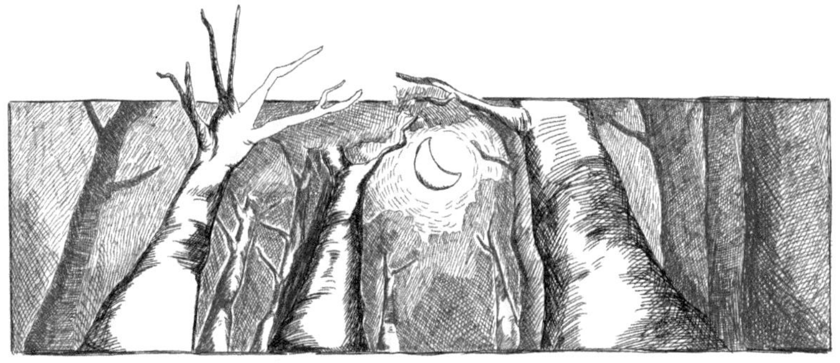

"May the Deep Wood be blind to your way"

— A Common Saying

I T IS ALWAYS NIGHT in the Deep Wood.

It was said—if you glimpsed it from the corners of your eyes—you'd see the forest writhe, only to freeze when you spun to look.

It was also said the Deep Wood hates an uncovered face. If you were to bed down without draping a veil over your features, you'd wake to find the forest's vines reaching for your neck and coiling about your arms.

The Deep Wood had eyes that followed as you waded through its undergrowth.

The Deep Wood breathed and stretched its high branches at the rising of the sun.

Something new grew there every day, so the stories go. The Darkest Forest only lets the cruelest of its children survive in its shadows.

Folk said a lot of things. What surprised Richard Aterox was that no one had thought to mention the bugs.

He slapped his neck. The bloodsuckers had followed him like hungry children all morning, nestling into his fur and biting his ears as he picked along the path he imagined in the brush. "Three days," he wiped his mouth, tasting salt. "Three days and not a drop, you hear? I haven't touched it."

The wineskin in his pack sloshed, disappointed.

The lone mouse clomped through a copse of reeds gathered like beetles over a muddy trickle of water. He wobbled in the slick earth and swung out his arms, half falling, half dancing to keep his feet. In the end, he sloshed into the reeds with a sticky smack and soaked his already muddy trousers.

Richard sat a moment, feeling the cold eek into his legs while gnats whirled circles around his eyes.

"Not a drop," he said. "Not even a sniff. I promised. Not till I find that blasted tree."

Find the Tree. Report back. Become a hero. That was the plan.

Richard crawled from the dying stream and scraped off what mud he could. The coolness of it he liked (a nice break from the shimmering oven the Deep Wood seemed to favor) but he knew it would cling horribly as it dried.

"Not a drop," he said again, stepping into the weeds and setting his face to the prickly hills ahead. "Nothing 'til the Tree. Then it's back to Border Town and back to proper meals and proper beds. I never want to see another nettle again."

The wineskin sloshed in his pack, agreeable.

He kicked the mud from his boots and leaned into climbing. His stomach gurgled, but Richard couldn't bear thinking of food. He'd eaten the last of his rations… two days ago? He'd been chewing on blades of grass and tree bark. The stuff only made him thirsty. And while there was plenty of water to find in the Deep Wood, it was best to boil it first. The Deep Wood is not kind to visitors.

"Curl-bark and sawgrass," his sister had told him before he left. "If you run out before you find it, you can survive on that." Then Kathryn jabbed him with an ink-stained finger. "Don't eat anything else. Not fruit or berry. I'm serious, Richard. Folk who went in there and tasted the stuff didn't come back right."

The sawgrass he could manage if he was desperate, but the bark was like gnawing cobblestones in an alley. And (like alleys) there was usually something with too many legs lurking beneath when you peeled a strip from the trunk.

What made this little trip worse was the fact the Deep Wood was colored with berries. Waves of warm blues and dripping reds, with bright shouts of green and orange scattered like the shot from a blunderbuss. Richard had spent many an hour weighing the risks of popping a few berries into his mouth to quiet his belly. The deeper he went, the more there seemed to be. High above, Richard spied fruit the color of a sunset, so heavy they bent the branches they hung from.

Sawgrass was bitter. Curl bark tasted like rotting cheese. All the while, The Deep Wood taunted him with poisoned fruit and the wineskin in his pack sloshed, sloshed, sloshed.

Then he crested the hill and saw it.

For a moment the mouse stood there. Leaning, holding his side, and blinking away the gnats swarming around his head as the mud on his clothes dried in the baking air.

Then Richard threw himself into a prickly bush and landed with a crunch.

Folk who journeyed the Deep Wood had spoken of the Tree like it was liable to pluck you from the ground if you wandered too close. And, looking at it now through the skinny arms of the bush, Richard understood that fear.

The thing even had something of a face, a squashed sneer in the warp of the gray bark. It stood alone; its growth stunted. The forest seemed to arch away from it like it was some unclean thing. Not a blade of grass or patch of moss was to be seen. A mire of dirt—skirting the Tree some forty yards deep—only made the place seem more forsaken.

Richard wasn't one to believe ghost stories—that was Kathryn's failing if she had one—but looking at it now... he felt a chill despite the smothering air bringing his whiskers to droop. He set his chin on his knuckles.

The wineskin sloshed in his pack, neglected.

"It's one thing reading rumors," he said, "Actually seeing the bloody thing is something else." Richard chewed his lip. Studied the hunched branches and the gouges near the trunk. Fresh soil, piled like graveyard dirt, circled the Tree's base. Kathryn said this place would be abandoned. She'd told him the chances of finding whatever proof of what had gone on here were slimmer than flax. Even Jonathan had agreed.

"That place is going to be close to twenty years abandoned," Jonathan had said, fanning through pages upon pages of notes. "If you find anything, it'll be rotted away to nothing if it was left in the open." Then the mouse pressed his glasses to his brow and said, "If you're lucky—very lucky—you might find a scrap of clothing, a shoe, or—heaven bless us—a bloody manifest in a nook somewhere. Anything that could tell us where the mice went on from there."

Richard inched from his hiding place, rolling his head to keep the tree in view. Any folk who called this forsaken place home… Well, he wasn't exactly eager to shake hands with them. But it wasn't the Tree's reaching limbs that gave him pause. It wasn't the gray face in its bark or the swamp of mud threatening to swallow any who ventured too close…

It was the window.

There were only two ways to get glass in the Middle Kingdom. The first was to trudge to the Salt Cliffs on the coast and spend a small fortune. The glass was brittle, and a break in transit was not rare. Some folk thought to simply bring in the sand from the Salt Cliffs and heat it themselves closer to the city. Many wished this had worked, but the closeness of the buildings in Green Hill proved to be disastrous when a fire broke out after only a few years of glassmaking.

The other way was to find it. Wild Glass, they called it. It proved stronger, clearer, and sharper than the manufactured variety. No one knew where it had come from. Often, you'd have to dig for it, and sometimes you'd stumble across it quite by accident and discover you've lost a toe or two tripping over it. The stuff was expensive to get, dangerous to find, and a whopping eighty-six percent of the stuff was dug up right here in the Deep Wood.

It was so much trouble to harvest, that most folk didn't even bother with glass anymore—of any kind. They barred their windows with wooden shutters, and with blankets come wintertime. Glass was for folk who could afford it. Glass was for the elite and the prosperous.

And none in all of Green Hill had more than Richard Aterox.

So, when Richard, weary from weeks of hard travel and wearing as much mud as he was clothing, looked up and beheld that window... That useless, impossible window, so far away from the pomp of the city, Richard smiled and found the clasp for his pack.

This was the place.

He plucked the cork and brought the beautiful, blessed wineskin to his lips.

But movement among the tree's lower limbs made Richard jump. He sprayed the beautifully dry wine from his mouth and ducked back into the prickly bush. He hid away in the dead leaves and crooked branches. Someone was out there. Someone was climbing *out* of the Tree.

A voice came over the muddy bog as rough as sand. "Did this one have a name?" he asked.

Richard bobbed his eye nearer between the leaves and spied the shape of a rat—a lithe fellow with long, sinewy arms—drop into the muck from the tree. He carried a pair of shovels.

As Richard watched, another rat shambled down and kicked up spackles of mud as he got his feet under him. He lurched a head shorter than the shovel-hauling rat and carried a load over his shoulder.

"How should I know?" The smaller rat sneered into the trees above, squinting like a bug slithering from under a stone. He licked his lips. "It's too hot to bother with digging. I say we just take 'em a little farther out and burn 'em."

"Fire's not allowed," the other rat said, already crossing the mire in long, squelching steps.

Richard watched as the other rat squinted his face into a sharp frown at the other's back. He spat into the mud.

"We'll be dig'n all day!" he called.

The tall rat didn't bother to respond as he paced through the mire. The other rat stayed as he was by the tree, scowling. "I said we'll be dig'n all day!" he called again.

But his fellow ignored him. After a moment of foolish quiet, the fat rat spat in the mud and waded after.

Richard watched as the rats wandered closer. *They're coming right this way,* he realized. Soon the rats left the bog for the somewhat more solid mud at the bottom of Richard's hill. Richard dared not move, afraid the smallest noise might give him away.

The fat rat shrugged his little burden to the ground and took up a shovel. *Who on earth were these rats? This place was supposed to be abandoned!*

The tall rat scraped out a gouge in the mud, roughing out the shape of the bundle they hauled out of the tree. "It's funny to think," he said. "They spend their little lives digging for us and then we thank them by digging their final little hole on their behalf. Some might even call that poetic."

"They should dig their own, miserable graves."

"No mouse leaves Dorgue's Tree," the tall rat said.

The other spat. "I'd rather burn 'em. Miserable wastes."

"Lou,"

"Don't 'Lou' me. Who in blazes is gonna see a fire this far out in the wastes? You tell me that."

"Dorgue says—"

"He says a lot of things." Lou peered over his hunched shoulder. The Tree watched over the little scene like a grim specter, its high branches like twitching fingers. "We're three years past when he said we'd be through with all this. I was count'n the days until we could cut their throats and finally be done with 'em. But no. Dorgue says a little more, a little more." The rat spat again in the dirt, leaning on his shovel, and looking on as the other dug. "He actually told me to grab a shovel and join 'em if I was so eager to be done with it."

The lithe rat gazed from his work. Moved his lips. "Lou," he said, "pick up your shovel. Before I beat you with it."

Lou showed his teeth. His knuckles whitened around his shovel. "Oh? So big mean Worth's too tired to finish up, then? Need Lou to give 'ya a back rub? Straighten your friggin spine?"

The rats stared each other down. The dim, quiet of the Deep Wood held its breath. Richard leaned forward.

Then Lou, with a throaty roar, swung his shovel, angling for the other's neck.

Worth moved. His arm lashed out, connecting with Lou's elbow. The fat rat screamed, flinging the shovel from his hands as he dropped, clutching his arm.

From his hiding place, Richard watched the fight like it was a play on a stage, transfixed. He watched the shovel tumble through the air, spinning end over end, coming closer and closer.

Oh, Richard thought, *that's going to hit me, isn't it?*

The shovel crunched into the bush, giving a fine hello to Richard's face with a musical *bong!* He saw a single bright spot—fuzzy and dull in his vision—and lumped through the scratching twigs. His arms twisted beneath him as tumbled down the hill.

Lou jumped like the devil himself had slithered from the dark forest.

Worth only crossed his arms and gazed down at the new mouse. He blinked.

"I've never seen this one before," he said.

Lou's eyes bugged. The fat rat clutched at his chest like his heart was liable to tumble out if he so much as sneezed. "Really?" he said. "Never seen? That's real good detective work, that."

Richard pulled his face from the mud. It was uncomfortably warm, but he was thankful he couldn't smell it. In fact, he couldn't smell anything. He tried to pat his face, but he'd gone numb. Felt like a dead hand brushing clumsy fingers at his nose. He rolled, still confused, and nudged into the shrouded body. Whoever it was had died thin. Small. Then a pang of reason thudded to life in Richard's head.

He crawled like a worm. Back up the hill. Back to his pack. Back to the bush. This wasn't what he'd signed up for, not by a bloody mile.

A muddied boot pressed into his back.

"Must have come from Border Town," Worth said as if chatting about the weather. He leaned to study the pinned mouse, grinding his boot deeper into Richard's spine as he did.

Richard heard the hiss of a knife springing from a sheath and felt the ice of the blade press into his neck, just under his jaw.

Richard froze.

"Should we..." Worth gestured to the wrapped corpse. "Double them up? Save us dig'n another hole."

Richard stretched to see the dead mouse, sewed into a bundle of brown sheets like a sailor. How long ago did the last kid go missing? Fifteen years? Had they been here all that time? At last, he found his voice. His tongue had gone numb, but his nose was beginning to wake: a buzzing sting growing into his skull.

"Please," it came out as a croak. "I'm just...just passing... I didn't mean to..."

"Mean'n and do'n are different things," Lou said, showing his crooked teeth. "No one comes here. No one leaves." He twisted his considerable weight to kneel and collect his shovel, grunting as he did. "Cut his throat, Worth. Toss 'em in with the other sap."

"Please," Richard said again, "Please, I just want to go."

"Can't help that," Worth said. The knife was ice at his neck.

This wasn't how it was supposed to go. This wasn't what Kathryn had told him he would find. The tree was supposed to be long abandoned; a ruin to pick through. Richard gritted his teeth and growled deep in his throat. "Wait! Wait! I can replace him!"

The rat blinked. Then looked to the dead mouse dressed for his grave. Richard felt the knife leave his neck as the rat considered.

"No, no, no, no!" Lou said as he saw the wheels in Worth's head begin to turn. "No outsiders. No new blood. That's his orders, and there's no breaking his orders."

Worth frowned, crossing his arms over his chest. "What happened to 'Dorgue says a lot of things?'"

"It's one thing to light a little fire he'll never know about. You wanna march in there with some Border Town oaf!"

"Wouldn't hurt to ask," Worth said. "Dorgue was just saying how short we were getting on workers."

The lithe rat lifted his boot from Richard's back and pulled him standing. The rat's fingers were like knives on his shoulders.

Lou's eyes nearly popped from his head. "You're crazy! You're ACTUALLY crazy!"

"Why? We'd only be asking. And if he says no, we can just kill him, no trouble." He patted Richard's shoulder, all brotherly. "Besides, this is quite the moment. We've never had a volunteer before."

Worth took up his shovel and pressed it into Richard's hands. He waved to the corpse lying alongside the shallow pit. The rat smiled.

"Dig."

THREE

"Some children run away. It is no business of Green Hill should a child not return in time for dinner. They are delinquents. Future trouble-makers. Our city does not need them. They are better off not found..."

— Head Bishop of the Garden, Steward of Green Hill

BRYCE WOKE WITH A sour taste in his mouth. When he reached to take hold of his bed-roll, he couldn't find it. When he stretched to see if it had tumbled from his bunk, he found he wasn't in his bunk. He lifted his leg to stand, but his knee came to burning life. Then he remembered... He wasn't in the burrow. He was still in the old tunnels.

Still in the dark.

Bryce clapped his hands to his ears and pulled them down the sides of his face. He shook. If he had missed roll-call... if the rats knew...

It'd be goodnight, friend. The Long Goodnight.

But how long had he been out?

Bryce brought a hand to the tunnel wall and felt its unknown face. He'd fallen, he remembered. He… lost the knife. Bryce pressed against the wall. He dug his nails into his palms and ground his teeth.

Stupid! Stupid! Stupid!

What would the others say? Did he even bother to go back? If he missed call, he'd just be stumbling back for his execution. He'd be better off dying in the depths of the deep places. Folk hear voices down there, a little voice said in his mind, Strange voices. Old voices. Bryce shivered. He hated the old ghost stories. Once they came to mind, nothing but the warmth of a candle could drive them out again. Bryce squeezed his eyes shut hard enough to see flashes.

He breathed… breathed… breathed…

Bryce limped from the wall. He toed past the hole in the floor and down the little slope to the crossways. He walked like a soul inching toward the ax; head down, shoulders slumped, and tail dragging. His fingertips brushed at the wall, following the turns, light as a cobweb. He followed the way back, back, back… His foot thumped a jutting stone. He pawed through the fissure and found empty air.

The tunnels he knew were just beyond. Bryce stood a moment and lifted his ear to the dark.

Listened.

If he was late, he'd hear the noise of picks and shovels, the breaking of rock, and the slush of buckets. He'd hear the rats rake their whips and the harmony of a hundred souls toiling together.

Bryce only heard the puff of his breath. His heart quieted.

Not too late. Not too late.

The mouse set his head on the cool of the stone and shivered. The sweat under his fur had turned to ice and he could taste salt on his lips.

Bryce ran, quiet as the ghosts that roamed the old tunnels. Even in the perfect dark, the pads of his feet knew where he was and knew the turns to make. His years spent in darkness were better than any teacher.

He saw the haze of a candle ahead and slowed. His feet knew the place well.

There used to be more than twenty burrows. Now there were only four. Bryce's burrow was known as The Sticks. Why the rats called it that, none of them could say. But this burrow, with its lone candle waving its thumbnail of a flame, was Candle Hall.

Something was wrong with Candle Hall.

The wide, mouth-like gap in the wall with its little dot of light looked like an eye. Bryce forced his feet to slow as he came on it. Underfoot, he felt a sharp crunch. Bryce jumped, his breath leaving him as he clapped his hands to his mouth. He pressed his back to the wall. Pulled air through his nose. He pried the stone from his foot, more of a splinter than a pebble. In the dim light, he spied the dull shine of blood on its point. He turned it over in his hand. Thousands of them littered the ground, stretching out shivering tails of shadow. Bryce blinked. His mouth dropped as his eyes darted from shard to shard.

This wasn't here before, Bryce thought. Had Candle Hall done this on purpose?

Bryce stared into the dark maw of Candle Hall, past that little prick of light. His heart spun in his chest. They'd laid this out after they'd snuck by. Which means they had seen them. And if Candle Hall knew, then the rats would know in the morning, sure as spit.

How had the others gotten by? Surely Vincent's group had come across this.

Bryce squinted, searching for any path through the splinters. He tried to scoot his feet into the mess to scatter them away, but they sang as they clinked into one another. Bryce bit his tongue at the noise. He raised an eye toward Candle Hall.

Listened.

He waded another stride, then another—wincing at the noise.

He stood center of the burrow's mouth, shoulders hunched to his ears. Bryce dared a peek at the candle dancing in the dark. Such a small flicker of light. The rats never allowed their burrow a candle. Candles were for good mice, the rats would say. And the Candle Hall mice would smile at them all, hands squeezed to white at their chests.

The rats even gave Candle Hall more food. Bryce had seen them gorge themselves, grinning their dinner at the others, while some of them hardly picked at the mountain on their plate. Bryce sometimes heard them vomiting in the secret of some tunnel. Heard them weeping too.

Bryce inched another stride, dragging his feet. The noise of the shards scraped like claws at his ears. One of them angled just right and sliced the side of his foot. Bryce bit his lip. A knuckle popped in his clenched fist. He was almost free of the candle's light.

Movement by the candle. A shadow, like a hand fluttering over the flame. Bryce could just imagine it: one of the Candle Hall mice watching him sweat, smiling a sick smile as he blinked the candle as if to say, I see you.

Bryce leaped the last of it, praying it was enough. A sharp jolt to his heel and a prick to his toe a step after was all it was. Bryce bit the wall of his mouth and pounded on, each step a scream in his leg, ankle to hip.

Bryce left the shaking light of Candle Hall far behind. He ran, ignoring the pain from the shard in his heel or the sparks in his knee. He ran as if every last one of them charged after. He ran as if Garrow, with his swollen face, reached just behind, eager to break him over his knee. And Dorgue… He was just ahead. Quiet and smiling. A long knife flashed in his pale fingers.

Bryce ran, not thinking. He gasped great blasts of breath and his eyes stretched wider and wider, desperate for light. Any light at all.

He ran into Vincent's hands and jumped.

"Would you hold still, it's me!" Vincent hissed. He pulled Bryce's scratching hands from his face and pinned him to the wall. Vincent whispered in his ear. "Relax! You're gonna wake up the whole burrow. We can't trust all of them, you know that. Just STOP KICKING, please."

Bryce froze, his hands still grabbing at Vincent's face with iron fingers. Vincent puffed.

"Let go. Of my face."

Bryce pried them away. His arms folded up—spent—and he followed the wall to the ground as Vincent did his best to keep him from braining himself on the rocky floor. "Sorry," Bryce said.

He said it again. And again. And over and over till Vincent took him by his shoulders and shook him.

"Relax," Vincent said. "You're good. You're back. You got away. It's alright, you got away from him."

"I lost the knife."

"Lucky for me you did."

"I lost the knife, Vincent. I dropped it. I fell through the floor like an idiot and I dropped it."

Vincent pulled Bryce's ear. Snapped his fingers. "Bad mouse. There, you feel better? Lesson learned. Now, are you hurt? I smell blood. Why do I smell blood?"

"Where're the others?"

"They're sleeping like a bunch of fat worms, now hush and tell me where you're hurt."

Vincent found the stone splinter in Bryce's foot and flicked it away to the dark. He ripped a rag from his jacket and pressed it to the wound.

"Where'd you get that?"

"Candle Hall. They scattered them out. Thought you must have passed them by too."

"No. They must've after we ran through." He clicked his teeth. "We'll get 'em one day. I promise. We'll get 'em. Anywhere else?"

Bryce bit his lip. "My knee. I busted my knee good."

This quieted Vincent. He crossed his arms. Re-crossed them. Vincent took a breath and sighed. After a time he said, "Will it show?"

Bryce shut his eyes. Even though the dark was the same either way, he couldn't bear to look at Vincent. Would it show? Already his knee felt as stiff as a shovel's pole and ballooned large as Garrow's wobbling neck. It felt numb now. He couldn't promise that come morning.

"I can hide it." Bryce's voice croaked. He heard a slosh and Vincent pressed a water-skin into his hands. Bryce drank in long, greedy pulls.

"You made it back is what's important," Vincent said. "I don't think Garrow ever saw us. And he won't speak up to the others that we got the better of him. That we grabbed his knife. He'll be trying to sniff us out." Vincent sighed. "That might get... interesting."

He helped Bryce to stand, pulling his arm over his shoulders. Bryce's knee woke up then, sending white sparks flashing through his vision.

Bryce forced his leg to bend. To walk. If Garrow saw him limping… The rat would corner him in a dark tunnel and that would be that. So Bryce gnawed at the side of his mouth and imagined the pain away. Far, far away.

The burrow was warm when they ducked in. The sounds of two hundred mice in fitful sleep covered any shuffle they made as they inched to Bryce's bunk.

Bryce was second in the stack, his bunk nothing but a hollow dug out from the wall with a thin blanket and a fresh jacket wound into a pillow. Vincent helped him in.

"We only have maybe an hour before call," he said, voice close and small in Bryce's ear. "Sleep deep as you can. I'll see if I can get someone to swap kitchen duty for you. I think Simon's on kitchen tomorrow."

Bryce didn't hear much else after that. Even as he curled against the wall, Vincent faded. He buried his mind someplace cool. Some place without thought. As Bryce fell away, he dreamed of green.

Richard's arms kept a heartbeat. His fingers curled, still remembering the work of the shovel. His legs quivered in his steps and each breath only made his chest tighter. The musty bag pulled over his head didn't help.

"Watch your feet," Lou said, the rat's hand firm on his shoulder, but he didn't give Richard a chance to do so. His foot caught on something—a root or a clump of dirt, Richard couldn't say. All he knew was the ground rushing to meet him and the flash that came from his swelling nose.

"I said watch it, fool. We're not even heading down yet!"

Richard clenched his fists. Felt the loose dirt fill them and felt the sweat trickle down his face. They hauled him up again, blind and shaking, as he let the dirt crumble from his fingers. A little here, a little there. Every couple of steps as they climbed. Up and up and up, until he felt polished wood underfoot. Stairs now. The way became so steep, his thighs burned with the effort. Then they stopped.

The rats stood on either side. For a time, neither moved.

"This was your idea," Lou said, keeping his voice hushed. "You talk to him."

Worth had spoken not a peep the whole way. His only sign was the noise of his knife as he sharpened it in long, dry flicks. Richard heard the click of a boot on wood as Worth left his side and two sharp raps at a wooden door. They waited.

The door opened with a click.

A rush of warm air like a held breath met them. The dead air under his hood shimmered, and his damp fur wilted like leaves in summer. He wished again for his wineskin, left alone and forsaken in that bush at the edge of the mud pit. Even through the bag, Richard could smell the thick aroma of herbs that came with the heat. Strong enough to water his eyes. Heavy rosemary. Jasmine. And something else. Something bitter, like the scent of decay under rotting, gray leaves. It was a smell like the snakeskin that hung in his Father's study; that old, molted thing. Richard imagined a snake coiled inches away, but that was a silly fear. No reason for his breath to catch.

All the snakes were dead, you see.

Still, he writhed at the smell and backed from the door. He came up against Lou's muddied jacket. The rat seized him and pushed him to his knees. Richard hissed from the sting of it.

A voice spoke. Quiet. Slow in its cadence. It said, "Have either of you heard of the wild beasts that roam the marshlands to the North? They are known to leave 'gifts' for those who happen to feed them. Dead things, fish, and such. Sometimes their neighbors. It's quite the nuisance."

Richard heard Lou working his mouth, starting and stopping. "Yes," he said. "I... I can imagine so. Sir."

Richard heard the lonesome pop of a fire somewhere in the room beyond. His stomach quivered as if a spear point hovered over the base of his skull. Invisible, but he swore he could feel it.

The voice spoke, "I only bring it up because it is with some annoyance that I behold the dead thing you've dropped at my door."

Lou stammered. His sharp grip, again, pawed at Richard's shoulder. "No, no, it wasn't me. It—"

"You are saying I'm mistaken?"

Richard could feel the air chill.

"Forgive me," Lou loosed his hold. Tightened it again. "Worth... well, he thought... you see—"

"Stop speaking. I hate your voice."

Lou's mouth shut with a sound like a stone plopped in the mud.

The speaker said, "Mr. Worth. Tell me what this is. Please."

If the tall rat was unnerved, he didn't show it. "Found him snooping outside while we dealt with the other one. Had him dig the grave. Thought he could prove useful."

"Ah. So it's still alive. Let it speak for itself then. Take that sack from its head, it will never leave this place."

Richard felt the bag drag over his face, pulling at his fur and ears. He blinked at the rat leering down at him.

He was old. Fur that may have been a deep rust had tinged to a muted gray. His hands, thin and skeletal, folded before him like a priest. His cloak (like a dark priest) hung from his thin frame and ended in many, many wrinkling folds over his feet. One eye clouded over but the other stood bright and sharp. An eye as gray and cold as a blade.

The old rat smiled. "Good evening. My name is Dorgue. Welcome to my Tree."

The room beyond was like many Richard had known in Green Hill. A small space with a bookshelf filling one wall and a snapping hearth on the other. A window—that impossible window—let in what light the Deep Wood allowed and shone down on an ancient-looking oak desk, almost as deep as it was long. A bucket and rags sat on its face. Richard caught a coppery smell wafting to join the jasmine and rosemary.

"What brings you to my tree then?" Dorgue said. "Speak and choose your words well."

Richard swallowed. He tasted hot blood on his lip and drew the back of his hand over his mouth.

"I... I was just passing by..."

"Liar. You're days from the nearest road." Then to Worth, "What was he carrying?"

"Nothing but himself. The fool's half-starved."

Dorgue's bright eye cocked back to Richard. His gray face tipped. Thinking. "Why have you sought us out?"

"I didn't!" Richard made to rise, but Lou forced him down again.

Dorgue lidded his eyes. "You can not make me believe you are lost. If you were, you'd be dead. The Deep Wood does not share, you understand. It does not offer gifts, such as yourself."

Richard spat out, "I was hunting for Wild Glass!" A lie. A good lie, he hoped. He flicked his eyes to the window. Maybe the rat caught it, maybe not, but it was worth the go.

Dorgue raised a brow. His thin shoulders shook as he chuckled. "Wild Glass? There hasn't been any seen this far into the Deep Wood for nearly thirty years. Years." He gestured to the round window, the same color as his dead eye. "That's the last bit I've found in a good while."

Richard licked his lips. "I just... I wanted to look. There has to be more somewhere, right? Perhaps a bit farther on?"

Dorgue shook his head, laughing. It snapped Richard's mouth shut and dried his throat. It sounded young. Wrong coming from Dorgue's aged face.

"Farther on," Dorgue said. "Yes, yes. You've come a long way, young master. My question for you is this," the rat leaned close. The rosemary was on his breath. "How badly do you want that glass?"

They went down now. Lou, keeping his death grip on Richard's shoulder, and Worth, back to coaxing a hair's breadth edge to his knife. Richard kept his feet as they went, watching his steps. Someone had dug little hollows in the walls and set candles inside to light the way. It was dim, but it was better than nothing. Reminded Richard of the cellars beneath Green Hill. Fewer spiders though. These tunnels were dead.

The descent spiraled like a narrow stair, sometimes wide, sometimes not. When they came to a space wide enough to breathe, Lou peered over his shoulder at the lithe rat keeping the rear.

"That must've made you feel good," Lou said. His teeth were clenched. "Watch'n me choke like a fish in a gutter."

Worth kept silent. His knife hummed over the whet-stone, singing like a tine.

"You didn't care if this welp got gutted or not. You wanted to watch me make a fool of myself."

Another dry scrape. Another musical ring.

"Old Lou, the fool. Old Lou, the noisy bum. Old Lou, the dumb sod."

"You said it."

The fat rat lashed like a drunk with fists as clumsy as bricks. Richard ducked away as the knife flashed and the two tore into each other. Worth twisted. Lou rumbled and roared. Three strikes and the fight ended. Lou stumbled away, clutching at his face as blood seeped past his fingers. The rat's mouth quivered, showing every tooth. "Curse you, salt tail!"

Worth shrugged from the wall and rubbed at his swelling eye with a hand. He cleaned his blade on the sleeve of his jacket.

"It's just a scratch," Worth said. "It'll heal over fine. Let it remind you every day you're a fool." He pointed the tip of his knife to Richard. "See to him. We still need to catch Fletcher before he leaves for the tunnels. Or do you *want* to ride the hoist all the way down?"

Lou tore his hand from his face, wild eyes burning. A red line from jaw to temple glowed like a lightning bolt. He spat. And spat again.

"Hang the hoist!"

But the rat fell in line, spun Richard around, and set to walking once more. Not another word was spoken.

Richard had seen tussles in the city, everyone had. But the Red Guard kept them few. The folk who march the city streets with their wide shoulders and staves usually proved more than enough to keep the peace: a handful of rats and mice and stoats. A shrew too, if he recalled. Richard knew most of them. Good folk all, even the rats, but these two had ice in their veins.

The way down grew darker, the candles fewer, until the rats stumbled just as much as Richard. They slowed. Worth took up a candle from the wall and passed it to Richard before the turning path turned to complete dark.

"Light the way," he said.

Richard didn't argue. It was like walking under a moonless night, under a sky without stars. The sharp slap of their feet and the sputter of Lou's breath were the only noises to be heard now. What air he could get tasted used. Old. Then at last the curving descent ended and Richard trod onto a level floor.

It was a wide room, cube-like in shape but not quite. Dug in a hurry, Richard suspected. A legion of rats looked up from their breakfast: a gray, dribbling mash in a bowl. Four tunnels led out and away, the largest lit from within with hazy torchlight. Above them, an iron chandelier that hung like a twisted arm. He could taste the oily, bitter smoke.

Several rough-hewn tables ran the hall's length, and here sat the rats—maybe fifty, maybe less. Each eye drifted to Richard.

Lou snatched the candle and marched for one of the dim tunnels. A rat called at him in a snipped voice.

"Take a tumble in the bath, Lou?"

The cut running the length of Lou's face arched like a bowstring. He showed his teeth in a wet hiss and stalked from the room, his little light wobbling in the dark till he turned from view. Snickers followed him, bouncing on the walls like pebbles.

Worth pushed Richard forward.

In the hall, one rat stood out from the rest. His coat was a dull gold. Even sitting down, he dwarfed the other rats around him. His arms were like boulders. His eyes found Richard.

"No," he said, the rat's voice a rumble. "Not now. Not tomorrow. Not EVER. You tell that sorry whelp of a cuss that we'd sooner eat one of his precious workers than take in another one." He stabbed a finger down the lit tunnel with its oily smoke. "They are the last batch! That's what he said. That's what he promised. How many more does he have up there? By all means, bring 'em down. I'll skewer 'em and boil 'em alive!" He slammed a knotted fist. Every bowl on the table jumped. A sleeping rat jerked awake.

Worth crossed to the table and peeked into another's breakfast with a crooked finger. "It's just the one mouse," he said, pulling away the bowl and bringing a spoon to his mouth. "No need to work up a huff, Fletcher."

The rat called Fletcher blinked. "One? One? What's the point of dragging only ONE down here?"

Fletcher pushed from the table, upturning the bench and the other rats with a crash. He jutted his scarred face with its white, crossing lines into Richard's. He puffed hot air.

"The runt's hardly standing! Look at his arms!" The rat thumped Richard's shoulder with a hand as big as the mouse's head. It was like having a rock hurled at his chest.

"He's a volunteer," Worth said.

"He's wobbly as pond scum! Never lifted a load in his life." Fletcher crossed his arms. "If he lasted the day, I wouldn't know whether to cheer or cry."

Richard kept his tongue. Physically bit his tongue. He had enough trouble without making enemies on top of everything. Richard had never been good at groveling, and he didn't trust his words with his nose feeling like an off-kilter wagon wheel. Words had always been Kathryn's thing.

She'd host the dinner or fundraiser or what-have-you, hating every minute of it, but Kathryn excelled under the pressure. If the folk of Green Hill needed the big wigs to improve the orphanage or shore up a channel twisting through the city, Kathryn was the one to poke at the machine and get it moving.

It was Richard's job to pick the wine. He wondered what would pair with the gray mash Worth shoveled like a chore.

Fletcher caught him staring.

"Hungry are you?"

The rat snatched a bowl from the table. The slobbering oaf he'd pinched it from blinked slow, wondering where it had gone. Fletcher held the bowl under his chin and spat, then offered it to Richard with a winning smile.

"A little thing like you needs what energy it can get. Go on, have a bite. You never know where your next meal will come from."

Richard couldn't even look at the bowl.

Fletcher grinned wider and tossed it back to the rat at the table. "Suit yourself, then. Follow me. I'll show you where Hell is."

The slobbering rat took up his spoon and finished his breakfast, smacking loudly.

Richard remembered when he was very small and Kathryn lost her patience with him: a rare honor. She decided a game of 'Hide and Seek' would be the perfect thing to get him out of her hair. At least for a little while.

"I'll count," she said. "You run along."

He decided against hiding in the library (Kathryn would see him) and Father's study was off-limits back then. He spent most of his time in the kitchen, anyway.

He remembered sneaking downstairs and cutting through the servant quarters. He tumbled past Old Jethro, an otter with a broom of whiskers fanning out from under his nose, fetching a sack of something from the cellar. Richard passed a trio of maids: two shrews, and a mouse gone ancient after the shrews were hired on. They chided him. Something about silver. Richard didn't remember and didn't care for the shrew sisters' chiding.

The kitchen was quiet (lucky!) and he stuffed himself into one of the deep cupboards with the ginger and the dried figs, the aroma sharp and soothing all at once. He had to get beneath one of the burlap sacks to fit and tucked his legs into his chest and eased the door shut with his toe. Richard beamed. Kathryn would never find him here.

Then Jethro set a box of something by the cupboard door and Ricard was trapped. He tried to wriggle out, to force his legs at the door as he pressed his face into the back of the cupboard, but all he got with that was sawdust in his nose. He was too afraid to call out. What if he got in trouble? And as the hours went by and he heard the dim sound of his name called over and over again, he was only more sure he would get in trouble.

He was in there for a day.

When one of the maids found him, she screamed and collapsed as if dead.

Father called back the guard, and the search quieted, but most of Green Hill knew about it. The whispers of the kidnapping of Richard Aterox spread over the city, a story the gossips sopped up like stolen ale. When his mother squeezed him with her shaking arms and his father scolded him with his tired eyes, Richard didn't mind so much being in trouble anymore. Anything was better than that dark cupboard.

So when Fletcher led Richard into a dim room with a planked, wooden floor, and the smell of gray sawdust filled his bloodied nose, Richard felt that little fear awaken in him again.

The Hoist was a little room built over a dark abyss. Richard walked out on a rough, wooden floor. The boards creaked at every step. In the room's center were two holes set side by side. A pair of elevators with rickety platforms hung over the drop. Ropes hung from the rafters, looped end-over-end, and led to pulleys and gears bolted into the walls with levers jutting out like fingers. Elevators, Richard thought. He had seen such machines used for repair around the city, but these lifts were bowed from years of strain. They squeaked as they swayed.

Fletcher gave one a kick.

"Always like to test 'em," he said. "Just in case the rope decides to give up the ghost."

Fletcher tugged a lever on the wall. Another, he wedged up then down. The lift bobbed in the air, lines shivering tight.

Slowly, it dawned on Richard what this place was. What this room meant. How deep underground were they... and how far down were they yet to go?

That fear fluttered, fluttered, fluttered.

"Digging," Richard said. "This whole time..."

The lift itself was like a rickety basket, Richard thought. Only, it didn't have any sides to keep you from tumbling off into the dark. The arms of the basket were iron gone red with rust and they met together in a box of gears and levers. Fletcher stepped onto the lift. The monstrosity groaned and stretched under the rat's weight, but it didn't move up or down. He reached and gripped a metal release painted angry red. He cocked his head to Richard.

"You've two options, Volunteer," he said. "Either you step too, nice and easy, and we can go down together. Or I can beat you till you forget your name and haul you down like a corpse. Which will it be?"

Richard climbed onto the lift and Fletcher pulled the release.

They dropped into the abyss.

Richard managed to grab hold of the lift's rusted arms before the light left. He strained his neck, stretching to watch the room with its ropes and gears and levers shrink farther and farther away. He watched that little square of light till it died, leaving him alone in the dark with the rat.

"You still there, Volunteer?" the rat said. He had to yell past the rush of stale air around them "Didn't fall off, did you?"

Richard swallowed. It was hard to breathe. "Yeah. Still here."

The rat laughed. "Maybe that was a mistake. Taking a tumble would've been an easy way out. There's still time if you change your mind. Plenty high up."

Plenty high up. The little worm of rot in his belly grew. This place was never a stop along the way for the kidnappers. They didn't sell the mice on from here. Kathryn had been wrong. After they'd brought them here, the mice never left.

He thought back again on that game of hide and seek. For a long time, he blamed himself for the sickness that visited their mother months later. Richard's time in the cupboard had left her drained. Shaken. Even in the weeks that followed, she looked like a ghost wandering the halls of the big house.

"It's because of the others," his sister had told him.

Richard could remember wandering into the library during the quiet hours of the afternoon. Kathryn was up the ladder, her finger gliding over the book spines. Searching.

Richard stared up at her. "What others?" he said.

"The other children. Mice folk are vanishing all across the Middle Kingdom. There are rumors of a league of kidnappers, but Father and Councilmen Bishop say that's… unlikely." She found the book and drug it out from between its fellows. Didn't look to have many pages, but the book was wide and unwieldy. Kathryn tucked it under her arm and tip-toed down the ladder.

She said, "They are telling everyone the children ran away to become highway folk."

Richard frowned. "Robbers? Like Saint Sansa?"

His sister wasn't one to laugh or joke. The most Richard could hope for was a raised eyebrow, which he got then. "Hardly," she said. "Highway folk are cutthroats, especially the bands roaming farther north. I'm sorry to say Richard, but Saint Sansa's just a story."

"I know that," Richard said. He padded to her side as she opened the book on a cherry wood desk. The smell of ink wafted thick from the pages, numbers, and letters arranged in tidy columns. A ledger of some sort. Richard asked, "But why would someone want to run away and join a bunch of murderers?"

Kathryn shrugged. "Kidnappers. Runaways. I've even heard whispers the snakes have returned, but they're only rumors, Richard. Not answers.

Richard thought of thieves hiding on the road, of thugs gathering in dark taverns, and of the snake skin hung in Father's study. Above all, he thought of his mother, racked with worry. Fresh guilt bloomed in his chest. The world was a darker place than it had been this morning. "What if they aren't rumors," Richard said. "What if they're all true?"

Kathryn lifted her eyes from the pages of the ledger. Her eyes were a blue so dark they were almost black, the color of a storm at sea. "Bones have a way of being found," she said.

Those words rattled in Richard's mind for years. And as the lift fell deeper and deeper into the earth, Richard understood at last where he had found himself. He'd discovered the center of all the rumors.

This wasn't an abyss.

It was a grave.

FOUR

*It is estimated over seven-thousand died in the tunnels be-
neath Dorgue's Tree. I've no comment on Richard Aterox's
effect on the number, positive or negative.*

— Jonathan Quick, The Sunday Circular

R ICHARD COULD SEE LIGHT again. It was just a pinprick, far,
far below. And as they came closer, it didn't get much bigger.
Richard tried to make sense of the space, but it was like descending
into a black ocean. Fletcher worked the release above his head and
the lift bounced once in the air then shuddered as it slowed. At last,
Richard could see the ground, made orange by a pitiful candle. It
rushed to meet them.

His heart skipped once or twice in his chest. They were still falling
too fast. They'd break to pieces.

Fletcher pulled hard on the red lever and the lift squealed. The
ground came quick but the lift settled, just kissing the cave floor as

they stopped. A candle flickered, and another rat appeared from the darkness. His belly preceded him into the light.

"Oh, gore, not another one of the devils," the fat rat said. His face was a twisted purple, and his right eye puffed large and swollen from under his brow. Sticky blood matted the fur of his snout. Richard could smell him.

The lift shook as Fletcher stepped from it. "What in blaze happened to you?"

Garrow smiled, showing gray teeth. "Tripped. Clumsy me."

"You smell like a gutter."

"You spend the night watch'n the site. We'll see who stinks then."

Fletcher pressed into Garrow's space. The fat rat turned away, not meeting the other's eye.

Fletcher glared, eyes flashing orange with candlelight. "Anything happen last night while you drank yourself to oblivion? Any ghosts come visiting?"

"Real quiet," Garrow said. "Not a peep."

"And how much of your watch did you miss? If I ask the workers, will they say your snoring kept them awake?"

Garrow huffed. "They'll say whatever you want them to say."

"You have watch again tonight."

Garrow's fist turned at his side as if reaching for a knife but then thinking better of it. His swollen face fought the spreading sneer, but he couldn't keep it out of his voice.

"Is there anything else?" Garrow said.

Fletcher glared a moment longer, then cocked his head to the lift. "Get the others down here. Don't let me see you again today."

Richard studied Garrow as he lurched into the lift. His tail dragged and his ears, dry as snakeskin, laid flat on his skull. His swollen, wobbling eye found the release, pushed it home, and the lift thumped the ground. High above, Richard heard a squealing, and the ropes hummed and twanged.

The lift bobbed into the air. Fletcher called up, "If you're late tonight, you'll wish Dorgue skinned you!"

The fat rat didn't respond. He stared out into the dark, not seeming to be looking at anything.

A little scream started somewhere in Richard's mind as he watched the lift shimmer away into the dark. He breathed deep. Hugged his arms. The smell of figs and ginger came sharp in his memory.

That was his way out. It was going away.

Fletcher took up the candle. "You must have questions," the rat said. "Feel free to ask them now."

Richard's eyes never left the square shape far above, even as it faded to shadow. He wet his lips. "Why are we—"

Fletcher's hand came fast. The left side of Richard's face exploded in teeth-clicking pain, driving him to the ground. Richard coughed and spat blood. Fletcher knelt at his side, the candle flame wobbling in his grasp.

"Here is the first rule," Fletcher said, his voice a puff in Richard's ear, "No questions. You ask one, then it's the whipping post for you."

The rat took hold of Richard's arm and forced him to his feet. Richard quivered. The floor seemed to be slanting sideways. He tried to speak, but his tongue lolled in his mouth, feeling like a bug worming around his teeth.

"Here is the second rule," Fletcher said and pulled Richard into a march. The mouse's feet dragged and stumbled.

"You do as we say," Fletcher said. "You don't talk back. You wake when we say wake and sleep when we say sleep. You're here to dig, Volunteer. And if you slow us down...if you prove to be a distraction…" Fletcher's grip tightened on his arm. This brought Richard back somewhat. He blinked up at the rat.

Fletcher said, "It's been one delay after another. I don't care what Dorgue says. If you so much as spill a bucket, I'll cut your throat and bleed you where you stand. Is that understood?"

Richard understood.

Fletcher glared ahead like the dark was a beast needing to submit. Richard had seen such looks before. This rat had been a soldier once upon a time, Richard was sure.

He'd visited Green Hill's barracks on occasion with his father. They'd watch the soldiers train, mice, rats, stoats—the mink that scared Richard witless—all sorts. They would pause in their sparring and salute from that dusty field outside the city walls. Richard liked to salute back. His father only ever dipped his head.

Richard had spent many days there in the training yard, visiting with the soldiers and no doubt making a nuisance of himself. As he grew, he'd talk them into teaching him. Small things. Self-defense; how to wriggle out of a hold and such. Much good that did him now. Even if he could escape from Fletcher's side, where would he go?

The way out was gone.

They came to the wall of the cave, rising forever up into darkness. Fletcher's candle revealed the messy mouth of a tunnel. A three-legged stool sat overturned and splintered just within. Fletcher pulled Richard along without so much of a pause, stepping past the wooden fragments.

"Tripped." Fletcher showed his teeth. The candlelight threw a mask of shadows on the rat's face. "The drunken fool's going to take a bad step too many one day."

The tunnel was just large enough for Fletcher to walk upright. The rat's ears brushed the ceiling.

"This leads to the burrows," he said. "There's an offshoot just there, it leads to the mess. Those are the only places you're allowed. Any questions?"

Richard almost asked if the rat had inherited his winning charm from his mother, but the image of Kathryn's shaking head forced Richard to hold his tongue. Fletcher smiled.

"Good," the rat said. "The Volunteer can learn."

He pulled Richard deeper in, passing another mouth-like hole in the wall. This one Fletcher would have to stoop to enter. The rat nodded to it as they passed. Richard spied the shine of eyes looking out, hungry for the candlelight.

"This is Isolation," he said. "The older ones stay there."

Richard moved his mouth to speak, but he swallowed his questions before they could jump into words. Older ones?

But they were already moving on.

The tunnel turned and Richard saw light ahead. Faint, but as glorious as sunlight in all this dark. They rounded the bend and the next burrow sneaked into view, little by little. Richard's feet stumbled at the sight that awaited him.

Mice, maybe twenty with many more in line behind them, stood at the ready at the burrow's mouth. They had their own little candle, set on the cave floor. At Fletcher's approach, the mice bowed. They wore rags over thin, wiry bodies. They were like skeletons.

Richard's breath caught in his throat.

The rat, Fletcher, didn't bother to even glance their way. "Here's Candle Hall," he said. "We reward the good down here, they get more kitchen work than anyone. Serve well, and you'll earn a place among them." Richard recognized the routine in the Rat's voice. He could sense the scorn as well.

One of the mice spoke up. His fur was gone in long, ugly patches revealing skin scarred silver. He kept his hands folded before him, much like the old rat upstairs. He had a hoarse voice. "We await the day with courage, sir," he said.

Fletcher walked on, never acknowledging the mice he'd called "rewarded". Before the light left them, he saw their eyes flick up from the ground to meet his— some were frightened, some were empty and roving, but most of them were cold. Cold and… jealous.

Richard knew the look well enough but to see it here was ice in his gut.

He smelled the next burrow before he saw it. His stomach coiled.

It was a tiny space. A square room. The scent of old blood and sweat hid beneath the aroma of herbs. Richard saw other mice—seven, he counted— staring out from their bunks with wide eyes and small faces. One mouse, with plain, brown fur matted around his neck, hid his face as they stepped inside. The pitiful thing was missing a good chunk of his lip and his teeth showed through like white flecks of stone. He covered himself with a club of a hand wrapped over with thick gauze.

"And now, Hospital," Fletcher shone his candle further in, "I have a deal for you Volunteer. Tell me what you see."

Richard looked. The others looked back. One was larger than the others. His fur was coal black and held his head awkwardly before his hunched shoulders. He had a gray bandage tied over his eyes.

"I see sick mice. Injured mice."

"Guess how much digging they do."

Richard bit his lip. He didn't know how much of this was a tour and how much of it was the rat's excuse to shake him up. Surely they didn't send these folk out to dig. He saw one had a leg in a cast from ankle to knee.

"They don't," Richard said.

The rat nodded. "That's right. It would only cause delays to send them out. They work the kitchen. Process laundry. Everyone in the Tree gets a turn at the easy jobs, but Hospital is special. They won't touch a shovel till they're able," he called at them, "Do ya?"

"No sir," they said. Their voices were dull. Unfeeling.

Richard felt a quiver deep within him. His skin writhed where the rat held fast to his arm, bruising him. "What is…" Richard stopped himself. Rephrased. "You mentioned a deal."

"That I did."

"You want to put me in here."

"It'd be best for everyone. Best for you. You're not ready for the dig site. You'd slow things down."

"I'm good at surprising folk."

The rat smiled. "I gave you a chance at the lift. To jump. To make it clean and simple for everyone. This is your last chance. If you clog up the work I'll make you suffer, Volunteer. You'll suffer worse than even them."

"I'll work the hardest."

"You haven't worked a day in your life, don't lie to yourself." The rat turned to face him. Knelt till they were eye to eye. Fletcher said, "Here's what I can do: I'll break your arm—a good, clean break—and you can stay out of the way. I'll even let you pick which arm."

"I'd rather not."

"You'll be worse off. I promise. Last chance."

Richard bit his tongue. He wasn't going to let this rat scare him into letting him… He took a breath. Didn't trust his voice.

Richard shook his head. A strong no.

The rat sighed. His lips moved into a scowl. "You'll regret it," he said. "You will."

Fletcher led him on, leaving the others in the dark. Richard kept pace, his eyes on the ground. He could feel their eyes on him.

He couldn't look at them.

FIVE

"Everyone knows the song."

— A Common Saying

BRYCE DREAMED THE LANTERNS at the dig site burst. Brown, brittle glass peppered his face. Bubbling oil stuck to his skin. There was no pain. He simply faded like paper burned to ash.

Then there was nothing. A deep nothing. And then Something Else.

Deepest Dark... an eye watching... a breath.

Bryce opened his eyes. Gavin had him by the shoulder.

"Fletcher's coming," he said. His voice was hushed. Bryce strained to hear him over the others stirring in their bunks. Gavin said, "Vincent told us you messed up your knee. You're not hauling buckets, are you? I'm down in the mud today if you wanna swap."

That was the worst job. Buckets. All day marching up and down the slick gangways, his fingers turning raw, rough ropes cutting into his palms. They all took turns, but the rats had favorites.

Bryce said, "Vincent's gonna see if Simon will trade me. He's in Kitchen today."

"Kitchen for Buckets?"

"He might."

"If he doesn't, I'll trade with you. At least you won't have to walk as much in the mud." Gavin drummed his fingers. Thinking. He said, "How's your leg? Can you move it?"

Bryce tried. The night before, he'd seen flashes at every step. Now everything stuck stiff. Still swollen. The dry rubbing in his knee felt like bone grating bone.

"Hurts," Bryce said. He took hold of Gavin's shoulder and swung out of his bunk. He kept his bad leg tucked, foot brushing the floor.

It was always a good idea to be out of bed when Fletcher came to gather them in the mornings. The rat wasn't kind in waking them. Fletcher often carried a whip and liked to use it.

Bryce lifted an ear. "You heard Fletcher?"

"Yeah, he was talking to someone. Farther down the tunnel. Sounded all chummy. Like, stab you in the neck chummy."

Bryce didn't get a chance to ask who. All conversation and movement faded away at the first hint of light from the tunnel. Bryce could see the others. All of them were out of their bunks and at attention. Mice crowded the space.

Gavin kept close at hand, lending his shoulder to help Bryce stay upright. Vincent stood farther in. He was in the middle of giving Simon a heated glare, which the smaller mouse ignored in his quiet, respectful way.

Bryce couldn't blame him. He wouldn't want to trade away kitchen duty either.

The candlelight grew and Fletcher stepped into the mouth of the tunnel.

It was easy to believe that there wasn't anything beyond the tunnels. Yes, Bryce and the others dreamed of a life outside and away from Dorgue's rats, but most of them had no memory of what life was like before. To Bryce, it was just a few feelings. Warmth. The smell of cinnamon. A few snatches of a song—no words, only half a melody—something to hum as he worked.

It was Vincent who remembered things. He could talk about trees, grass, and the wind, but the colors were always changing. How could a tree be green one day and orange the next? How could the sky be black and blue and pink? Well, Vincent insisted that they had, and that was that. It was nonsense to most. Even Bryce thought he made it up sometimes—butterflies, berry-picking, dancing flowers—just to keep up their spirits on the worst days. The world outside was a land of fairy tales. Of magic and story.

Bryce especially hoped the dancing flowers were real.

So, you can imagine the shock of seeing Richard Aterox in the mouth of their burrow, with his swelled nose and hunted eyes as Fletcher loomed behind him.

All was still. No one even dared to breathe.

This mouse was not like any of them. His fur was clean. His ears were not notched or cut. He stood straight with his arms folded before him and his mouth flattened to a line as his eyes darted from face to face.

Fletcher kicked him and the mouse dropped to his knees.

"Meet your new brother," the rat said. He leaned on the carved stone of the burrow's mouth. "You can call him Volunteer. Everyone say, 'helloooo Volunteer.'"

They did. Bryce sneaked a look at the other mice in the burrow. Gavin's frown was drawn deep over his eyes, buried in thought. Vincent's mouth was already working, silently gaping and clamping shut. The others looked as if they'd seen a ghost.

Fletcher held up his candle. The shadows jumped. The mice jumped too. "See that he gets the run-down," the rat said. "I'm not wasting any more words on the idiot, and we're already late for count. Everyone, file in."

That was all they got. Here's a new face. Don't panic. Everyone, file in.

They filed in. Gavin took hold of his arm. "Walk straight as you can, I'll help."

Bryce shrugged him off. "I don't think we have to worry about that," he said and nodded to the others shuffling after Fletcher. "No one's looking my way."

And it was true. Every eye was focused on the new guy. Yes, if Garrow hung around the dig site he'd pick Bryce out quick enough, but until then, all the attention was going to be on one mouse.

For now, Bryce was invisible.

"I'm still not sure if I'm awake," Gavin said. "You think it's a trick?"

"How?"

Gavin shrugged. "Dorgue hears about... an incident. He needs to find out whose fault it is and sends a snoop."

"So, he's got a bunch of... secret Candle Hall mice we've never heard about?"

"Heck of a coincidence after... well, you know."

Bryce missed a step and had to reach for Gavin's shoulder. Did Dorgue have some mice they didn't know about? Just in case he needed some fresh faces to spook out the bad ones? Was that even possible?

"How would we tell?" Bryce asked.

But Gavin didn't seem to hear. His eyes were fixed on the back of the new guy's head. "Vincent always says to wait for changes. To listen for any skip in the rats' routine. If this isn't Dorgue spying on us…"

Gavin frowned. While Vincent was content to spend days counting how often a particular guard walked their rounds on the gangway, Gavin's patience extended to taking the time to find a rock with enough heft to leave the rat wondering 'what had happened' and 'why is my eye bleeding'?

Vincent often thought out loud, laying out ideas and then arguing them to pieces in the same breath. Gavin, meanwhile, would be collecting stones.

They crowded out into the tunnel. They passed Hospital, who limped after them, smelling like medicine. Candle Hall joined with shining greetings that Fletcher ignored. And Isolation brought the rear, silent and dragging. Bryce thought about joining them. His knee sparked like a dying candle flame.

Light ahead. The rats had lit the lamps, their version of a sunrise. The tunnel opened like an eye and dried mud crunched like pottery underfoot. Bryce lifted his face and followed the shaft up—past the lowering lifts, past the swaying walkways—as far as he could see. He could hear the rats' voices echoing in the dark above.

Did Garrow watch from somewhere up there? Bryce was afraid to scan the walkways. What if their eyes met? He'd see Bryce's shock. Then the rat would be certain.

The new mouse took it all in with wide eyes and a mouth flattened into a line. He spun around, hands curling into shaking fists that opened and closed at his sides. If it was an act, it was a good one. Bryce looked at the rats gathered around the dig site.

The first lift shuddered to a halt an inch from the ground. More rats piled off, keeping a hold of the ropes lest they started to swing. Once the lift settled, a rat called up, "Slack!" and the lift thumped to the ground, raising a billow of dust.

"You lot line up!" Fletcher ordered the mice, as the second lift floated to a stop behind him. Another party of rats stepped from it, stretching, and tasting around their teeth for the last of breakfast.

A normal morning.

Bryce stepped in line next to Gavin. He saw Vincent and Sampson a couple of heads down, but none of them shared any looks. They were at the dig site now. Too many eyes here.

The new mouse frowned at the line. He moved to join one end of it, but Fletcher took his arm and pushed him toward Bryce and Gavin.

"No, no. You go over here," he said. The Volunteer tripped on his own feet and sprawled in the dirt. Bryce backed away like he was poison. The rats near the lift laughed, but Fletcher only grimaced.

The Volunteer's knuckles were white as he pushed himself to his feet. His eyes flicked between Bryce and Gavin. There was a panic growing there. Panic and fury.

"We're already late this morning," Fletcher growled as he yanked Richard upright again. The rat pointed a finger in Bryce's face. "You're his friend today," he said. "Buckets, both of you. Teach him the ropes. If he dies, it's your fault."

SIX

"I hide a knife at my side, for a smile means many things."

— A Common Saying

T HIS WAS BAD.

No. Wrong word. This was disastrous.

Richard ducked as a whip cracked overhead. Fletcher bellowed. "Two lines, you worthless worms! Can't you count? GET IN LINE!"

Richard got in line.

At least he wasn't in the dark anymore, Richard thought. Warm light the color of torches made his eyes squint. Oddly enough, it reminded him of home, of the glow of street lamps and windows come sundown. But this wasn't Green Hill, and the orange glow of the torches did not cast a cheery scene in the cavern.

And yes, it was a cavern. On the way down in that rickshaw of a lift, Richard had sensed the large space, but even in this new light, he had trouble grasping it.

In Green Hill, there is a tower called the Garden Spire near the heart of the city. It rises hundreds of feet into the air and could house all of Green Hill's citizens if you told them to hold their breath and squeeze in.

But this place...this *monument* dug out by hand...

It *dwarfed* the Spire.

A rat ambled by, counting them one by one. He had a hairless and pocked face. Clicked his teeth now and again, too. Nervous tick, most like. He stomped to their line's end and nodded to Fletcher, who bellowed out, "YOU LOT ARE ON BUCKETS."

The mice knew where to go and Richard did his best to mirror them. Some mice were excused and filed back into the tunnels. Richard recognized them from Hospital and one or two from Candle Hall. Must be the kitchen work Fletcher had been raving about. Everyone left in Richard's line watched them leave; some with envy, some with hate dripping from their eyes, but the worst were the ones who stared ahead, hollow, and empty as the line moved.

Then Richard saw the dig site. A hole, center of the cavern, like an impossibly deep lake drained of water. Cranes and rickety scaffolding circled it like stitches ripped from an open wound. Richard tried to swallow, but his throat had gone dry. The sight of that pit descending into the dark was... *wrong*. Vulgar. A thing that shouldn't be.

And yet there it was.

Stuck...Can't get out...

Richard looked away from the monstrous pit and stretched to see up and out. Rope walkways strung the expanse overhead, criss-crossing like dust-covered webs. He saw guards up there as well, patrolling or otherwise busy with some errand or another. Richard thought he spied Worth on the walkway. The lithe rat looked his way and gave him a nod as if to say good morning.

Creep.

The mouse Fletcher had bullied into guiding him along, gave him a nudge and whispered, "Stop looking at them."

Richard knew a good idea when he heard it. Problem was, knowing and doing were different things.

In the new light, Richard could see the walls of the cavern rising up and out to freedom. It would rise fifty feet only to cut in like a terrace, then stretch up another impossible distance and cut in again.

It's like I'm standing in a telescope, Richard thought.

There were more walkways higher up, but these were dark. No rats patrolled them.

That's the way out.

The idea was like a golden coin in Richard's mind. Except, this coin sat on display behind shop glass, iron bars, and at least fifty tough-faced rats armed with whips, clubs, and knives.

Richard's line ended at the lift that had brought him to this hell. It bowed under the weight of the day's tools. He recognized the rat passing out the shovels and buckets. Richard had nearly shared breakfast with him. Some of the gruel still clung on the breast of his scratchy doublet, but it had gone dry and crumbly. The rat stood hunched, quick in his movement, and deep in a pattern of shovel, bucket, shovel, bucket, as he serviced the two lines.

Richard got his bucket. The rope handle was stiff and prickly, and the inside was painted dark with tar.

His assigned friend got his too. He blinked, slow and resigned. Dots of sweat stood out on his forehead. He turned to join the crowd marching toward the dig site, trying to hide his limp as he went, but not doing the best job of it.

Richard watched him go.

Another crack of the whip and Richard scurried after. He came alongside the mouse and asked his name.

"Bryce," he said.

"I'm Richard."

"Alright."

Richard nodded toward the pit. "What's down there?" he asked.

Bryce's eyes darted to his then away again. "The dirt," he said. "Dirt's down there."

No kidding.

Richard scanned the mob around them. Buckets and shovels were pretty much split in half, he guessed. Every mouse moved with their faces set toward their feet. Fletcher kept the rear, spurring the stragglers on with his tree-trunk arms folded over his chest.

"Yeah, dirt. But what else?" He leaned closer, "What are you digging for?"

Bryce frowned. His eyes grew to saucers. "Shut up," he hissed. "You'll stir trouble with that sort of talk."

"You're not *already* in trouble?"

He shook as if struck. Bryce opened his mouth. Closed it. Then his eyes hardened and he pressed close. "I still have my feet," he said, voice harsh. "Used to be a mouse everyone called Cave. He didn't care about trouble, so Dorgue cut his feet off and forced him to dig. He lived ten days like that before fever took him."

Richard blinked. "They...*his feet?*"

"You make trouble for the rats, then they make three times as much for you." Bryce shuffled ahead, mouth determined. "Don't talk to me."

And that was that.

Richard looked back at the rats with their whips and their scowls. Cut off someone's feet? What good would that do? Why in blazes were all these mice here and not scattered to the four winds like they were *supposed to be*? Like Kathryn *said they were*?

Richard had a mind to grab Bryce's shoulders and shake the answers out of him if he had to. Not tactful. Not what Kathryn would do. But she wasn't here, and Richard was a hundred miles under the earth breathing rotting air and mud. He'd do whatever it took!

But they reached the ramp and all words left him. He looked down into the depths. Into the pit.

Long way down.

More terraces, like the shaft up, but closer together, and going down. The ramps and scaffolds flowed in something of a spiral, but not really. It looked ready to snap to pieces at a sneeze and was so coated with mud that Richard could hardly tell it apart from the dirt.

Only two or three at a time could work in the tiny space he spied at the bottom.

He felt fluttering in his stomach. In his toes. Then the dumbest thing came to mind...

Harvest time.

Back then, Richard was young and his mother was still alive, but not by much. She was bedridden and the rattling in her breath made the doctors nervous. And she wouldn't take leeches, which made them petulant. In the end, Father sent the doctors away. Mother was tired of the attention.

Richard had been tottering at her bedside when the coughing started. At first, she'd cover her mouth with her hands. Next, she'd use hankies. Then she had a wastebasket at her bedside full of them, all tainted red.

Father called the doctors back after that.

Richard blamed himself for his mother's sickness. The stress he'd caused after his disappearing act in the cupboard had brought it about, he was sure of it. The episode aged mother, and she fell ill shortly after. So, Richard became a rain cloud, roaming from room to room. Not speaking, not eating, and hardly sleeping. The day the Harvest Fair put up their tents outside the city gates, they forced him out.

"Have fun," his mother ordered. Her face was drawn, and her eyes were glassy, but she managed to turn up the corners of her mouth into a smile. "Go find some mischief. Laugh. Run. Don't come back until you see that first lucky star in the sky."

"Yes'm."

She smiled bigger, but she kept her teeth hidden. They'd gone to color. "Bring me back something pretty," she said.

When the maid clicked the door shut, he could hear his mother cough. Sounded like choking.

Richard remained a rain cloud as he walked from Green Hill and its noise. He passed through the wide Century Gate and down the sloping hill for which the city was named. Below he saw thousands: half the city emptied out, he reckoned. Never had he seen a Harvest Fair bigger, before or after.

The smell of bonfires and merry food returned his childhood to him like a flower in want of water. For a moment, the smell of oily medicine and the papery sound of sickness were banished. Richard enjoyed himself. He forgot his worries.

One tent housed a troupe of shrews that wore shining masks and put on dramas. In another was a rat who ate fire and spewed it out overhead with a sound like thunder. Richard saw a short mouse wearing a tall, pointed hat who could guess whatever number you held in the front of your mind and did wonderful things with cards.

Then, as the day turned to evening, he came across a little crowd. In its center stood the fool.

A mole, all dressed in colors and bells, with happy and wrinkled eyes that never opened above a wide, painted smile. He did tricks, like the mouse with the pointed hat, but the mole's tricks were better. By far.

He could make things disappear and reappear. He could pour a flagon of ale into his cap, only to set it right back between his ears without a drop to be seen. He could make a ball float on the palm of his hand, vanish it behind his fingers, and point to the startled stoat in the crowd who found the very same ball in his coat pocket.

But the fool had hardly begun.

A juggler carried a chest into the circle of folk. It was the sort of chest you might store clothes in for a long journey or use to lock away a keepsake or two. He struggled with it, comically drifting back and forth before letting it fall with a heavy thud before the fool.

He clicked the chest open, and the fool folded himself inside, letting the juggler slam the lid shut and lock it with a golden key.

Another juggler happened by, carrying a chest a little larger than the first. Together, they locked the first chest into this one.

Then another juggler, and another chest.

And another.

And another.

The thought of the fool, so packed in that he had to force his head between his knees to fit, made Richard's hands shake in his armpits as he hugged his chest. He could smell the ginger and figs in the air. All the worry he'd been running from came upon him all at once. Him trapped in that stupid cupboard. His mother dying in that sunless room. All of it his fault.

But then everything was alright.

One last juggler and one last chest; this one so large, not even all the jugglers (five of them!) could lift the mole sealed away under all those locks. They struggled and heaved and arched their backs with the effort of it.

And so, the fool—the very same who'd been folded up and packed away—waddled out from the audience, with his bells jumping and singing, to help them lift and lock it.

The crowd roared, laughter shook the air, and Richard clapped and clapped till his hands stung.

The strangest feeling filled Richard from toes to ears. It was like a shaking, a lightness in his chest, and a spin to his walk.

Deepest relief conquered the black dread that had been hovering over his heart. He had gotten out. He'd *escaped*. But Richard never found out how the fool had done it.

Now, here he was, trapped in a different sort of box. No way out. Sinking deeper and deeper as that same old dread returned to suffocate him. Looking that long way down, past the scaffolds and dirt and lines of mice as they descended, he couldn't breathe. Couldn't move.

A whip cut an arc in his back. Felt like someone had clubbed his spine with a board. It burned worse than fire.

"Keep on!" A rat screamed. He had a scabbed nose and a twisted shoulder. His whip shrieked again, slicing Richard's arm as he scrambled away. The mice around him scattered, their feet bouncing the ramp. The third strike missed Richard's knuckles by inches and shot the bucket out from his grasp. He fumbled to catch it.

"We chop up clumsy fingers here, *Volunteer*," the rat said, grinning as if the thought of maiming Richard's hand would prove a particularly delicious thing to brag about.

Richard scooped his bucket into his arms and ran as the smiling guard raked the air once more.

The ramps leading down were made from rough wood and had some grip, but the slick mud coating them forced Richard to slow and choose his steps wearily.

They were sixty feet down before the scabbed-nosed rat ordered a halt. Richard risked a peak over the side. Four levels from where he stood, the base of the pit looked like the open mouth of a corpse. Richard saw mice down there, coated head to foot in dark mud the color of ash. They worked by torchlight, their forms casting weird jumping shadows as they jabbed into the mud with poles twice their length.

Loosening the clay, Richard thought. He stared up the way he came, past the scaffolds, past the terraced slopes of the pits, past the wooden walkways, and into the darkness that hung over all like a starless sky buried deep within the earth.

They dug all of this... with sticks and shovels.

The scabbed-nosed rat ushered them from the scaffold and onto the grime of a shallow terrace. Richard watched as other mice continue down the scaffold into lower levels.

It was getting hard to breathe.

The rat whistled for attention. "We're gonna need more elbow-room here in a couple of days, so we're collapsing this level down," he said. "Lot of dirt to move. The sooner it's done, the sooner we break. Your reward awaits you."

"Our reward awaits us," mice echoed.

Figs and ginger. Dust and smothering heat. His heart spinning, spinning, spinning...

He thought of that cupboard, crushing him smaller and smaller. He thought of his mother, laying on her death bed as father wasted away in a chair at her side. He thought of his sister, losing weeks of sleep, and pacing the dark halls after everything had finally ended.

He thought of his Father at the window.

That big, glass window.

A hand found Richard's shoulder. Someone spoke, but he couldn't hear it. Couldn't breathe. There wasn't any air this far down, none at all.

Richard wasn't stupid, he knew he was panicking. He also knew the rats would notice before long and hit him again, maybe even kill him. But he didn't care.

He was trapped in that cupboard. Locked in that chest, except he didn't know how to magic himself out again.

Stuck... The way out... I can't...

A voice in his ear, "You need to breathe. You need to breathe or I'm going to hit you, alright? What's your name?"

He pulled at Richard's face and forced him around. Richard saw an eye the color of the forest at night. Eyes the color of the Deep Wood.

"You hear me, guy? What's your name?"

Richard swallowed. He tasted metal and his empty stomach didn't appreciate it. He felt light and sick.

He wished he'd eaten the gruel.

"Richard," he said, "My name is Richard."

The mouse nodded and let him go. He knelt to take up a shovel. "I'm Vincent. Now that we're friends, can you catch for me?"

The mouse pushed his shovel into the dirt and wedged out a thick brick of sludge. He nodded to Richard's bucket. "Hold it out," he said.

Richard did. His bucket slurped the mud from Vincent's shovel like it was alive. Richard felt his mouth sour.

"If you toss your dinner, please do it in your bucket," Vincent said, digging his hole wider and passing the mud to Richard. "The rats don't like us adding to the pit."

Richard took a breath. Took another. *The fool got out,* he promised himself. *He got out, and you'll get out too.*

Two other mice worked nearby, the one with the limp and another with boxy ears. They worked the same as Vincent and himself, albeit faster and all with the briefest glances at their work. They eyed him. They eyed Vincent.

Vincent ignored them.

"You smell like the Deep Wood," the mouse said, adding more mud to his bucket. Richard tried to lift it.

"I said, you smell like the Deep Wood. Is that where you come from?"

Richard bit his lip, took another breath, and stuck to his story. "Yeah. I'm from the Deep Wood."

"Near the river?"

The bucket was full now. Richard gripped the prickly, rope handle, lifted it, and got a hand under to cradle it at his chest. His cheeks puffed with air.

"Yeah," he said. "The river. We go fishing."

Vincent nodded, continuing his shoveling. His mouth shook. "I'll...dig a little pile here," he said. "Then when you come down again, you can scoop it up. That's what you'll be doing most of the day. Scooping."

Richard's hands burned and he had to remind himself to breathe. He asked, "And how long is that? The day, I mean."

Vincent kept his face at his work. shrugged. "We go till they say stop."

If walking down the angled ramps had been tricky, up was worse. The mud sloshed beneath his boots and Richard sucked in his breath, expecting his legs to slip out from under him and send him tumbling down into the pit once more.

Panic rose in his mind, but Richard did his best to ignore it. Pushing it away. Swallowing it. Sending his mind someplace else.

He thought back to the Harvest Fair.

Young Richard had spent the last of what light was left searching through the wildflowers that grew in the fields around Green Hill. He still needed to find something pretty to bring back for his mother.

As he padded back, returning to the echo of the city, Richard thought over the fool's trick. No matter how he puzzled at it he couldn't make sense of how he'd done it. All he had gotten for his trouble was a headache but there was one person, Richard thought, who might know the secret.

When he returned home, the windows were dark, and he stole through one of the side entrances near the garden, thinking the less trouble he made, the better.

He found Kathryn in the library.

Richard shared the whole thing with her; how the fool had folded himself away, how the jugglers had locked him up in larger and larger crates, and how he'd appeared in the crowd like magic.

Kathryn had pushed from the table and ran her hands over her face. Her eyes were rimmed red. She hadn't slept well in those days. None of them had.

He watched as his sister thought, her storm-colored eyes drifting closed and her mouth flattening to a line. Richard waited. The only sound in the sleeping house was the pop of the fireplace and the mournful thump of the library's grandfather clock.

At last, Kathryn sighed, pressing a knuckle into her brow. Then she looked his way and gave him a sad smile. "It was magic," she said.

Even at that age, Richard knew a story when he heard one. He never could get the truth out of Kathryn.

Drove him crazy.

When Richard, at last, stepped from the rickety scaffold and onto the solid ground of the dig site, his mouth hung like a dead flag. He stumbled, bucket sloshing over his chest. The mud was cold.

Others were looking at him. Sidelong glances that reeked with pity. One of the mice, the fellow he'd seen from Candle Hall who had bowed to Fletcher, gave Richard a sly smile. White scars crisscrossed his back and he carried his shovel propped over his shoulder. The scarred mouse laughed. A short chuff through the nose.

Richard's ears laid flat against his skull and he *seethed*, vision going red. *No one laughs at Richard Aterox.* He set the bucket down, spine aching from the effort. "*Hey*," Richard called out, his voice rough and out of breath. "Hey, you!"

A hand found Richard's arm but he shrugged it away. The scarred mouse was ignoring him.

"*What do you think is...so funny?*" Richard said.

The other workers looked up at the commotion. Some froze, expecting a fight, but the scarred mouse kept on his way. And Richard *knew* he'd heard him.

Richard showed his teeth. "Don't walk away from—"

His next step found unsteady ground. He was too weak and too close to the pit's edge to stop himself. His boot scraped a wide swath of mud, stealing his balance, and the yawning mouth of the pit filled his vision and the world

spun

around

him...

An arm snatched his sleeve and yanked him back from the drop. Bryce dragged Richard from the edge, face strained and bum leg dragging.

Richard shook and his stomach quivered like a fish drawn from a river. He toppled over, clinging to Bryce who pushed him away. Richard sat in the mud, hands shaking.

"*Get your bucket,*" Bryce hissed.

Richard swallowed, heart pounding in his throat. He looked back to the rickety scaffold and the mice filing to and from it. How many more times would he have to make that climb? Ten? Twenty? A hundred? Bryce said something. Repeated it. Richard blinked away the fog and listened hard.

"—don't try to pick fights, they're gonna make an example. Get up before someone sees you."

Richard looked past Bryce into the crowd of mice. He spied the scarred mouse talking with his head bowed to one of the rats. "What's that one's name?" he asked.

"Said, *get up!*" Bryce kicked Richard's thigh, but there wasn't any heart to it and Richard was too dazed to care. He forced himself to stand.

"He a friend of yours?"

Bryce frowned and followed Richard's gaze to the scarred mouse from Candle Hall. "He's not the friend-having type," Bryce said. "Steer clear of him."

"We'll, what's his name?"

"Said, steer clear, *okay?*" Bryce marched to join the line again. "Don't fill your bucket so high. But don't let the rats see. They'll beat you for it."

"Is that what you do? For your leg?"

Bryce shook his head. "Nothing wrong with my leg."

Richard collected his bucket and fell in line.

The lifts met them at the end of the line, their bases bowed under the weight of excavated dirt. Two rats stood by, keeping a hold on the lines leading up to the Hoist. One of them had a wedge of wood in his mouth and chewed it like cud. His teeth were green. He looked bored.

"Dump it and head down for more," The rat said. He rattled the woodblock from one side of his mouth to the other. "Busy day. Bizz-*ee*-day!"

Richard upended his bucket and watched the sludge roll out. Other mice shouldered past. One mouse, Richard saw with some surprise, hefted *two buckets*.

The others headed back down to the dig site and Richard watched them go. The line of hunched mice followed the path toward the pit beneath a dark, unfeeling abyss.

Stuck.

No way out.

Richard closed his eyes. Breathed deep.

"*Magic,*" Kathryn had said after he'd returned from the fair. After he'd asked how the mole's trick was done. She had smiled and looked at the flower he clutched in his hands.

"What's that?" she asked.

"For mother," Richard said. "She wanted something pretty from the fair."

"It is pretty."

"I didn't have any more money."

"That's fine."

Richard yawned wide. Blinked little blinks. "She's asleep?"

Kathryn nodded.

"I can give it to her in the morning," Richard said. "And I can tell her about the mole and his trick."

Kathryn said nothing.

It wasn't until the following day that Richard learned what had happened. That as he was picking flowers, his mother, Margarett Tull Aterox, struggled through one final breath, and shut her eyes forevermore.

SEVEN

— Entry from journal at Aterox Estate, Author Unknown

BRYCE DIDN'T SEE GARROW up in the walkways, but that didn't mean the rat wasn't there. The swaying bridges crisscrossed the expanse of the dig site all the way to the top. All the way to Dorgue.

Bryce hefted his bucket. The new face, Richard, was huffing and gasping somewhere below him like he was drowning in mud instead of hauling it.

Bryce dumped his bucket at the lift. The mud overflowed and Teague, gnawing away at his block of wood, looked ready to ride it up. He picked a splinter from his green teeth.

"Last call for this one," he said. "I'm calling a break."

The mice with their buckets gave a hearty sigh, Bryce among them. His knee didn't feel like his knee anymore. Just an angry lump of bony flesh. It stung. It burned. Bryce needed a break.

He carried his empty bucket with him to join the others sitting at the edge of the pit. Bryce peered down at those still hauling full buckets and saw Richard lagging behind. His tongue hung low from the corner of his mouth.

A rat called down. "Break! You lot come get some water."

Mice in the lowest circles let their shovels drop where they were and hurried up after the others. Breaks didn't last long, and it didn't do to waste them climbing all the way to the top. Bryce remembered days when he'd tripped up or upset one of the rats and missed a break. He'd been so thirsty he ended up popping a rock in his mouth and sucking it. He still did sometimes.

Richard drug himself up the ramp in a shamble. Vincent stood at his left, helping to heft the bucket. The new mouse's eyes were wild, white saucers that roamed the cavern seeing nothing.

Bryce sat on his bucket and stretched his leg in a way he hoped wasn't noticeable. Gavin came to his side.

"Sorry we couldn't trade," he said.

Bryce shook his head. "Not your fault. If Fletcher says 'buckets', there's not much to do about it."

He risked patting his knee. It was like touching a nerve with a shovel-blade.

Gavin said, "I've been thinking. Maybe you could fake an accident and get into Hospital. You'd get some medicine for your knee."

"And it'll be Dorgue who gives the medicine." Bryce shook his head. "No thank you. He'll sniff me out quicker than Vincent sniffed Gar—Well, you know."

A rusty squeaking filled the air and the mice turned to see the hulking shape of a cart as it wheeled out from the tunnel. A few mice from the Isolation ward pushed it. Bryce shivered to see them. Those older mice with their drooping faces and voiceless mouths scared Bryce. They scared him a lot. He was afraid that would be him one day; pushing out the water cart, passing out dented tin cups, and dipping a ladle into the barrel to draw out the water. Looking for all the world like a body without a soul…

Bryce didn't like thinking about it.

As Bryce and Gavin sat with their water (it was warm, but oh so good), they watched the others. Everyone had gathered on the top level and sat in groups, some large, some small. The cavern filled with hushed conversation.

Bryce spied Sampson. He cracked some joke and the others in his circle covered their mouths to hide their laughter.

Vincent stuck close to the new one, Richard, who had gulped his water too fast and now sat on the ground clutching his stomach.

Gavin nodded. "What do you think of him?"

Bryce didn't know. Had Dorgue sent him? The panic he'd seen on his face had been genuine, but him arriving the day after they nicked Garrow's knife? The day after Bryce *lost* it?

Bryce said, "You first. Think we can trust him?"

Gavin sat a moment, thinking. He took a sip. "Don't know yet. My gut says Dorgue sent him down as a snoop, but I might just be hungry."

"You're always hungry."

"Of course, I'm always hungry. I'm a genius." He tapped his noggin. "This much brain needs food to work proper. Right now it's stuck thinking about carrots when it should be mulling other things."

Other things. Like getting the knife back.

Bryce laid his head in his hands. A busted knee wasn't a proper enough punishment. He should've snapped his leg like an old shovel. He should've busted his head open on a rock.

should've, should've, should've...

Gavin batted his shoulder. "We'll fix it," he said. "You fell. We're lucky you're not worse off. Dropping something is the least of our worries, Bryce. *The least.* Don't worry, we'll find it."

"When, then?"

"Soon as possible, I'd say." He dropped his voice further. "Tonight, even."

"Do we risk sneaking out so soon?"

"I don't think we can afford not to. If...*you know who* is on to us, we have to risk it. No choice."

Bryce nodded. They had hoped the rat would be late in noticing the missing knife—at least a day—that would have given them time to get everyone ready.

But then Garrow woke up.

But then Bryce lost the knife.

but then, but then, but then...

At most, they had only a few more days before Garrow felt enough pressure to do something stupid. Bryce risked another look up at the walkways, but the lumpy rat was not to be seen. Somehow that was worse than seeing him.

Where was he? What did he plan to do?

"We need to have another talk with the others," Bryce said, voice so low air hardly left his mouth.

"Got that right." Gavin finished his drink.

Above them, they could hear the rattle and whine of the lifts returning in the dark. It'd be another few hours before the next break would be called, and Bryce wasn't much looking forward to standing up.

Gavin tapped his mug. Looked at the rats already lining up to send them down again. "The secret place?" he said.

Bryce nodded and hid his scowl as he stretched upright again, taking up his bucket. "The secret place."

EIGHT

A WATCH IS IN EFFECT, BY ORDER OF GREEN HILL. ANY SUSPICIOUS PERSONS ARE TO BE REPORTED TO YOUR CONSTABLE. YOU ARE NOT TO ENGAGE. ALL ARE TO BE INDOORS ONE HOUR BEFORE SUNSET UNTIL FURTHER NOTICE. THIS IS A PRECAUTION.

BE VIGILANT. REMBER THE SNAKES.

— A notice, recovered from the office of Jonathan Quick

G ARROW SPAT FROM THE walkway.

In his years with Dorgue, he'd been good at two things: yelling at the sniveling mice till they wiped their eyes and just got on with their work, and drinking himself sick on the bitter acorn ale Luther distilled. The first swallow made you gag, but every pull after?

Bliss.

Made your mouth taste like rotting leaves, though. He spat again and watched it fall past the other walkways, down into the dig site, and down into the pit.

"Hope I hit you, you little cuss."

He scratched at his wobbling neck and pawed at his swollen eye, hissing through his teeth. If it weren't for Fletcher, he'd be down there right now sniffing the troublemaker out. And when he found him...

He dropped his hand to where his knife should be. Felt the empty scabbard. What were the devils going to do with a knife anyway? With thirty rats standing between them and the surface, what could they hope to do?

They could hope to die as painlessly as possible, is what. Not that they would. Garrow would drag their worthless bodies to Dorgue. Then he'd have all the acorn ale he wanted. Dorgue would reward him.

So long as the old rat didn't find out about the knife.

Garrow pillowed his face into the crook of his arm and growled. He couldn't just *kill* the mice. He'd need to find his dagger first.

He'd just make the mice tell him where to find it, he decided. Then he'd drag them up to Dorgue. Yes, that would work. Then the other mice would fear him even more than they did Fletcher. That'd be nice.

That'd be real nice.

"Good view from here?"

Garrow pulled his face from his arm to see Worth strolling his way. The bridge didn't even sway at the rat's step. Garrow grumbled.

"I can look from where I please," Garrow said and peered back down to prove it. He saw some scuffle far below. A mouse nearly took a bad fall into the pit. That would have been fun.

Worth eyed Garrow's swollen face and wobbly eye. Tipped his head. "What happened to you? You had watch last night, yeah?"

Garrow shrugged. His shoulders pressed into his jowls. "Took a bad step."

"Took a bad step."

"Yeah."

Worth settled in next to Garrow, resting his arms on the walkway's rope handrail. The lithe rat gazed down at the lit sight below. They heard green tooth Teague holler up, "Slack!" and a whirring began high above in the Hoist, like a horde of wasps.

"Working fast," Worth said. "I'm running the dump crew today. You wanna join? If you can't sleep, some fresh air will do you good."

Garrow huffed a laugh. The only air he needed was what he found in the neck of a bottle, and he said so.

The clack, clack, clack, of the lift as it struggled back up echoed throughout the shaft. Garrow could smell the aroma of the raw earth freshly disturbed.

The lithe rat said, "You saw the new one? The Volunteer?"

Garrow nodded. "Dorgue must be get'n itchy to risk a new face down here."

"You remember the first group."

"I remember cutting their tongues out."

Worth said, "I don't think the boss would risk that again. Unless he felt we're close."

"Where'd he find him?"

"I found him," Worth said. "He wandered a little too close to the tree. Left me little choice. It was bring him down or kill him."

"Fletcher seemed angry."

"Fletcher's always angry."

The lift wobbled into view below them. Its tick, tick, tick, and musical groan sounded like a ship in frozen waters. Worth stood, hopped from the walkway, and flitted onto the mound of dirt. The lift didn't even bow beneath his weight.

That wasn't allowed, of course, but when you were as light on your feet as Worth you could get away with it. If anyone else tried that stunt, they'd turn the lift into a carnival ride, the kind that spun you round, and round, and round—then splat! Nothing but a smear of mud and guts on the ground far below; both them and anyone unlucky enough to be beneath it. Dead.

No, not dead. Obliterated.

Worth nodded as he passed, rising above Garrow's head. "Enjoy the walk up," he said.

But Garrow didn't hear him. He gazed down at the scores of mice moving like so many ants. He licked his lips.

"Obliterated."

Escape was the only thing to do.

Richard ate at a long table of smooth wood. Despite sitting in a room with a hundred other mice, each holding their own whispered conversations, Richard had never had a quieter supper.

Dinner tasted better than it was: a potato eye blinking through a thin broth and a browned crust that shot crumbs at every bite. Richard had never cried on account of a meal, but he came close with that dinner. His hands shook as he brought the bowl to his lips. Every inch of him ached.

"You can take the bowl back in line for some water," Vincent said. The mouse had led him from the dig site and introduced him to the others, an act the other mice clearly had not appreciated.

The limping mouse who had pulled him back from his nasty fall was named Bryce. The quiet one with the boxy ears was Gavin. And the others at their table were all named such-and-such and this-and-that. Richard nodded. Drank his broth. The chunk of potato bobbed against his lips.

The others were skittish of him. And that was fine, he told himself. He could win them over. The fear was so thick in the air he could smell it over the sweat of the work. He was sure he smelled just the same, but if he could...act like he wasn't. If he could smile, then maybe... maybe they'd trust him.

He'd need friends if he was going to get out of here.

Vincent leaned close and kept his voice hushed. "He's from the Deep Wood," he said. "Just like I am."

"Yeah," Gavin said. His face was strained. Untrusting. "He tell you all about it?"

Vincent blinked. His mouth set. "I can smell it on him, fathead. He ain't lying."

"B-but the Deep Wood is juh-juh-just outside," another mouse said. He was smaller than the rest and Richard had not paid attention to his name. One eye was blue and the other was dark brown. He showed his hands, unstained from the work (he'd been in the kitchen that day).

"I thuh-think everyone s-smuh-s..."

(he clicked his teeth in frustration and dragged his lips over the word)

"SMELLS...like the Duh-D-Deep Wood when the fuh-first come here."

Vincent shook his head. "No. Even—" he looked over his shoulder and whispered smaller, "even the rats smell of the Deep Wood some after they go up to dump the dirt. But him?"

He clapped Richard's shoulder.

Vincent said, "It's in him deep."

Yes. A week's hard trek through the dark will do that. Richard set down his bowl. It was dry as a bone.

If hailing from the Deep Wood earned him a good standing, then Richard would be from the Deep Wood. And it wasn't a lie. He *had* come from the Deep Wood. It was too risky to speak of Green Hill anyway. If the rats found out…well, they might have more questions. Richard wasn't that curious to find out how well he could keep a secret, especially if the one asking the questions did so with a sharp knife.

So for now, Richard would be from the Deep Wood. He'd be the best friend these mice had ever had. And he'd get out.

He'd get out. He'd get out. He'd get out.

Richard eyed the stuttering mouse and tried on his best smile. "What was your name, friend?"

"Simon. And I'm n-n-nuh…" he swallowed, "NOT your f-friend." He crossed his thin arms. "S-s-smiles mean nutt'n, if the teeth are sh-sh-shhhharp! And sometimes it's hard to s-s-s-see if thuh-th-they are."

Vincent leaned further, the whole of his arms rested on the table. "Please," he said. "If we just—"

The table rattled and, for a moment, Richard forgot his calm. He jumped, looking at the hulking mouse at the end—*Sampson*, he remembered. The big mouse had slapped the table.

"Another time," he rumbled and nodded toward the mouse walking to visit them.

This one. The mouse from Candle Hall who had the gall to laugh at Richard Aterox. He did his best to keep his face flat, but he'd never been good at ignoring a smug look.

The scars on his body were silver with sweat and he walked crooked with his left foot turned in and dragging. He offered a small smile as he came to the table.

"Hello," he said. His voice was hoarse. "I have come to welcome our new brother." He stretched an arm toward Richard, palm up. "My name is Bard."

He took the offered hand. Bard's grip was strong.

"Richard."

"Well met," Bard said, taking back his hand and looking it over, like Richard was some dirty thing from the street. His eyes shifted to the others at the table. "I trust the day's work was good for the blood?"

Richard wasn't used to folk asking how his blood was doing, but the others at the table seemed to know how to respond.

"Our blood is strong," Sampson answered. "And how goes it in your Burrow?"

Bard's smile ticked a little wider. "We fare well under the care of our masters," he said, "Each day brings us closer to our grand reward."

Richard's ears perked at that. "I've heard that a few times," he said. "This reward or yours, what is that exactly?"

The mice at the table turned to stare. And not just their table. A hush came over the dining hall as others cut short their little conversations to strain and listen in on a tastier one.

Careful now, Richard thought. *You don't want the rat's special attention. Lay low.*

Bard blinked at the question, and for a moment, Richard thought he had stumped him. Bard said, "Our reward is for our good masters to decide, both in measure and method."

"Oh, I see. Saint Sansa only brings sweets to the *good* little boys and girls, right?"

Another breath of silence. Bard's eyes dropped to half-lids. "It is not our place to question. Dorgue is wise beyond time, how can we expect to understand his reasons? We owe our lives to him. All he asks, is we trust him."

Gavin rolled his eyes behind a hand.

He smiled a tick wider. "Our masters have placed you in The Sticks, yes? The dark burrow?"

Richard looked to the others at the table. Most of them kept their gaze firmly in their bowls. Vincent and Sampson were the only ones to remain staring at Bard (Gavin too, but he hid it well).

"That's me," Richard said.

"Hard work, living so far from Dorgue's grace. You may have friends, yes, but they carry rebellious thoughts so deep in their minds, that it takes all the more labor to drive it out. Much better to bend the knee."

Don't hit him.

"Bend the knee, huh?" Richard asked.

"Yes. To Dorgue and his great work."

You could cause a lot of trouble here. Let. It. Go.

Richard smiled. "So what did you do then? Did you have to sing him a song? Bake a cake? I don't bend the knee to *anyone*."

More eyes flicked his way. Richard knew he should stop, but this mouse… He was so *full of it.*

Bard crossed his arms. The scars lining them were wide. "Dangerous words," he said, "Some ears remember better than others and more still remember things a mite *worse* than they actually were."

"Oh, I know a few folk like that. Good friends with one." Richard glared through slits and a smile. "You wouldn't happen to be *threatening* me, would you?" Richard's voice carried a little farther than he would have liked. The rats on the edge of the room took notice.

Vincent placed a hand on his arm, but Richard shrugged it off and stood from the table. The others looked from their bowls and stared at Richard in rapt attention. Gavin especially. The mouse with boxy ears looked from Bard to Richard, a smile playing at the edge of his lips.

Richard said, "Was there anything specific you were going to *remember* me saying, or would you like to brainstorm a little? Cause I have a few good ideas you might take a liking to."

The smile on Bard's face was dead. Richard could see the confusion in his eyes. No mouse had ever spoken like this, not in all their time in the Tree.

Rats were coming their way, passing between the tables.

Don't draw attention. Don't cause trouble.

Too late for that now. He took a step for Bard. "You have anything to say then? You seem to have gone awfully quiet all of a sudden."

Bard held his ground. His smile at last left, replaced by a grimace that slithered into being like a slug from under a stone. He said, "Our reward awaits us, you filthy dirt licker."

Richard punched him. Hard. He heard a dry *pop!* and his arm went numb from fingertips to elbow.

Blood gushed from Bard's nose and his eyes blinked wide as saucers. It was the sort of face Richard had seen visiting the training field and only happened when you smacked someone hard enough. This was the first time Richard had ever done it.

Bard's grimace twitched. He wobbled, like a tree deciding how to lay, and toppled back, landing with an ugly thud on the floor.

The effect wasn't immediate. The dining hall kept its silence. For a few moments, at least.

"MURDERER!" someone shrieked.

"THE POST, THE POST!" from another.

The dining hall erupted then. Mice from every table called out, some furious, some excited, some confused, all loud. The mice at Richard's table only looked on in shock. Vincent stared with his eyebrows raised and Gavin held both hands over his mouth, choking on laughter.

It was the rat with green teeth, Teague, who got to Richard first. He smiled wide. Splinters stuck out from his gums.

"You're the volunteer, eh?" he said. "Making friends?" He carried a short club, the kind made perfect for breaking skulls.

Richard had never felt a panic so true. His blood left his face and the shiver that had begun in his hands had spread up his arms like snake poison. He could feel his dinner spinning in his stomach.

The rat came at him with the club.

So Richard dove at him.

It was crazy. Richard didn't know what he was doing. There was no knowing anymore. He'd turned into a beast. The taste of metal was in his mouth and the rat struck him and struck him.

He heard screaming; his own and others. In the end, it took two of the rats to pry Richard off of Teague, and four to keep Teague from using his club to make good on his skull breaking.

The rat spat. Blood oozed from his shoulder and a nest of scratches covered his chest. His neck looked like a bruised apple and he hissed through his green teeth.

"I'LL GILL EM! LEGGO YOU SLOGS! LEHMEGO! I'LL TAKE HIS EYES! I'LL EAT 'EM!"

Richard understood somewhere that one of the rats (gruel rat, maybe) had him locked in place with his arms twisted around. But this was far away. All Richard could see were green, snapping teeth.

Then Fletcher thundered into the room and all fell still.

Every mouse dropped into their seats. Every face turned to their dinner's gone cold or empty before them. Even the rats who held fast to Teague jumped. The green-toothed rat was the last to notice the hulking figure of Fletcher pushing past the tables with eyes like pin-pricks and fists coiled at his sides. The mice he passed cowered at his approach, some slipping to hide beneath the tables. Fletcher paid them no mind. His eyes were set ahead, planted firmly upon Richard.

So far so good.

The hulking rat came to a stop beside Teague and the rats still gripping his arms.

In the quiet, all Richard could hear was the puff of his own breath. And in those moments, as his mind caught up with the rest of him, the pain in his wrist came awake.

The bone is split. Right down the middle. A sharp, hairline fracture. Either side twisting from its mate, marrow screaming. Twisting. Twisting.

Fletcher waved a hand and the slobbering, gruel rat dropped him. Richard fell to his knees clutching at his arm. His hand. His wrist.

fire fire fire fire

Keeping his eyes set on Richard, Fletcher said, "Care to explain yourself, Mr. Teague?"

Teague scowled and let his arms hang loose at his sides. A trickle of blood dripped from the fingers of his right hand.

"Won't my fault," he said.

"The Volunteer bit you?" Fletcher asked, his voice dangerously steady.

Some green escaped Teague's grimace. "A scratch," he said.

If Fletcher was happy with that answer, Richard couldn't tell. Richard tasted bile pawing the back of his tongue, but he held his gaze. Couldn't drop it now. Couldn't show fear.

The whipping post for you

Richard wanted to scream.

"And who's this?" Fletcher nudged a boot at the groaning mouse sprawled like a spider on the ground. "Gave good, little Bard a knock on the noggin?"

Teague nodded once. "He did."

"He did," Fletcher said. "Damaging a valued worker. That's an issue, Volunteer. I warned you about delays."

"But he doesn't do much digging, does he?" Richard heard himself say. Then he heard, "Candle Hall. Like you said this morning, they get more kitchen work than anyone. Kitchen isn't digging, sir."

Richard saw the change in the rat's eyes then. A blink. A tick of the brow. At Fletcher's side, Teague's scowl stretched into a green smile.

"Got a tongue, this one," Teague said. "You won't talk so good if we snip it out. Fit right in with Isolation, then. You'll—"

"Take him to Hospital," Fletcher said.

Teague blinked. He jut his teeth. "To *Hospital*? To the mud more like! You heard all his questions. Let me dunk 'em till he can't walk straight."

"You'll take him to Hospital."

Teague growled and spun to face Fletcher. The blood on the rat's shoulder had turned his fur into a shell that cracked as he raised his arm. "We should rip his GUTS out! We—"

Fletcher moved fast and Teague's nose broke like a carrot.

Fresh blood dotted the floor. The rat's mouth stretched in a shriek and his teeth pointed to the ceiling like fenceposts.

The silent spell in the dining hall snapped and mice ran over each other as they left in panicked waves. Only the ones nearest to the rats remained as they were, afraid the rats would reach to grab them if they moved.

Teague dropped his head between his knees and howled. Fletcher pointed to the rat just behind Richard. Gruel rat.

"Take him to Hospital." Fletcher smiled. "Dorgue will see to him."

This rat didn't hesitate.

NINE

"Aterox lied about many things."

"State them for the record."

"The Snake war, the hurricane, those bumpkins screaming in the Deep Wood. He knew more than he let on. Just look what he did after the death of his wife. Something was eating at his soul."

— Notes from the Posthumous Trial of Damian Aterox, 18th Sovereign of Green Hill

ALONE ON HIS COT, Garrow pressed the cool cloth into his eye and hissed at the sting. He'd find those guilty sods tonight. No doubt one of them had the knife hidden away in their bunk. But who?

Garrow had plenty to choose from.

The Sticks was most likely. Plenty of degenerates there. There was Sampson, who'd had his hand crushed under the lift a few years back.

The mouse had a stink eye. Big fella too. Might think himself big enough to take on ol' Garrow.

Hugo was another. Red furred lout. Talk about a stink eye. But then there were plenty of stink eyes in The Sticks. Garrow could take his pick!

He doubted anyone from Isolation would have the nerve. Too slack-jawed. And Hospital was too bedridden to do more than wet themselves. Besides, with all of that medicine spread over their bodies, Garrow'd smell them coming long before they showed their scrawny faces.

And Candle Hall, what a circus they were. With their 'yes sirs' and 'await the days'. Some of the idiots even meant it. And the ones that didn't...well, folk said there weren't no snakes left in the Deep Wood.

Garrow begged to differ.

Once the work was done...Candle Hall would be the first to go if Garrow had his way. But did they have the gall to steal his knife?

He dabbed his eye again and the pain came fast like a wasp-sting. How could anything hurt this much? He slapped at the frame of his cot. Vented. Waited for it to pass.

His eyelid had gone fat and purple—edging on black—and looked more like a grape than an eye. It hurt too much to sleep and Garrow didn't dare drink. Too much to do. Pain would keep him focused, anyhow.

Just gotta hurt the thief twice as much. He thought this as he stood and fetched his belt. His candle.

Garrow snuck from his room and ambled toward the Hoist. He could hear the *clackclackclack* of the winch as he stepped into the wooden room. The floor creaked beneath him.

Lou stood at the switch, watching the sharp whirr of the mechanism above—all those gears and bony cogs spinning like corks in a faucet. An angry cut ran the length of Lou's face and bent like a bowstring as he scowled. He pointed out Garrow's eye.

"You look like you had your face kicked in," Lou said and coughed into his sleeve.

Garrow imagined picking the squat, little rat off the floor and tossing him into the workings over his stupid head. Lou'd get all tangled and the Hoist would keep up its work like nothing was amiss. Nothing at all.

Lou hacked again into his arm and spat ugly on the floor. "Caught something digging graves outside. Some nasty pollen or such. Bloody, Deep Wood!"

Garrow said, "Ain't nothin' worth see'n out there, anyhow. What with winter inch'n close." He stepped to peer into the darkness. He could see the shape of the lifts as they rose. Long way down.

"Thought you had watch *last* night," Lou said. He wiped his mouth and held another cough in his throat. Sounded like a dull saw running over dry wood.

Garrow smiled. "I had a cousin once upon a time," he said. "Coughed for a month before he died of a bloody mouth. He would've made it just fine had he taken a vow of silence. A year at the minimum, doctor said. But no, he talked and coughed and talked and—"

"*You mind your own cussed business!*" Lou screamed. His voice tore, and he doubled over as he hacked, spit dribbling from his mouth. He didn't get his fool breath back until the two lifts bobbed up into view.

Fletcher and the others stood like soldiers, grim-faced from the fray. And some (Fletcher most of all) were sprinkled with little flecks of red. They shook the gray dust from their fur and stomped onto the creaking floor of the Hoist. Garrow stood aside as they filed out.

This was routine.

Boring, tedious, routine.

As rat after rat stomped by, Garrow saw Teague step from the far lift. He had a gush of blood drying down the face of his doublet like the pebbly vomit of a drunk. He walked with his head tipped back in the air, neck stretched and bobbing as he pressed his fingers stoutly into his snout.

"I'll *gill* 'em," he said, more mumble than talk.

Fletcher barked from the head of the room, his face a storm. "Stop your whining! You'll get your chance. If the mouse doesn't gut you the next time."

Another rat, Boil (who matched his name very well), snickered from the mouth of the tunnel leading out, "Maybe he'll knock out a few of your choppers. Do us a good favor, yeah?"

Lou, still wheezing at the switch, laughed and brought up a fresh bout of coughing.

Garrow frowned. "What in blazes happened?"

Teague glared, his green teeth showing. "Dat slime *Volunteer*. Guhm at me 'ike a serpent."

"Came at you like a wet skitter-bug, more like," Fletcher said. "You let your fool guard down and got your fool face broke."

Garrow chuckled, wincing as his eye throbbed. "New fella broke your nose?"

"*He gib!*" Teague said, pointing at Fletcher and showing more and more teeth. He marched toward the rat, bloody face still set skyward. "*You guhda gilledme!*"

"And you needed to take orders!" Fletcher's voice, with nowhere to go, thundered in the tiny space.

Teague's mouth clicked shut. The other rats, still lagging behind, made a hasty exit as the hulking rat steamed. Then Fletcher smiled a small smile.

"I don't care if the Volunteer defies you. I don't care if he spends the rest of his short life cursing you behind your back and sneaking slate into your food. But if you ever defy *me* again," Fletcher turned to leave, "I'll twist your neck like a dry twig."

Garrow, Teague, and Lou watched the lumbering rat march out. Their ringing ears sounded all the louder in the new silence. Garrow had known Fletcher to be something of a lit fuse, and this wasn't the first nose he'd broken, but he seemed somehow...*more.*

Lou cleared his throat in his sleeve and rubbed an absent thumb over the scar forming on his face. "Well, he's chuffed, in't he?" he said nodding ahead. "Never seen 'em so...chuffed."

Teague snorted and patted at his bent nose with a careful hand. "I'd still gill 'em," he said. "Ib I ehva get 'em alone..."

"Well, Sansa's blessing on you then," Garrow said. He lumbered onto the lift and waited for the swaying to stop. "Those mice run together. We made 'em that way. They hardly go anywhere alone."

He reached for the release and— Wait. He'd said something very interesting. Garrow paused to find it again. He chewed the side of his mouth...

"What are you wait'n on?" Lou said. He stood ready by the switch. "Too high and mighty to pull the lever yourself? Afraid to get a little grease on your hands? I bring the lift back up when you hop off, you fat tic. Not'n else."

"Shut up you twit, I know what I'm doing." Garrow pulled the release and the lift wobbled before lurching into its slow descent.

They never go alone, that was true, yeah? How many of them had he been chasing that night? How many knew where his knife was stashed? He grinned. The more who knew, the easier it'd be to find.

Then the lift jolted as if kicked, coming to a stop. Garrow clung to the moorings with his head level with the floor. A child's view.

Dorgue stood in the doorway of the Hoist, cane in one hand and a dark bag slung over his shoulder. The tilt of his head favored his non-cloudy eye. He smiled at the room.

"Going down?" Dorgue said.

Hospital was quiet. The other five occupants kept in their beds. And in the dark, Richard waited.

His bunk, carved into the wall, was a good deal taller than the ones he'd seen in the other burrows. He could sit up and the blanket he'd found waiting was soft. He was sorry to dirty it.

Did they bathe in this place? It had been a while for Richard. Bathing in the Deep Wood...wasn't recommended. If he got back to Green Hill

(not if, *when*)

filling a tub with steaming water would be the first thing he'd do. He'd soak for a *day*. Maybe two days. But thinking of getting clean just made him feel *dirtier*. If he got out

(not if, *when when when*)

he'd break every record crossing the Deep Wood to civilization. And, despite the sparking fire in his wrist, he thought he'd made good progress so far.

Those mice had been *enthralled*. All it took to be a leader was to stand on your feet when others could only sit on their hands: that's what Father had always told him.

Well. He'd stood up tonight, and taller than anyone else he'd seen in this pit. So far so good. Now, if he could focus on keeping his dinner where it was and stop shaking.

Dorgue will see to him, Fletcher had said.

What did *that* mean? Fletcher had seemed angry, sure, but nowhere *near what* Richard was expecting. He hadn't thought of it at the time (pushed it from his mind, more like) but he should've paid a visit to this whipping post by now. Part of him was relieved.

Another imagined Dorgue could be worse.

A good deal worse.

But this was fine. He was fine. All Richard had to do was get through it. Another day, maybe two, and Richard would be free as a skitter-bug. He'd be *fine.* Everything would be *fine.*

But that dirty little question came to mind: *how?*

Yes, he could survive another day. Maybe *more* if they put him in the kitchen on account of his wrist. *Yes*, he was confident he could get the other mice to trust him. He could be a leader. And *yes* Richard would grit his teeth and soldier through any beating they might send his way. He was an Aterox.

But *how* to get…

Out?

His thoughts roamed over the day's events. He pictured the walkways over the dig site as they faded into darkness above. That was the path, he knew. *But how to walk it?*

He wished he could ask Kathryn, this had been *her* idea, after all; going into the Deep Wood chasing ghost stories. Well, he'd *found* them, hadn't he?

He could hear Kathryn in his head. *Falling into the same pit as someone else doesn't count as finding them.*

"Technicality," he said, surprised at his own voice. He blinked in the dark.

Had he fallen asleep? It felt like it. He moved in his bunk, mindful of his hand, and stretched his eyes for light. Any light at all.

And then Richard could *see*. An orange glow shimmered on the tunnel walls beyond the mouth of the burrow. He heard a scratch, the dry rasp of a snake twisting over river stones, and the tap of a cane as the old rat crept closer. Closer. And then he was here.

Dorgue stood in the tunnel's mouth. The lantern in his grasp cast an orange light. The other mice of Hospital kept still. Made no sound.

Dorgue smiled at them, his dead eye colored by the flame. "You are my favorites, you know," the rat said as he entered. A wooden hook had been set in the ceiling, and he stretched to hang his lantern.

Dorgue said, "There is magic in setting something *right*. In mending what's broken."

He unslung the bag from his shoulder. It was a dark bag. Richard heard the musical *tink* of glass inside and Dorgue dropped it onto Richard's bunk, flipping it open. The husky smell of leather billowed to fill the space.

"You knocked over poor Bard?" Dorgue asked. "Knocked him flat?"

The rat turned his thin smile to Richard. The shadows on his face were deep under his eyes.

Richard said, "Is he…"

"Alright?" Dorgue finished. "Yes, yes, he's fine. We're a hardy sort here, I'm sure you'll find." He pulled out a sealed jar and a roll of gray gauze. The rat looked to Richard's arm.

"Fletcher told me you clutched your wrist like a sailor on a line. Here, let me see it." He held out his hand. Richard expected to see a tremor in the old rat's hand, but it was steady as stone.

Or still as a corpse, Richard thought.

Dorgue waited.

Richard set his wrist in the rat's palm.

"Tell me when this hurts," Dorgue said and began to squeeze. Immediately it hurt, and Richard said so.

Dorgue tilted his head. "No, it doesn't," and squeezed more.

A burning blossomed in Richard's arm. He sucked his breath. "It does! It's—"

"No." The rat's hand became a clamp, closing tighter and tighter. And then, as Richard began to see colors dancing and as the room turned to white, Dorgue let go.

"You didn't start to sweat till the end there," the rat said. "It's a fracture, but only a little one. Hairline."

Richard clutched his arm to his body. His fingers pulsed and felt ready to burst, and his wrist…he could *feel* the fracture now. He knew exactly where it was. It glowed with bubbling fire.

A wave of nausea came then, and Richard threw his head over the side of his bunk until it passed.

I'm dying, I'm dying, some part of him cried, but Richard ignored it. Waited for it to be over. He tried to think of the fool, of Green Hill and open air. Of water so cold it hurt your teeth.

He tried. Really, he did.

"That's unfortunate," Dorgue said, sidestepping the mess. "Dinner's a long way off, you know. Shame to waste tonight's."

Richard wiped his mouth. His hands were shaking. "I'll live," he said.

Dorgue smiled. "*That's* the spirit. Whatever doesn't kill you, eh? Perhaps you were a gift from the Deep Wood after all."

He set the sealed jar by Richard's side and disappeared elbow-deep into the dark, clinking bag. "Open up that," he said, "and smear the cream on your wrist."

Richard took up the jar. It was round and made from rough clay, and its top was sealed with clear wax. It twisted off like the crown of an acorn.

The aroma wafted up like a heavy fog: rosemary and jasmine.

And something else.

Dorgue pulled a scalpel from his bag and cut a length of the gauze. Looked as easy as cutting air. Hardly made a sound. Bryce caught a glimpse of the blade as it flashed in the meager light and sucked in his breath.

The rat winked.

"My window might have been my most promising find, but I've other prizes to show for my work." He held up the scalpel. Set into the elegant, polished wood winked a shard of wild glass. Richard's mouth dried. That blade could slice through bone and marrow in one swing.

"Nothing cuts better," Dorgue said, reading his thought. "Quite the trouble to set it, though. Not to mention shaping the thing. The only thing that can cut wild glass *is* wild glass, you know."

A chill eked into Richard's arm and it already began to numb, but he hardly noticed this. His eyes remained locked on what Dorgue knuckled over his fingers like a wand at a birthday party.

Wild glass had never been the safest of materials to work with. Each shard was all too eager to open your hand and sop its blood. Few blades had ever been made. To fasten the stuff to a hilt and carry it on your person, took courage. Courage and many spare fingers in the making.

He *couldn't* be seeing what he was seeing. But he was.

The rat vanished the scalpel back into his bag and took up the gauze.

"A fracture like you have can only be bound and rested," he said. "The cream will soak into your skin, invigorate the marrow, and help some with the pain. Here, give me your arm."

Richard didn't have a choice.

The rat rolled the length of the gray gauze round and round his forearm, from wrist to elbow. At the last, he dabbed a finger into the cream to help keep the cloth in place. It was tight and woke a dull ache, but Richard thought he'd manage. Dorgue lent back his arm.

"Maybe you'll think twice before striking out against your own kin," Dorgue said, wagging a finger, as if Richard was a child who'd climbed the cabinets for a cookie, instead of busting someone's face.

"Your brothers are all you've got now, and I love each of them *dearly*," the rat said. "This is all new to you, so I'm lenient. But if you hurt one of them again…" The rat pouted. Shrugged his shoulders. "You only need *one eye* to dig. And some get by just fine with none at all!"

Dorgue pointed to a mouse, nearer to the burrow's end, a larger fellow with a band of yellowing cloth tied over his eyes. Dorgue snapped his fingers.

"You work just fine, Mr. Kip?"

The mouse straightened, his mouth twitching at one side. "Plenty fine, sir. Plenty fine."

"You chop potatoes, yeah?"

"I chop potatoes."

"*Gooood lad!*" Dorgue beamed. "Obedience is rewarded here, but so is *disobedience*. Both in kind. And if you cause further trouble—make us fall in our workloads—I might have to reconsider your position as a volunteer in this tree."

Dorgue's hand flipped from his bag. Richard saw a glint of amber light, but he was too late to dodge. The wild glass drew an inch-long, slash down his cheek.

A tally mark.

Richard clapped a hand to his face and recoiled, bashing his head on the bunk's wall. The rat held the blade before his face.

"That's strike one. You won't get a strike *two*, I'm afraid."

Richard took his hand from his face and stared at the blood on his palm. It had smeared with the grime in his fur and turned black.

Dorgue reached once more into his pack. "I almost forgot," the rat said, talking as if he *hadn't* just tried to cut Richard's *face* off. He pulled a little vial from his pack and set it on Richard's bunk.

"This is for the pain when it comes. One drop in water, no more, and that will numb it some. *Don't* drink it straight. Do you hear me, Volunteer? Look at me. *Do not drink it straight.* There are better ways to *un*-volunteer yourself. Much better ways."

Richard took it in his hand.

Sealed with a cork, the liquid inside looked to glow red, but that was a trick of the rat's lantern, surely. There was enough for a swallow at the most. Even drinking it by drops, the stuff wouldn't last long.

Dorgue reached to take down his lantern, sending the shadows moving in a way that gave Richard a headache. The rat paused at the burrow's mouth. Turned his dead eye to Richard.

"Sleep well," he said.

Then he left.

TEN

Secrets are best kept by knives.

— A Common Saying

ONE FOUND THE SECRET place just before rounding on Hospital. It was Gavin who discovered it. They'd only known about it for about a year and—so far—had risked meeting there only a handful of times.

Leaving the burrow at night was always a risk. Another mouse could notice and go to the rats. It had happened before over smaller sins. Or Candle Hall itself could be watching and setting traps like they had the night before.

But the biggest reason they didn't often meet at the secret place: it was a bit of a squeeze to get in.

After all had quieted and the muted snores had fallen into their final rhythms, Bryce felt a tap on his shoulder. He opened his eyes to darkness and leaned heavily on Gavin's arm to unfold from his bunk. His knee sparked once or twice. His leg was stiff. The others shuffled along with him as they left the burrow, he didn't know how many.

Then his mind played a trick. Bryce felt like he was repeating the night before; following after Vincent to steal Garrow's knife.

How much can change in only a day…

They didn't go far. Gavin brought them to a halt with a click of his fingers. After a moment, he brought Bryce's hand to a grip on the wall and patted his shoulder.

"You first," he whispered.

Bryce gritted his teeth and climbed.

Digging in a downward direction lends itself two problems. First, every day the journey to get the dirt out of the hole stretched a little longer. And second, as the chore of moving the dirt grew, so did the chore of getting everything you need down there to start with. The hour-and-a-half wasted lining up and passing out tools wasn't ideal for anyone, rat or mouse. So, as the hole whittled farther down, so did the burrows.

Every few years, Dorgue called a break to the work to have the mice dig out new homes and seal up the old ones. Bryce could still remember that first burrow. It had seemed enormous, as cavernous as the dig site even. But as the years went on the burrows didn't need to be as big. Fewer bodies to take up space, you see. Someday, it would just be a handful of mice down so deep and air stretched so thin, that they'd have to take turns breathing. Bryce couldn't stand the thought.

That's why they needed to get out soon. Every day lost was another few inches added to their prison.

They needed the knife. They needed to plan. So the secret place came in handy.

As Bryce climbed, the holds came easier. Then his nose found the little space beyond, just hidden from any torchlight that might shimmer by. He had to stretch to reach it, but then he twisted his way up and in. If he had any claustrophobia, it had been driven from his heart long ago. Dorgue's tree was good for that, at least. He found the small space comforting. Here no one could get him. Here he could hide.

Then Bryce popped from the dusty floor of the forgotten burrow and shook the cobwebs from his ears. The place had been sealed off from the main shaft, yes, but some of it was still open—a little pocket of space in the dark.

Stubbed candles rattled across the dusty floor as Bryce crawled from the hole. His fur felt chalky from the cloud he'd stirred crawling in. The others followed close behind and Bryce heard someone stifle a sneeze.

The last one up spread the blanket he'd brought from his bunk over the seam in the floor.

A spark jumped in the dark.

Vincent had cut a corner from his vest and reduced it to strings and ribbons. This he sparked a stone over till he had an ember, and from that ember, they lit one of the stubbed candles.

The space was cramped. The mice he saw in the new candlelight had to sit hunched to make room. Gavin and Simon kept near the covered crack in the floor. Ed, a small mouse with dowdy, white fur mostly coated in the dark mud of the pit (he'd dug that day), settled next to Bryce. Sampson was too broad to make the climb to the secret place, so a red mouse named Hugo had come along in his stead. Vincent set the candle center of them all.

"We'll make this quick," he said, "Some of us will have to sneak down into the old tunnels, and we can't waste any time."

Ed, Simon, and Hugo all shared a worried glance. Ed spoke up. "Um...why do we have to go to the old tunnels?"

Simon's mouth twitched. "Duh-d-did y-you get the nuhuh-knife?"

Bryce wanted to sink into the stone and dirt around them. They hadn't had the chance to talk about any of what had happened with others. Couldn't risk it. He wished more than ever he had just clocked his head on the way down and been done with all of it.

"We stole the knife from Garrow," Vincent said, choosing his words. "Then we lost it. But it's safe. It's in the old tunnels."

Hugo sighed long and ugly. "Why in the blue heck did you *lose it*? You get mud in your eyes?"

Bryce shook his head. Raised his hand. "It was me. I dropped it."

Bryce could feel their eyes on him. Hugo opened his mouth, but then closed it again and crossed his arms in a huff.

Ed's brows dipped as he mulled over Bryce's words. His lips rolled in careful thought. "Um...where exactly did you...uh, drop it?"

"Could you find the place again?" Gavin asked.

Hugo muttered through his whiskers. "He'd better be able to."

Vincent shushed them. "Yes, yes, we'll get it back. That's not what we need to talk about," he said.

"Yeah, the new guy." Hugo shrugged his shoulders. "He bopped Bard right between his stupid eyes. So I like him."

"But do we *trust* him?" Gavin asked. "Vincent and Bryce were with him all day, what do they think?"

Bryce wasn't sure. Yes, Richard had nearly killed himself doing the work and his show over dinner had been real enough. But then Fletcher hadn't whipped him for it. Now he was in Hospital and kitchen duty.

Not a bad first day. It might have been a *great* first day. But had it been on purpose?

Bryce looked to Vincent. "You said you smelled the Deep Wood on him?"

Vincent nodded.

Ed pursed his lips, wrestling for words. "Um…what does the Deep Wood smell like?"

They fell silent for the answer. Even Hugo looked up from his grumbling to frown at the rust-colored mouse sitting at their head.

Vincent blinked. Bryce could see his eyes working through it, zipping from one side of his face to the other as if the answer were hiding on the dark side of his nose.

"I can't…put a word to it," Vincent said and pressed his knuckles to his forehead. "It's like…my Maw and Paw. Like feeling warm and…safe." He nodded, sure of it. "The Deep Wood smells like safety."

They had been so focused on Vincent's words, on imagining what it might be to remember such a place, they didn't notice the intruder till the blanket thrown over the seam in the floor jumped like a ghost, nearly catching light on the candle.

Bryce scrambled back, spraying pebbles. Simon jumped, smacking his head on the low ceiling and sending fresh dust down on all of them. Gavin shot an arm down into the seam. Hugo ducked behind Vincent.

The rats had found us, Bryce thought. They'd pull them down, drag them to the dig site, and hold them under the mud till everything went away.

And that'd be it.

Gavin's face strained as he struggled with whoever was beneath them. Simon got his senses again and rushed to help, but ended up standing uselessly by, batting his fists against the sides of his head as he stuttered.

Vincent pushed between them and reached into the floor. "Keep your voices down, it's not them. It's NOT them!"

Vincent pulled the dust-covered mouse up to join them. "I told you," he said. "He smells like the Deep Wood."

Vincent hauled the new mouse into the room by the scruff of his neck. Dust and cobwebs clung to his ears and his arms swung loosely at his sides. He swayed, blinking at the candlelight.

Richard smiled. "Smell like the woods, eh?" he said. Then he laughed.

Hugo marched from the wall and got in his space. Shoved a finger at his chest. "How did you get here?" he said.

Richard chuckled and waggled his fingers at Hugo's nose. "*Magic*."

Gavin pushed the two apart and looked into Richard's eye, stretching the lid down with his thumb.

"His pupils are confused. Dorgue gave him some of his loopy juice" he said.

Vincent nodded. "Yeah, I can smell it. You're supposed to take that with water, a drop at a time."

"Yeah. *Yeaaaah*." Richard tossed a hand at Vincent's shoulder. "Only took a drop. Just a taste. Works great! Hotter than hellfire though."

Hugo crossed his arms, eyes bugging from their sockets. "How did you find us?" he asked.

Richard shrugged. "Couldn't sleep. Too much to think about. Heard someone moving around. Followed you. And I must say, you have a lot of fun things to talk about. A lot of fun things. Am I repeating myself? Can I sit down?"

Vincent helped him to settle and Ed fixed the blanket over the hole once more. He smoothed out the wrinkles and eyed Richard, the cogs in his head turning. "Uh...your arm...is alright?"

Richard smiled wide and held his arm out for the others to see. The bandages wrapped around his wrist and forearm had begun to harden into a shell.

"It hurts. It hurts a lot, but Dorgue's stuff is…making me not care so much about it. You could probably…sock me 'cross the jaw and I wouldn't even…bat an eye."

Richard smacked his lips. Looked into the candle flame. For a time, everyone kept silent. They studied the mouse before them, shivering where he sat, but his face looked content and his eyes remained half-lidded.

Bryce's heart still stumbled to catch up at Richard's sudden entrance. How much had he heard? Bryce set his forehead into his knuckles. If he *was* with the rats…

Richard twitched as if waking and chuckled. "I'm…I'm hungry," he said, giving the room a toothy smile. "I want some fish."

They looked among themselves, confused. Vincent leaned closer, brow dropping in memory. "*Fis,*" he said. "I…I remember *fis.*"

"No, no, no, no," Richard said, waving his hands. "Fish— S, H —Shh. Like that. Fish."

Vincent tried it, sounding the word slowly. "Fish."

"Yeah, that's it," Richard laughed. "Catch it, gut it, fry it in oil and lemon. The best."

But then his laugh grew sour. Richard's face twisted into a deep frown. Shadows flowed over his face. He let out a sob and dropped his head into his hands.

"I'm so…I'm so *hungry.*" He pulled at his ears and shook his head in a fit like he was trying to tear them off. Ed stepped in to settle him down, but Richard pushed the little mouse away. He stood to pace, still clutching at his head.

"This was just supposed to be a…*a survey*! Get in, get out. Weren't supposed to be *rats*! Weren't supposed to be *you*. You lot ought to be scattered to the winds. Frost Marshes to the north, Gob Desert to the south. Sold to caravans and mines and…wherever else the scum-faced traitors would've made a profit. Food, in some places. The Wastes, maybe. There're *crazies* out in The Wastes."

Richard made to stretch to his full height, but his head clumped against the rocky ceiling. He twisted and met either wall of the burrow with his hands. Richard's fists shook and his teeth bared in an ugly grimace.

"There's. Not. Enough. *Room.*"

Vincent placed a careful hand on his shoulder. He spoke softly. "Breathe, remember? You gotta breathe. Just sit back down and we can talk. Watch the candle, there. Don't knock it over."

Richard dropped back to his place against the wall, knees tucked into his chest. He wasn't smiling anymore.

"I hate that stuff," he said.

Gavin nodded. "Messes with your head."

"Can't stop thinking about fish."

Bryce leaned forward. "Is it…like eel? We get that sometimes. The rats—"

Richard shook his hand at him. "I don't want to talk about that. I want to talk about this knife."

As one, the mice shushed him, pressing fingers to their lips.

"Will you whisper!" Hugo hissed.

Richard threw his hands in the air, "who's gonna hear us?"

Hugo threw a pebble at him. "*You did!*"

"Only because I wedged myself into that blasted crack!" Richard bit his tongue. Opened his hands. "Look, it's been a long day. So, hows-a-bout we start over, yeah?" He held a hand to his chest. "My name is Richard At—," he blinked. Smiled. "*Towner*. Richard Towner. What's yours?"

They went in a circle, starting with Gavin. They got stuck on Simon, but once they got to the last mouse in the room, he kept his arms crossed and mouth shut. Vincent answered for him.

"And that's Hugo," he said. "He's not as grumpy as he looks."

Gavin nudged the frowning mouse. "Naw, he's worse. Aren't ya, Huey?"

"Don't call me Huey."

Richard seemed to not hear any of this. His chin hovered over his chest as he tapped his fingers, repeating each name. "Right. Are there any more of you? I mean…" he waved his hands, "Is there anyone else you trust? Or is this it?"

The mice shared a look.

"Um…" Ed struggled between deciding whether to frown or smile. He settled on a raised eyebrow and a stern mouth. "We aren't sure we trust *you*…exactly."

Ed nodded toward the covered entry. "On account of you…spy'n and all…well, I'm sure you're a nice guy, Mr. Richard, knocking Bard flat and such…but you haven't made the best…" Ed frowned, searching for the word.

"Impression?" Richard guessed.

Ed squinted. "Ain't that when you fall and make a dent in the mud?"

"Th-that don't mh-matter," Simon said and leveled a finger at Richard. "Trust or nuh-not, You are a lul-luh-lul—"

"Liability?" Richard guessed again, brow raised

"Yes," Simon answered, his face stormy. "Eh-everyone here we nuh-know."

Vincent nodded. "Yes, their strengths and weaknesses. What they'll do under pressure. What they won't. I don't deny Richard is new to us, but he's new to the rats too! He surprised them. They don't know what to expect of him. We can use that!"

"To what end? *What are you talking about?*" Hugo said. "You wanna sic him on Fletcher next? Or Worth? That stunt won't work twice!"

"That isn't what I'm saying."

"THEN WHAT—"

(shhh!)

"*...then what are you saying?*"

Vincent pinched the bridge of his nose. "I'm saying what choice do we have but to use what we got? Yesterday, it was just us making a break for it. Today, we have a mouse who *lives* in the Deep Wood. He can guide us through. All of us."

"We still haven't decided if we trust him!" Hugo said.

Gavin crossed his arms. "I thought you said you liked him."

"That was before he leaped into the room like a *jack-ghost!*"

Richard placed his hands on his chest. "So sorry. Next time I'll sing softly and make scratching noises."

"What are you even talking about?"

Richard grabbed hold of Hugo's collar and pulled him nose to nose. Hugo jumped, but he was too surprised to get away. It happened so fast, like the strike of Fletcher's whip, that the others could only look on with gaped mouths.

Hugo struggled. "Let...Let GO of—"

Richard growled. "Shut. Up. Alright? Just...shut your mouth for two seconds."

He shoved him into Gavin, whose eyes were squinted into slits. Watching.

"I went through a lot of trouble to find all of you," he said. "This tree is in the armpit of the Deep Wood. There's nothing to eat except what you bring with you and if you step wrong, it's *you* who gets eaten."

"What are you saying?"

"I'm saying I don't belong in here. *You* don't belong here. And if those rats think I'm gonna spend another day in this mud-hole..." He closed his eyes. Took a deep breath. " Now, I don't expect you to understand, but there's air up there. There's sky and trees, and even if the Deep Wood tries its level best to skin us as soon as we poke our heads out..." Richard pulled at his ears again. Took another breath.

"All the same. If I don't get out of here I'm gonna self-destruct. So what's the plan? Come on, I'm not a snitch! If you don't believe me, then go ahead and kill me now. If I found your secret hiding place and I *was* a spy, you think I would have barged in?"

"You're not helping your cause," Gavin said.

"You're not—"

(shhh!)

"*...You're not helping yours.*" Richard pulled at his face. Stared at the ceiling. "You stole a knife, I've gathered that much. How long can you keep that secret?"

Hugo crossed his arms. "That's none of your—"

"Your window is closing, smart guy! This situation is a ticking clock! How long until the rats raid the burrows to come looking for it? A week? *Tomorrow*? You can't expect me to believe you stole it without knowing you had to move fast after you did. *So what was your plan?*"

Hugo's face burned like he held a flame in his mouth. He held Richard's gaze. "Alright," he said. Hugo pointed to Vincent. "You say he's from the Deep Wood."

"Yes."

"You say you trust him?"

Vincent bit his lip. Scratched his neck. "If he's lying, we're already dead."

Simon spoke up. "Let's v-vho-vote!"

Vincent nodded. "Alright. I like that. You like that, Richard?"

The mouse stretched his face, feeling the cut on his cheek. "I think I've spoken my peace well as I could," he said. "Can *I* vote?"

"You just keep quite a moment longer. *If you can,*" Hugo said. He faced the others. "All for?"

Bryce watched them. Some, like Ed and Vincent, had their hands up with no hesitation (though Ed might have been watching Vincent to see how he would vote). Simon struggled a moment but then voted yes.

That left Hugo, Gavin, and Bryce; two of which had their arms stoutly crossed.

The others were watching him. Vincent's face was blank. Hugo's was steaming. Ed was picking his nose.

They were looking at him. Waiting.

Bryce didn't know what to do. Didn't know what to think. He didn't know if he could trust this new mouse. He couldn't even trust himself! He was the idiot who lost the knife, who dropped it like a fool!

Richard was looking at him. Studying him. He kept perfectly still, hands cupped before him in thought, but his eyes were wild things, like glass and fire. Bryce thought back to the dining hall, Richard lunging at Bard and coming at Teague like hellfire burned beneath him.

There had been nothing thinking about those eyes. They had been void. They had been brutal, and terrifying.

And pointed at the rats.
Bryce raised his hand.

ELEVEN

We can hear the ones of old. We live in their towers. Did they ever leave? Can you hear them? Can you?

— An epigraph, found beneath the foundations of the Century Gate

T HEY DECIDED TO SEARCH for the knife that very night and took along the candle from the secret burrow. Vincent had tried to argue that Bryce should return to the burrow, but Bryce couldn't accept that. It was his mess. He'd help clean it up. Didn't matter that his knee crunched like salt ground between two stones. He was gonna get that knife back. They'd wasted enough time.

The climb down and hike past the burrows went smoothly enough. Richard kept knocking into him in the dark, and when they crept past Candle Hall, nothing moved in the light of their little candle and no surprises waited for them on the tunnel floor. All the same, Bryce held his breath until the candle glow vanished behind them.

They stood before the gap in the wall; the drop into the Old Tunnels. Even in the dark, Bryce could feel the space beyond. The cold he felt in his bones could have come from the ghosts that hid in the dark places, creeping through cracks in the rock like nightmares between dreams.

(We have your blade. Looking for it? Want to trade?)

Bryce shivered.

Vincent sniffed the air. "I don't smell anything."

"No guard?"

"At least not Garrow. Still, best be quick."

Hugo crossed his arms and scowled into the dark. "This is as far as I go. I'm on buckets in the morning. I'm no good to anyone if I fall over dead."

"That's fine." Vincent slipped through the gap.

Ed and Hugo returned to the burrow, Ed with only a grumbled mention of *good luck.*

Bryce pushed the ghost from his mind and followed after Vincent. The air in the old tunnels was musty and made his throat sore. Richard found them in the dark and Gavin took the lead.

After a little way, they felt safe enough to light the candle. Once the spark turned to flame, the space came to life around them. The shadows stretched and reached for them as they walked. Richard especially looked unnerved at the sight. He stared ahead but the candle's light only went so far.

"It's like...walking on the bottom of the sea," he said.

Gavin made a face. "*Sea?* I thought you were from the Woods."

Richard raised a brow. "I've been around," he said. "Here and there."

Then he smiled. "So will you, and that's a promise."

"Let's just focus on where we're standing, for now," Vincent said. "We're nearly to the crossways, yeah?" This he asked Gavin.

The mouse nodded. "Not far. Bryce, you said there was a drop?"

Oh was there ever. Bryce was glad he followed at the back of the group. "You should see it fine with the light," he said. "Just…be careful."

Richard pointed to Bryce's leg. "That what happened to your knee? You fell? Bit of a hazard, this place. Must be easy to get lost…"

"There used to be a rhyme," Vincent said. "Back when Dorgue was more…liberal in the work, he had the mice digging in all directions. They say—"

"Who says? The rats?" Richard placed his hands on the rocky wall of the tunnel. "You're telling me Dorgue had these passages…dug out?"

Vincent frowned. "Well, yeah. How else would they get here?"

"They could be natural."

Gavin squinted. "*Natural?*"

"Natural caves. I mean, look at this," he ran his hands up and down the seams of the wall. "How far do these go on?"

Forever. Bryce had heard stories of mice who'd gotten lost and never came back. Of rats who never came back. But then…if they did go on and on…

"Natural tunnels?" Bryce asked.

Richard let his hand drift away from the wall. He sniffed the thin chalk clinging to his fingers. "Maybe. If we explored enough, we might even find a way back up."

Gavin barked out a laugh. "You don't think we know this place? I've been here my whole life, guy. I've explored miles of these tunnels."

"So why haven't you gotten out through here? Follow the tunnels back up?"

"'Cause I don't wanna starve to death. These tunnels twist and loop like weaves in a blanket. You might follow a tunnel up to find it drops down twice as far! And when you double back, you'll find more passageways than you remembered. Then you're left guessing. Only takes one wrong guess to ruin all the rest."

Gavin brought the candle up to peer around the next bend. The light danced on his face as globs of wax dribbled down his fingers.

"I'm good at feeling my way through," he said, "but not that good. Not to the top."

Richard twisted his lip. "Well, can't fault me for asking. You're the guy with experience."

Gavin huffed "Experience got nothing to do with it," he said. "You gotta keep your ears in the air."

They arrived at the crossways, where tunnels mixed and tangled in unknowable directions. It unnerved Bryce how nothing ever changed down here. He could have been gone a day or ten thousand years and the crossways would have remained unchanged. No air to move the dust, no hands to smooth the walls. Unbreathing dead things, these tunnels were.

Gavin held the candle high. "You remember which passage you took?"

Bryce did. The one to the left, angling up. The one that looked like a stretching mouth.

"Well, this is a lovely funhouse," Richard said. "How far—"

"I don't know." Bryce pushed past him. "Let's just find it."

The space forced them to move single file. Vincent had to duck to get in. The others felt their ears brush up along the ceiling as they climbed, and it *was* a climb, steep enough to bring out a sweat. Then the tunnel leveled out and Gavin forced a halt.

The hole gaped in the floor before them. It was an odd shape and hugged the wall on the left. If Bryce had just walked closer to the right, he would have missed it altogether.

Dumb, stupid luck.

"I imagine this is the spot?" Richard called from behind, trying to peek past Vincent's arm.

Gavin inched past the drop, letting the little candle cast its light down. He said, "Unless there's some other hole farther on, I'd say this is it."

"It is," Bryce said, and moved to look down. By the candle's light, Bryce could just make out the level below. Vincent and Richard crowded in to steal a look.

"Can we climb it?" Vincent asked.

Bryce shrugged. "I did last night. Who wants to go first?"

"No need," Gavin said. "Only takes one pair of hands to find a knife." They stood aside as he scrambled down, keeping a hold of the candle with his free hand. He shimmied far as he could, hung by his arm, and dropped. He landed on his bare feet with a clap.

"See it?" Vincent called down.

Gavin roved the floor with the candle, crossing in and out from view as he searched. Every second that ticked by was another weight dropped on Bryce's soul. *What if Garrow* had *found it? What if they returned to the burrow empty-handed?*

Gavin came to a stop, a circle of light in the dark. He huffed once. "Maybe I could use a few more eyes."

"I'll do you one better," Richard said, working off his shoe. "How big was this knife? Rat-sized, I imagine. Pretty big?"

Vincent nodded, his brow creasing. "What are you getting at?"

"This."

He dropped his shoe through the floor. It thunked at Gavin's left and jumped like a cricket into the dark, end over end. Gavin tried to follow after with the candle.

"That won't possibly work," Gavin said, as he vanished from view.

Richard took hold of Bryce's shoulder as he lowered himself down into the floor, his face twitched once or twice, but Richard managed to clamber down until he trusted gravity to do the rest. He followed after Gavin into the dark.

Vincent looked at Bryce from across the drop. "You wanna go down?" he said.

No.

Yes.

Bryce rubbed his face. Even sitting as he was, his knee was on fire. He almost wanted to jump down again, as if repeating the fall would correct it somehow.

Vincent said, "I could lower you down and Gavin could catch you."

"We'd only have to climb back up again."

Vincent nodded. Peered back down into the space below. "They'll find it," he said. "It couldn't have gone far. You don't happen to remember which way it bounced?"

Bryce couldn't even say which way *he* had bounced. He shook his head. "If Garrow had it...we'd know, right? He'd gloat."

"Oh, certainly," Vincent said. "He'd wear it on his belt and march down the line with his drunken smile. He didn't find it, Bryce. It's wedged in some groove, here or there." He held out a hand. "Come on, I'll hoist you down."

Bryce took his hand and ambled down through the floor. He was hardly over the lip when Gavin shimmered into view beneath them.

"We think we found where it went," he said and wiped his mouth. "We might have a problem."

Richard was down a shoe. His good shoe. The one with the fresh laces. Now he'd have to hobble like some drunk until they found it again. *If* they found it again.

Just their luck to find out these blasted tunnels went even deeper. He pointed out the twisted gap in the wall to the others. It looked more like the bloated roots of a tree than rock. There was something of a slit leading farther in. They only found it because Gavin had been gliding his ears along the wall and heard...*open space*, or whatever. Richard hadn't heard anything until he stuck his head into the narrow twist of an opening. Like cramming your face into a sea shell.

"How could it have gotten in there?" he said. "It's not even opened towards the rest of the room!"

Vincent got down on his hands and knees to look. He sniffed. Closed his eyes. Another sniff.

"I smell your boot," he said.

Richard crossed his arms. "*No*. You smell the boot currently on my foot. I'm standing right next to you!"

"Take a few steps back then," Gavin said.

Richard rolled his eyes, but he complied, stomping a few paces away. He leaned against the far wall and crossed his arms. Too quickly though. He winced as he loosed the grip on his wrist. He wanted some more of those drops.

"How's this?" he asked. "far enough?"

Vincent shoved his face into the wall. One of his ears twitched. A moment passed.

"I smell it the same," he said. "Your boot's down there."

"And the knife?" Bryce asked.

"Well, I can't smell the knife, but it's worth going down to see. If only to fetch Richard's shoe."

"Can you see how far down it goes?" Bryce asked.

Vincent shook his head. Looked to Gavin, who spent a moment in thought.

Gavin said, "Couldn't see far with the candle because there's a turn, but it *sounds* like it opens up. Should go at it slow all the same. Could end in another drop. How close did Richard's boot smell?"

"It doesn't smell so close that I'm pushing my nose into leather, but it doesn't seem that far either. A few yards."

"A few yards," Gavin repeated. He set his face. "Alright, I'll crawl in and get a feel of it."

He passed the candle to Vincent.

"You're going in blind?" Richard asked.

"I can't crawl with the candle," he said. "I'll be careful. Besides, it might not go on too far." He shuffled onto his belly and wriggled his head and shoulders in. He kicked as he worked his way around the turn.

His voice came muffled. "We might be able to pass it through."

"Pass what through?" Richard asked.

"The candle," he said, sounding far away.

Richard looked to Bryce. To Vincent. "Should we...hold on to him? In case there *is* a drop?"

Vincent shrugged. "He's fine."

"What if he slips and bashes his head in?"

"Gavin's the best in these tunnels," Vincent said. "If anyone—"

Gavin's legs slipped from view like the wall had slurped him up like a noodle. The opening echoed with a whoop and a thud as he landed. The Mice crowded the hole, pushing the candle through for light. Vincent called down.

"Gavin, you alright?"

They held their breath. From within, they could hear him stir. They heard the echoey slap of a hand on rock and a groan. Richard stared into the gap in the wall. He listened.

"...didn't fall far," Gavin said.

far far faar faaaar

"Big space. I don't... You need to see."

see see seee seeeeee

Richard crossed his arms. Re-crossed them. "I'm not going down there," he said. "There's no way I'm going down there."

Vincent was already scooting in. Feet first. He smiled up at Richard. "Don't you want your shoe?"

"What if we can't get out again?"

"Gavin said it was all right."

"Gavin landed on his head."

"All the more reason to go down." He passed the candle to Bryce and shimmied in.

Richard and Bryce stood alone. The candlelight shook in Bryce's grip.

Richard said, "We aren't going to follow them. Are we?"

"Probably."

Richard moved his arm, felt the ache there, and crossed it again. "Your leg alright?"

"It's fine."

"Liar."

"It's *my* leg. I can say when it's fine or not."

Bryce knelt to look. He cupped his mouth. "Everything alright?" he said.

They waited for Bryce's voice to die away, then listened for the answer. Vincent sounded quiet.

"Come down," they heard. "You won't need the candle."

Richard never had much experience with caves and caverns before volunteering at the point of a knife to venture down into Dorgue's horrible tree. Stories of the deep places of the earth were strange and 'juvenile', according to his sister. Odd places, where salt-tails hid their treasure and witches conjured the dead. Strange places. Ghosts lived in them.

Once he'd read a story about a cave an adventurer found in the desert. Days of no drink had turned his lips to paper and when he found the cool space between the rocks, he crawled in, eager to leave the sun. He crawled down, down, down. His only company was what his voice bounced back to him.

But the longer he stayed in that place, the stranger his voice became to him. He'd call:

My father and mother were silk traders from the North. They once killed a stoat whose silk was finer and buried him in the frost. Will I find them in this place?

His voice came back:

I have heard your stories for so long and I am tired. So very tired. Will you share your food with me?

The adventurer called again:

I lied to my love, promising to return to her arms, but I knew this journey would kill me, yet I went at my king's behest. Will I find her in this place?

His voice came back:

I am so very tired. How long must I sing this song? There are only bones to hear it. When will they sing with me?

The adventurer called:

Not until their flesh grows new.

And his voice:

I am so tired. I cannot hide my face.

The story haunted Richard long into many nights, and it was this story he thought of when he crawled into Vincent's waiting hands and saw the cavern twinkling around them. Richard thought the dig site had been big. This place...

All of Green Hill could fit down here.

The colossal granite shelf they found themselves on dropped off into pure dark a yard or so away. All around them, formations of deep crystal rose and vanished in columns. There were hundreds and they were chaotic, laying over each other and looking ready to fall at any moment. Astonishingly beautiful.

Could rocks sing? Could they hum like children? At first, he thought he was imagining it but when Richard pressed his palms to his ears it was there too. He could feel it in his teeth. A shaking.

Gavin stood at the very edge of the shelf, looking up into the lazy twinkling beyond the mammoth crystals. His mouth gaped.

"Are those stars?"

Richard studied them. Of course, they weren't stars, they were still underground.

Yet...

Richard shook his head but the humming remained, quiet and constant. "Did either of you find my shoe?"

Gavin blinked and the spell broke. He turned to face them. Lights reflected in his eyes. Dots of blue.

"Not on this shelf," he said. "Think it tumbled off. But it couldn't be too far if Vincent can smell it."

"I still smell it." Vincent roamed the edge staring down into the blackness. The 'starlight' above gave just enough for them to see one another, but anything beyond clung to its shroud. Vincent squinted. Sniffed again.

"It's just down there. I don't know how far of a drop it is."

Gavin leaned over the edge. Chewed his lip. "Maybe Richard could toss his other shoe?"

"Maybe you could land on your head again."

"No need for that," Bryce said. He scooped a handful of loose pebbles from the ground and let them slide from his palm into the abyss. They listened as they fell, peppering the granite with little pops.

"Maybe eight feet," Gavin said. "I could hang down and drop."

"Feel for holds first," Vincent said.

Richard crossed his—no, that hurt. He let his arm be. It felt like he had a slow clock ticking away within the seam of his arm. He breathed, ignored it, and walked from Gavin and Vincent as they fussed at the shelf's edge. Richard faced one of the columns.

It was cool to the touch and perfectly smooth. When he took his hand away, thin flakes came away with it, sticking to his palm. They were fibrous but hard, like wood shavings. They crumbled in his hand.

Odd.

He could probably tear a chunk out. Take some back to Kathryn to see what she made of it.

Yeah.

Vincent called from behind. "Could you help us out here?" His head and shoulders were over the ledge and Bryce held fast to his legs.

Richard hurried over.

"Sure," he took hold of one of Vincent's legs and Bryce renewed his grip on the other.

Vincent said, "Alright, lower us down some. Little at a time."

Richard, at last, gathered what their plan was. "Wait, are you holding on to Gavin's legs?"

"His hands."

Gavin called up, "Can we hurry this up, please?"

No time to argue. Richard and Bryce inched them lower. Vincent's torso slipped from view before Gavin called up.

"I feel the ground!"

"Make sure it *is* the ground," Bryce said. "Is it flat?"

"Yes. Leggo of me."

The tension left, and they heard Gavin stumble and recover his footing. He shuffled in the dark.

"I think I'm on one of those rocks," he said.

"Crystals," Richard said as they reeled Vincent back onto the shelf.

"What?"

"They're crystals. They grow from rocks."

Gavin laughed. "Rocks don't do nothing but get in the way. They don't *grow*."

"Could all this be what Dorgue is looking for?" Vincent said, looking into the sparkle above them. "I mean...I've never seen anything like it."

Richard shook his head. "I don't think there's much use for this stuff. Some crystals are valuable, but... I don't know. It feels cheap, I guess."

Bryce's face fell. "So no then," he said.

Richard shrugged. "What do you think you're digging for? After all this time…you have theories, right?"

Vincent and Bryce shared a glance.

"That's where a lot of us differ," Vincent said. "Some think we're digging something up—"

"Morons do," Gavin called from below.

Bryce crossed his arms. A frown colored his face. "I'm not a moron. And I think it *is* a thing we're digging up."

"Moron."

"You can't get idiots like Teague and Lou to stand around as we dig up *nothing*."

"You said it. They're idiots."

Vincent cut them off. "Some say it's a treasure. Others say it's nothing. And some, like Gavin, say—"

"I'm just pointing out what Dorgue himself says," A dark shape tumbled through the air and clocked onto the ground next to Richard: his boot, scuffed and dusty.

Gavin said, "The rats always say, 'Nearly there, nearly there.' Where not digging up a *thing* we're digging to a *place*."

Richard took up his boot and shook out the pebbles. "Alright, what place then?"

"Think about it," Gavin said. "All this time digging down while the rats beat us with whips. Dorgue's the Devil. He's just trying to get home."

Richard smiled. Shook his head. "You don't…you don't actually think…"

"Friend, we're digging down."

The thought of Dorgue digging to Hell honestly wasn't hard for Richard to picture, and he'd only met the rat twice. He imagined living down here your entire life with the only *'food for thought'* coming from the rats beating you down.

Vincent showed his hands. "Not all of us think that way," he said. "Me? I think the rat's insane."

"It's hard to get folk to follow crazy," Richard said. "How's he have all his help? Fletcher, Worth, and the other rats? You have to offer them something to keep them around."

"You're the big tough mouse with shoes. You tell me. The best we can come up with is treasure or Hell. And 'treasure' could mean anything, we don't know what's worth spending our lives in a hole digging to death."

"You don't have context."

Bryce's face squinted up. "What's—"

"Never mind." Richard rose to pace.

What's worth digging for out in the Deep Wood? The answer was clear.

Wild Glass.

If you found a good amount, you'd have a healthy fortune, provided you could move it without getting cut to ribbons. But Richard had never heard of anyone *digging* to find the stuff. It grew above ground as far as Richard could tell. Though, he couldn't deny he'd seen the rat waving the glass around like it was a gold-threaded doily at a garden party. He was showing off, but not with the fact he had wild glass...he was showing off he could work with it.

The only way to cut wild glass is *with* wild glass.

The window.

The scalpel.

The vial he'd freaking given to him.

Richard pulled it from his jacket. Its smooth surface glowed in the blue light of the cavern. Dots of color covered it like a spider's eyes.

"It doesn't matter what they're digging for," Richard said. "Or even why. All that matters is us getting out."

Bryce leaned over the edge and called to Gavin in the dark. "You've checked around where the boot was?"

"Yes. Did any of you check inside the boot?"

"It's already on my foot."

"But did you check inside it?"

"It's on my foot! I think I would have noticed if there was a knife inside it."

Gavin shuffled some like he was kicking pebbles. "Maybe we could use that candle after all. You think you could light it again?"

Vincent could. He worked another ember to life and had a flickering flame dancing on the stubbed candle.

"This won't last long," he said. "Best be quick," and stretched his arm over the space.

Warm light. Gavin stood some ten feet below, squinting at the candle flame. As it turned out, it wasn't another granite shelf he'd climbed down onto, but one of the mammoth crystal formations jutting out into the void like a bridge spanning a dark ocean.

Gavin moved to the edge of the candle's light and peered over the edge.

"Feel. weird underfoot," he said and lifted his foot to brush away the twinkling fibers that clung to his skin. "Sort'a crumbly."

"We're not here for that," Vincent said and stretched to hold the candle higher. "We don't have a lot of light left. See if you can—"

Bryce's hand shot out. A dull shine winked in the candle's meager light. "*There!*" Bryce said, "You see it?"

Richard strained to see. Between the dimming light and the child-like hum of the crystals, his eyes struggled to focus. Haze inched from the edges of his vision. Richard shook his head and pressed his fingers into his eyelids.

"This place makes me tired," he said.

Gavin padded over the bridge, edging into the dark. Then a sound like ice cracking across a vast expanse, a deep tear that echoed forever in the dark.

The bridge under Gavin's feet tremored as musical fractures zipped through the crystal. Gavin lowered his body and ambled along on all fours.

"It's right in front of me!" he called up. "I'm gonna try and grab it."

Vincent shouted. Something about the knife not being worth it. Richard couldn't really remember what the mouse had said. He got distracted.

Either by some trick of the light or a shift in the crystal formations around them, Vincent's candle illuminated just the right patch of darkness. In a brief blink, Richard saw it.

Sitting in a web of crumbling crystal and buried to the hilt like something from a fairytale...

Garrow's knife.

Cracks surrounded it and Gavin was only a few feet away.

The candle flame brushed Vincent's knuckle. He hissed, sending the stub tumbling and Gavin vanished into darkness.

The noise of the crystals grew. Richard thought it was like the musical sound of champagne. Like a thousand soap bubbles tearing into nothing.

Not good.

Gavin called from the dark, "Get ready to haul me up!"

Vincent growled, but he didn't argue and lowered himself from the ledge. Richard and Bryce grabbed his legs and held fast.

Below, the noise had evolved from "shop bell chimes" to "tree limbs tearing in the wind". Richard heard Gavin struggling.

"It's stuck!"

"*Then leave it!*" Vincent screamed.

Richard's shoulders shook. The warmth growing in his arm wasn't the good kind. Then the noise of the bridge collapsing echoed like a beast rising from the depths. Richard thought for sure Gavin was gone. That he'd fallen into the void, doomed to lose himself in the bowels of the earth. Alone for all eternity with no one to sing over his bones.

But then Vincent got *immensely* heavier.

"*Up, up, up!*"

They pulled. Richard stretched his neck, blasting air and sucking it back. They had Vincent's knees, then his legs. Once Vincent was more or less safe, all three focused on hauling Gavin out of the brink.

Between Gavin's teeth flashed a rusted and miserable blade. Its tip was gone, and though its edges pressed brutally against either side of Gavin's lips, they didn't cut.

The thing wasn't even sharp.

They laid out on the shelf and waited for the echoes to die.

Took a long time.

TWELVE

*I don't have anything else to say on the matter. It's done. I'm
sorry for everyone who was hurt, but I'm more sorry it had
to be done in the first place. We can only pick ourselves up
now... No, we haven't heard from Haven.*

— Kathryn Aterox, fourteen days after the Deep Wood event

ARROW WATCHED DORGUE LEAVE on the lift. Watched as the rat's lantern winked away into nothing.

"All quiet?" the rat had asked him.

"All quiet."

"*Gooood.*" Then Dorgue scuttled into the lift and gave Garrow a wink with his clouded eye. "Don't let the pesky little things get past you."

Garrow had kept his right hip turned away from the rat, his hand carefully placed.

"Wouldn't dream it, boss."

"No, you wouldn't, would you?"

Garrow couldn't breathe until the rat was gone.

Once he heard the echo of the lift settling and locking for the night—high, high in the hoist—Garrow walked into the tunnels. He didn't bother to bring his candle. He knew these tunnels as well as any mouse. In some ways, he knew them better. Garrow had done his fair share of digging at the start of all this. More than his fair share.

He remembered the days stretching into one another, the hours becoming meaningless. He remembered the sweat. The dark. The shouts of those lost in the deeper places as they followed their own bouncing voices deeper and deeper. They'd lost as many rats as they had mice in those days.

Idiots.

It was much better now. The little creeps didn't know how good they had it. Had they no sense at all? Did they *want* things to go back to how they were?

He padded at his eye and hissed.

"I can play rough too," he said.

If they had snuck to his post at the dig site, then they had to have come through *here*: at the switch between the tunnel to the burrows and the dinner hall.

He knelt to place his hands in the dust of the path. He felt the grit of the smallest flecks of stone and the crunch of dried mud. He let his fingers pick it up and coated them with it. He spread the stuff on his neck, his face, and under his arms.

He pat his hands together and rubbed the grit into his palms till they were rough like the bark of an oak. Perfect for grabbing.

Garrow stood center of the passage and let his arms spread. He shut his eyes. Listened.

He hoped all of them would happen by, but he'd settle for just one. Only took one to talk. He'd crumble once Garrow laid on some pressure. And if the runt had the gall to come at him with his own knife? Garrow smiled. They had probably cut themselves by now, the fools.

Movement.

Someone shuffling along the wall, the slap slap slap of bare feet, the steady breath of someone treading where they shouldn't... Garrow's lips spread over his teeth.

Little closer. Little closer, you imp.

Garrow moved, like a serpent angling for a strike.

And he had him.

Garrow ripped the mouse from the wall. He squealed, in pain and terror. Garrow hoped he'd broken his filthy arm.

The mouse writhed, but Garrow put an end to it with a slap. He heard the dirty thing's teeth click and the mouse went slack.

The mouse blubbered, speaking past the blood in his teeth. "M-master," he gasped. "Forgive me."

Candle Hall.

Garrow growled. "That depends on how sorry you are," he said.

"I have news...news for you..."

"And which one are you?"

"Bard."

Bard, the skinny mess of whip-scars and spit, the head of Candle Hall himself. Ran the place like some kind of sick church. Dorgue found it funny but Garrow didn't trust the crazy ones. There wasn't any rhyme to figuring them out. You beat them and they *thanked* you.

He shook the mouse. "Speak your piece, Bard."

He squirmed in his grasp like he was trying to point down the way.

"There were...others last night," he said. They snuck from their burrow."

"Like you are now?"

"I...I wanted to catch them. I wanted to know who they were before I told you, master."

Garrow bought that. Bard had done as much in the past; dragging out one of his own brothers for a sin he'd committed. All for Dorgue's praise and the music of the whips.

But Garrow remembered the days Bard had been thrown under the whip. He remembered them well. The fool had set fire to half the burrows. The smoke got so bad, that Garrow vomited soot for days. The mice had used the chaos well, running at the guards and stealing what tools they could get their grubby hands on.

But they didn't try to escape. It was like the thought had never crossed their minds. No, all Bard seemed to want was rat blood staining the ground and his fists.

In the end, the rats put out the fire, any mouse who had struck a rat was held under the mud, and Bard was whipped and drug before Dorgue. His body was such a dripping ruin of lines, that it shook Garrow to see him still alert, still moving. The fury in his eyes...

Then Dorgue took him up. All the way to his study, Garrow had heard. They were gone for hours.

Everyone assumed Bard to be worm food. Maybe Dorgue had even chopped him up himself, but then Bard rode the lift down alone. His body had been mummified in gauze and tape. The work froze to see him there, standing crooked on the lift. He risked step after shaky step as he moved for the dig site.

It was his eyes Garrow noticed above all. Set. Controlled. Absolute focus. No one knew what Dorgue had said to him and no one dared to ask the rat.

Bard was forever different. No more riots. No more revolts.

But someone had taken his knife. And here was Bard, sneaking around in the middle of the night.

Garrow said, "You know what I think? I think you're rotting meat. I think you're lying filth."

"I await the day with courage, master."

"Yeah?" Garrow pressed his thumb into the mouse's eye. Bard cried out in shock, then again in pain.

"You like that? Think that's funny? You blind one of my eyes, and think you can skip on back to your bunk? Think you can whistle while you work like *nothing happened?*"

Bard's hands gripped Garrow's palm. He breathed, ragged and fast. "I swear it. I swear it, master. Please, I know who. I know who did it. I can lead you to him and you can drag him to Dorgue. Dorgue will reward you. He will reward you."

Garrow dropped him.

The mouse cried out as he collapsed, landing in a heap on the ground. Garrow could hear him gasp in shock, no doubt clutching his eye.

"Still work?" Garrow asked. "Shame it's too dark in here to know. You have a good walk to get back to your burrow and your little candle."

Bard had gone quiet. Even his breathing stilled. He said, "I wear my suffering...with pride, master."

Oh, please. Garrow kicked him. As the mouse doubled over, Garrow searched for the knife.

If Candle Hall had it, they'd just as likely use it on the other burrows as on the rats. Couldn't have that. And if Dorgue found out, Bard would kiss his little church goodbye. His whole congregation could kiss everything goodbye.

More delays.

More setbacks.

More digging.

Bard didn't have the knife. Garrow took the mouse by his collar. "Tell me who snuck out last night. Tell me their names."

"I...I only know one," he said. "But if you give me time—"

Garrow slapped him again. "I only need the one. Tell me."

Bard told him.

THIRTEEN

A MEMORIAL TO THE FALLEN TO BE HELD BE-FORE THE GARDEN SPIRE IN GREEN HILL TOMOR-ROW MORNING, AT THE RINGING OF THE BELL. A CITY-WIDE MOMENT OF SILENCE TO FOLLOW.

THE SNAKE WAR IS OVER. THE SNAKE WAR IS OVER.

— Atticus Quick, The Sunday Circular

RICHARD FELT DEAD.

His head ached, his stomach held a quiver that made him nervous, and his wrist felt like it had an expanding spike of red iron in its marrow. He'd promised himself he wouldn't take any more of Dorgue's medicine the night before...

But that had been the night before.

They'd taken him to the Kitchen today, a barbarian ruin of wood and steam, and allowed the mice some water before the work began in earnest. Richard eased a drop from his little vial into the mug. It fizzed and bubbled, but the water eventually stilled and turned the slightest bit pink. He slurped the cup dry.

It burned.

After the last swallow, Richard found he had to strain to grasp the instructions the rat-cook shouted at him. Best Richard could figure: he was to cut vegetables. Or rather, *snap* vegetables. He saw no sharp implements in the kitchen, not even a fork. After a few hours, he'd worked his hands raw from breaking carrots into so many little pieces with his fingers.

The kitchen reminded Richard some of his own, but only in its busyness. The same iron cauldron he'd seen the night before in the dining hall, bubbled in the place of honor at the room's head. The walls and ceiling around it had gone black from years of wood smoke.

Richard was surprised to find the space didn't exist in a cloud. The wood they burned was dry and smoke was minimal.

That's not to say there *wasn't* smoke. There was. Richard had to blink away the stinging in his eyes on more than one occasion, and many of the others he worked with had dry coughs, especially the mute and tired mice from Isolation, the first burrow Fletcher had introduced during his guided tour.

The rat in charge of the kitchen was a bone-thin fossil. His skin hung from his body like the frills of a lizard and was as loud as he was old. He never closed his lips and his teeth peeked out like little eyes, all turned gray from tobacco. He leveled one dry look at Richard and shouted something about drooling.

Was Richard drooling? He patted at his face. Moved his lips.

He felt numb.

Loopy Juice, Gavin had called Dorgue's Medicine. Certainly was. It had played with his emotions enough last night to prove that. Had him sobbing like an infant over an empty stomach. Richard shook his head, snapped a carrot, and tossed it into the bucket at his feet.

Working at his left was one of the mice from Isolation. His face looked dead, but his hands moved fast as skittering spiders as he worked through the hill of carrots.

Richard had asked his name (at least he thought he had) but if the mouse had heard, he gave no sign.

Made him sad. Then it made him angry. Then Richard got frustrated that Dorgue's medicine could mess with his head so easily.

He breathed like Vincent had said.

In and out.

Don't let your mind wander, he told himself. A wandering mind invites mistakes. And mistakes could kill.

Richard tried to push his thoughts toward the knife hidden beneath a blanket in the Secret Place. He thought about the hunk of crystal he'd stuffed into the lining of his jacket. But mostly, he thought about Vincent's stupid, stupid plan.

Hours ago, before sneaking back to the burrow, Richard and Vincent sat in the dark of the Old Tunnels to have a little chat.

"Tell me again. Walk me through it," Richard said.

They were alone and the way back lay just around the bend. Bryce and Gavin had gone ahead at Vincent's insistence to hide the knife and get some much-needed rest.

Vincent sighed. Richard couldn't see him in the dark, but he could hear him rub at his face.

"There's not that much to it, Richard."

"Still feels like too much. Too much leaves room for mistakes. Now just...go over it again. I need to absorb it."

"Ok. First, we needed a knife—"

"We have a knife—a sad and crummy knife—but yes. Skip this."

"Next we need to get past whoever is guarding the dig site and hide in one of the passageways. There are a lot of nooks and crannies up there, plenty of places too—"

"I still don't understand this...Bryce told me the old burrows are always sealed up."

"Yes, but not every little pocket. There'll be places to duck into."

"Enough places?"

"Yes. Once everyone is hidden, we light the fire using our blankets. Lots of smoke."

Richard blinked. "And that'll work? Is that...is that a good idea? I mean, how much air do we even have down here?"

"That's why the rats will come. If we die, they lose all their workers."

"So the plan is to...smother ourselves and wait for the rats to run and *save us?*"

"It's one of the drills they practice. They'll come."

Richard shook his head. "So who stays behind to light it?"

A frown in Vincent's voice, "Stay behind?"

"*Yes*, who stays to light the fire? Fires don't just happen," he snapped his fingers, "you need someone to spark 'em awake."

"Yes, but no one is staying behind."

That was the third time Vincent had said this, each repeat becoming a little more desperate.

When it finally clicked what Vincent meant, Richard felt a jolt of panic, like he'd felt a fishbone disappear down the back of his throat.

"Vincent... do you mean *more* than just Bryce and Gavin?"

"I mean *everyone*."

The word hurt his stomach. How many was that? Three-hundred? *More*? And what about the problem mice in Candle Hall? *What about them?*

"Everyone means everyone, Richard."

"I thought you said we couldn't *trust* everyone?"

"That doesn't mean we don't give them a chance to leave! If you give them that, they'll take it!"

"And what about that Bard guy? You really wanna give him a chance? He'll stab us in the back before we even get past the guard at the dig site!"

"Anyone we leave behind is as good as dead," Vincent said. "If Dorgue wakes up tomorrow and he's missing more than half his workforce..."

Richard felt the cut on his cheek. His tally mark. *Strike one.*

Dorgue would kill them.

Right?

But what about what Fletcher and the other rats had said? About delays and setbacks? Surely killing those left behind would count as much.

Right?

"Their blood would be on our hands," Vincent said. "My pa always told me, 'if you can do good, *you do it*'. To stand by and pretend you can't is as bad as doing it yourself."

Richard was glad it was dark enough for the mouse not to see him roll his eyes. "Good way to get yourself dead," he said.

"Now, shut up and listen. Once the fire is lit and everyone is hidden, the rats will smell the smoke and come down on the lifts."

"And you're positive it'll be *all the rats*, not just some of them?"

"Yes."

"Because if we run into a single rat we'll only have one chance with our little blade, and if we run into two you can say goodbye to ever smelling pure air again."

"They'll all come running. The rats are terrified of fire."

"Alright, so they come running. They use their lifts. They don't see hundreds of mice hiding in the shadows because they're distracted with putting out the fire."

"Then we cut the bridge between them and us and we run."

"Alright…how long do we have to run to the top? When do they notice everyone pounding up the walkways?"

"We've timed it. It takes five minutes for the lift to come down with a full load of rats, and fifteen for those same rats to go back up."

"So we have fifteen minutes to run to the top."

"Only the mouse at the head of the pack," Vincent said. "Once he's up in the hoist, he can stop the lifts."

"Or he could cut them."

More silence.

"Yes," Vincent said, "We could…cut them. Then it's up and out. Into the Deep Wood."

And there was the last thing: The Deep Wood.

Sure, Richard had made it though, but he'd only had *himself* to worry about. He'd kept *quiet.* Three hundred mice trooping through the underbrush would raise a racket, and the dark forest would have more than just poisonous berries waiting for them. All one had to do was remember the Snake War.

Three hundred mice and a week's worth of forest? They might as well head North to Haven, at least the squirrels would only kill them. Maybe skin them for hats, but that would at least be *after* the killing.

The Deep Wood would eat them. Slowly. It would dissolve their feet and blow poison in their faces. They might even turn and eat each other.

Happened before.

Richard sighed. "You don't know those woods. Sending that many out with none of them knowing what to expect…"

"Then tell us what to expect."

"You can expect to lose most of them the first night. Or day. It can be hard to tell which is which."

"I think you'll find we're good at that."

"Doesn't matter. If something out there notices us—"

"And what's out there?"

"I don't know! Monsters? Devils? Folk who aren't careful are never heard from again. If they're found it's only in *pieces* or with a vine growing out of their skull."

"I thought you lived in the Deep Wood."

"I thought you did! Tell me what you remember. What stories did your mama tell you? What was her favorite threat to get you to eat your liverwort? *'Finish up or the Red Demon will steal you away?'*"

Vincent stuttered. "That doesn't—"

"You lived by the river, right? Where the sky could still sneak in past the trees? We're in the middle of it, Vincent. A good week's walk in the middle and it'll take some doing to get back out again."

The silence between them grew. Richard's final word echoed deeper and deeper away.

"I just want to see them again," Vincent said, his voice quiet. "I want to go home. I know this is a big thing we're asking, but we're tough, Richard. Through and through. We'd march through Hell itself if it meant leaving this place."

Oh, how Richard wanted to hit him. This mouse would get everyone killed with that sort of talk.

"Okay," Richard said. "What if only a few of us escaped? We could slip through the Deep Wood undetected. Move fast. Then once we hit Border Town it's a short wagon ride to Green Hill."

"It has to be all of us."

"I have powerful friends! We can have an army big enough to cut through the Deep Wood and knock down Dorgue's door in less than a month. An army, Vincent! Think of that! I'd like to see Fletcher go toe-to-toe with a hundred armed green cloaks. They'd chop him to ribbons. Less than ribbons! They'd bring swords and spears and arrows and—""

"You aren't *listening* to me," Vincent said. "If Dorgue wakes up tomorrow and finds a few of his workers missing—one of which is the strange new mouse from the Deep Wood—everyone suffers.

"Sure, fine. Let's say things go great and you get all three hundred outside and into the Deep Wood. What next?"

"You lead us out."

"Through the Deep Wood? *Three hundred mice*?"

"What's the problem?"

"Oh, well, let's see." Richard counted his fingers. "Everything in the Deep Wood is poison. There are things in there that'll tear us apart if they find us. And if we tip-toe a little too close to Haven's border the squirrels will fill us with musket shot."

Vincent remained silent. Richard waited.

Green Hill was their best bet. Just the thought of the army marching through the Deep Wood with grim faces and clicking spears brought a warmth to Richard's heart that he hadn't felt in an age.

And then Vincent spoke. "The ones left waiting… You haven't said how we will magically trick Dorgue into *not* knowing we are gone."

"We'll think of that! We have all day to figure that out. I promise we—"

"Don't make promises."

He heard Vincent stand. Standing was bad. Standing meant his mind was made up. Richard scrambled.

"There are monsters out there, Vincent. Real ones. If they find us, we won't last an hour."

But Vincent had heard enough. "I believe in monsters," he said. "I've lived among them all my life. If there is more to be found outside, so be it. You underestimate us. We'll lose no one when we leave this place. And we'll lose no one when we go outside."

Richard gritted his teeth. *Idiot!* "If you try to move three hundred mice out of here tonight…a lot more will end up dead than if we left some behind."

"But not because we abandoned them," Vincent said.

And that was it.

End of discussion.

Richard snapped another carrot and tossed it into the pile. He felt sick. He felt tired. He felt hungry. But little by little that began to fade away as Dorgue's Medicine worked its little miracle.

A numbness washed over Richard. But at the same time, he wanted to punch something. This old kitchen rat, for instance: leaning against the wall with his long, wooden spoon. Chewing his stringy tobacco. The rat spat a glob of black ooze at his feet. It dotted his boots, his legs.

"Dorgue got you on drops?" he said. "Feel'n light 'n dusty?"

Richard blinked. Shook his head. What had he been thinking about?

"If you're get'n restless, go to the storeroom and haul back some spuds. Just follow the path. Walk some of that stuff off. And don't even *think* of getting sick in my kitchen."

Richard had to duck to keep away from the next hunk of tobacco and spit.

He left the kitchen, keeping a hand ready by the wall should he lose his balance. The firelight faded behind him as the noise from the dig site echoed to him from the dark. The others were only a short walk away. And the storeroom was…

This way, Richard decided and followed a fork in the path.

His thoughts wandered to the twisting roads and alleys in Green Hill. Now *there* was a place a fellow could get lost. After the sun dropped below the walls, Green Hill became a different sort of place.

And Richard loved it.

If he closed his eyes, he could imagine walking one of the city's many alleyways, side-stepping trash as he snuck his way home. He could almost smell it.

Then Bard dropped on top of him and forced the wind from his lungs.

Richard's face met the gritty floor of the tunnel. His only thought was, *These drops are good stuff. Can't feel a thing.*

Bard ripped him from the floor and bashed him into the wall, pinning him. He hissed in Richard's face.

"Have you no *sense*?" Bard said. "Do you know how hard I've worked to build *peace* down here?"

Richard blinked. "Why is everyone…spitting on me today?"

The scars lying across Bard's face twisted. One of his eyes had swollen tight as a grape. He showed his teeth.

"You've no idea the importance of our work, no one does. Dorgue will lead us to glory, but not if you drag us all down into the muck!"

Some part of Richard understood Bard's fist cruising into his gut like a boulder, but distantly. His breath left him as he doubled over. Richard's chin bounced. Tasted blood. Had he bit his tongue?

Weeeeird.

Bard took Richard's ears in his fist and yanked him upright again. He said, "If you anger the rats, it will be *all* who suffer, don't you understand? Submit to them and our obedience will be rewarded. That fool Vincent has stressed things far enough as it is. The last thing we all need is some idiot outsider spreading chaos like it was—"

Something hit Bard like an oak ram crashing through a door. The mouse tumbled into the air before Richard could react. Then again, he wasn't sure he could if he wanted. React, that is. All that stuff in his head...he might have added a drop too many to his water.

A dusty mouse with the skeletal hands had Bard by the neck. They were on the ground. Rolling, as they bit and scratched.

Richard could only watch.

Bard growled out what words he could and threw his arms over his face as the stranger waylaid him, raining blows.

And then it was over.

Bard scampered into the darkness. He cast a final look, his eye catching Richard's. "You're not here for us!" he said and darted round the bend.

Richard had watched the entire ordeal from his place on the ground, laid out as if on a sofa in his drawing room rather than on rough and unforgiving stone. Bard's final retort bounced off Richard's skull like a dream just before waking.

He looked to the stranger, leaning heavy on the wall and heaving sputtering breaths. He wore rags. Same as everyone else, Richard supposed, but this mouse's rags were ancient. His arms and legs were thin but wiry and strong. All gristle. He turned to face Richard. Dark, sunken eyes. Slack skin without enough muscle to fill the empty spaces. He could hear him breathing like wind moving through an alley in the city.

He offered Richard his hand.

"Thank you."

The mouse's only response was a tired nod as he helped Richard to stand. He pointed down the way and mimed peeling a potato with his thumb.

Richard focused. "Right...potatoes. I guess we better go get them, yeah?"

He moved his jaw. Dabbed at his lip. Pulled up his shirt to clean the blood.

He considered the Mute. He kept glancing the way Bard had fled, off toward the kitchen. He lifted one eyebrow at Richard.

Who was this mouse? He from that other burrow? What had Fletcher called it...

Richard did what he could to shake the medicine from his mind. Easier said than done. In the end, he decided he was too tired to care and resolved to worry about it later. He reached to pat the Mute on the shoulder, missed, and got him on the second try.

"Lead the way, my friend," Richard said. "What do I call you? Sorry, never mind. How about I call you Donald, yeah? My best friend growing up was called Donald. He died in a caravan up north. Long Jacks got 'em all."

The mute didn't respond. All his focus seemed to be on keeping Richard upright and on the path. They walked as Richard yammered on.

"How long have you been here Donald?" Richard shook his head. "Sorry, keep forgetting. You're not so easy to talk to, are ya? Alright, how about this," Richard held up his fingers, "One blink for yes...and two for no."

The other mouse sighed but looked to Richard and gave him a slow blink, *yes*.

"Perfect. Your name wouldn't happen to be Donald, would it?"

No.

Richard deflated some. He supposed he could go through the alphabet letter by letter and figure it out, but that seemed like a lot of work. Donald was good enough for now. Especially if he didn't ask the mute mouse how he felt about it.

"That Bard guy a friend of yours?"

No.

"I guess he's not anyone's friend, is he?"

No.

Bryce stabbed his shovel into the wall. The mud that crumbled away was dark and lined with gray. It smelled.

Rot and mildew.

Overhead, a whip broke the air. Someone cried out. He didn't know who. Didn't want to know. All around the noise of work threatened to swallow him. Above, the groan of scaffolds. Below, the hungry gurgle of the dark soup at the bottom of the pit. Only a few mice could work there at a time—at least until they made the space bigger.

Bryce stabbed at the wall again. More clumpy dirt, but what hid beneath was the harder stuff, what he'd be gritting his teeth at for the next few hours. Working nearby, Gavin nudged him and tipped his eyes up. Bryce followed the glance.

Garrow looked from the lowest walkway. The lumpy rat's face had returned to something like normal, but his color was still like something you'd find under a stone after squashing a spider. He was too far away to tell if he was looking their way or not.

"Think he's searching for us?" Gavin asked.

"Probably."

"Think he has any idea who?"

"Probably not."

Vincent came sloshing down the scaffold. He was with the group marching down and was coated in the dark mud. He swung a bucket in each fist, a shine in his eye. As he passed, he whispered, "He's up there. You seen him?"

"Yes."

Bryce forced himself to face his work and not look. But when a hammer was held over your head, how could you not look at it? He stole glances from the edge of his vision as he worked.

Garrow had posted himself center of the walkway. Bryce saw the rat lean to spit. It landed somewhere in the dig site. Then Garrow lumbered farther along the rope bridge, lean, and spit again, watching as it fell.

Gavin made a face. "What is he doing?" he said.

Nothing good.

Bryce's bucket of personal worries was full enough without Garrow lurking above them.

Sweat made his palms slick. He had to pause in his work to get a better grip on his shovel. He remembered a time when the shovels were splintery, but the years had made them smooth.

Tonight. They escape tonight.

Bryce stabbed the wall. Stabbed it again.

First the fire. Then the bridge. Then the Deep Wood. That was the plan. The terrible, wonderful plan.

Stab. Slice. Stab.

No, first was getting everyone together. Getting them to go along with it. They'd have to deal with Bard.

Another drop in the bucket. Another worry for his collection.

Bard would be the problem. The others in his burrow, not so much. He was the zealot. The fanatic. But it wasn't always the case. Bryce remembered a time when they had been friends.

The shovels had been splintery then.

Bryce hoped when Bard saw the knife and heard the plan, that old light would return to his eyes. But then... Bard had never been the same after his talk with Dorgue.

His long talk.

Others had asked what the rat had said to him, why they hadn't held him under the mud like the others, but Bard would only ever shake his head and say, "Some things are not for us to know."

Vincent passed by again, his buckets full and dripping the dark mud. He turned his eyes up. Bryce thought he was checking for Garrow, but Vincent's gaze rose past the walkway, past the dark, past the Hoist.

Up and up and up.

Vincent looked toward freedom. Bryce wished he could imagine the same.

FOURTEEN

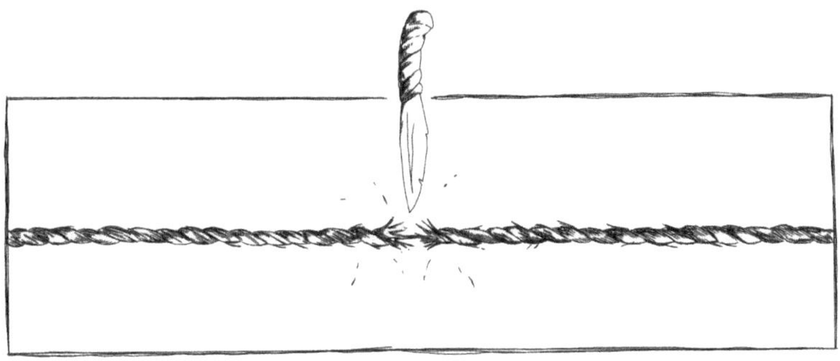

The Deep Wood always claims you in the end. It eats you.

— Thaddeus Keene, High Captain of the Long Walk

THE DROPS WERE STILL very much working. As Richard pushed the water trolly to the dig site, he could feel the vibration of the wheels as the bone in his wrist jittered against its neighbor. The pain was sharp as a winter gust, but it was like it was happening to someone else. He didn't...care. As he walked, trolly rattling ahead of him, he wore the dumbest smile. He might have even been humming.

The trolly was a rickety thing, with squarish wheels, an open barrel of water, and a little shelf of tin mugs that crashed at every bump and turn. Richard opened and closed his hand around the trolly's bar, flexing the bandage wrapping his arm. He could smell it too: sweat mixed with the high aroma of medicine. He caught hints of Dorgue's rosemary and jasmine.

As he wheeled the trolly into the rising spire of the dig site, the lifts were just beginning their long ascent. The space was lit by torches stood up on poles, and a few of the rats carried them as well—some up the walkways, some down in the pit. The space looked like a painting he'd once seen. A painting of hell, or some such, full of the tortured souls of the damned, aglow with the deepest reds and darkest blacks.

Haunting. Beautiful. And something else Richard couldn't place...

As his cart rattled, the rats watching over the dig site looked to see his coming. The call for water echoed down into the pit...

Bryce's knee had stiffened to something like stone, but the pain was not as bad as yesterday. He gave the wall they were collapsing one last stab and left his shovel there, jutting out like an arm reaching through the mud.

The mice all around him did the same, letting their tools fall from their hands and stretching their necks to look up and out.

Teague was down in the pit with them that day—most likely at Fletcher's behest. His nose was partly wrapped in a bandage, and what wasn't swollen, looked more like putrid fruit than flesh. The wood block rattled back and forth between his teeth as he gnawed. He spoke through a wet, twisted lip.

"That's *break*," he said and gave the whip at his side a hearty lash through the air, sending the noise of it bouncing up into the forever of the dark.

The scaffolds groaned as they started their trek back. Vincent walked at Bryce's shoulder, hauling full buckets of the gray slop from below.

"Three to go," he said.

Bryce took that to mean breaks for water. Three more until...
never again.

A hitch caught in Bryce's chest. Did he truly believe that? Could he see a day without the rats standing over them? A morning where they woke to daylight instead of the harsh flame of a torch? The feeling brought a shaking to his hands, and a certain horror as well.

And then Dorgue's voice in his head:

Without me...are you really YOU?

Gavin came up alongside, elbowing through the crowd, worry on his face. He nodded to Bryce. "You're not about to be sick, are you?" he asked.

Was he? Bryce rubbed a knuckle to his eye. There was a growing pressure there—the beginnings of a migraine, felt like.

Then Dorgue's voice echoed in his mind like Teague's whip.

Haven't I told you again and again? Your reward awaits you. Here, you serve a purpose. Out there, in the madness of the wider world...you mice are but a speck. Yet in my Tree, your efforts will change the world.

As they moved up and away from the mud, Bryce set his gaze ahead. He saw Sampson, standing a head taller than the mice around him; and Hugo, his brow stern and looking his way, searching Bryce's face.

They hadn't even had a chance to tell the others yet, Bryce realized. Should they? Was Bryce *happy* in knowing they'd soon charge for the outside or die?

The rolling in his gut told him no...

Garrow spied from the walkway as the mice filed from the scaffolds. Waiting. As soon as the mouse with his knife stepped onto level ground, he'd have fourteen seconds (give or take).

Garrow let his hand drift to this side and the fresh blade he'd nicked that morning and smiled.

Lou had been as pale as a gourd at breakfast. The short little spit had been so easy to steal from, and once Garrow had his knife back, he figured he'd hang on to Lou's for a little bit. See how long he'd squirm before making a fool of himself. Besides, it was time to start thinking about "adjusting" the available shares once everything was over.

Once Dorgue had what he wanted.

He watched the lift as it rose. Looked down to the growing line leading from the pit. The line often formed in a path that led directly beneath the lifts...

Sampson waved to Richard as he bounded from the scaffold. The wave was friendly, but the face was cloudy. Everything was cloudy.

Richard squinted.

The mice coming up from the pit looked muddy enough to hide in the street should they decide to lay still. Some part of him—the part smothered under Dorgue's medicine—laughed at that. Kathryn used to say as much after he'd come in from the garden on rainy days in late summer. Why Richard had liked running around in the rain as a child, he couldn't say.

Perhaps it was the thrill of requiring the attention it took to get clean again? Or perhaps all children are joyful idiots, and all they lack for bliss is a mug of cocoa and a warm blanket by the stove as their mother chided after their hair.

Look at you. A disaster.

Richard smiled.

Fletcher ordered him to a halt, a stone's throw from the pit. The rat crossed his arms and nodded to the sloshing barrel he'd delivered.

"Divvy that out," he said. "Don't give too much, it's gotta last."

The growing line of thirsty workers didn't seem to hear. They pushed against each other, coaxing the queue on, all the while eyeing Fletcher like the rat might lash out at a moment's notice.

Richard dipped the ladle, spooning water into a mug. The first mouse in line was one of Bard's burrow mates. He took his cup with closed eyes and thanked Fletcher with a hushed voice.

The rat pretended not to hear...

Garrow reached for the rope of the lift as the mice moved below. He checked the gangways overhead, biting his lip. He didn't see anyone. And why would he? All the rats' focus was on the mice, keeping them in line.

Garrow let the rope move through his grasp. The fibers felt coarse and sharp. They nicked the skin of his palm, but Garrow didn't move from his place.

He kept an eye on the scaffolds...looking for the right mouse. Looking for...

Bryce stepped from the scaffold. He saw Richard manning the water cart, looking as drunk as Garrow had been the night they'd stolen the knife. Under Fletcher's supervision, the mouse dribbled water from a ladle into waiting mugs. His eyes were glassy, and a stupid smile hung from his mouth, but every so often smile would slip and he'd shiver.

Would Richard be ready to escape tonight? To lead them through the Deep Wood? Bryce didn't like the thought of a drunk leading them through the jungle, forest, or whatever was waiting for them up there. Who knew how far Vincent's house would be? Hours? Days?

More?

All things considered... you lost the knife. It was Richard who found it again. Who's to say you won't be the one who gets everyone killed tonight?

Bryce tried to force the words away, but they were true.

He had dropped the knife.

Already, he had almost ruined everything. Luck was the only reason they had the knife now. Luck and Richard's boot.

And drunk or not, they needed him. He was the only one who knew the way.

All Vincent had said he could remember was gliding through air as cold as bare granite and watching the trees pass under him as he clung to the...

Well... He'd called it a monster.

Vincent had never been able to say much about it, and whenever he tried, his hands would begin to shake and he'd become sick. It was like everything in his being rebelled at even the thought of trying to remember that night so long ago.

Even the memory of his parents (something Vincent alone could brag of) had become...colored by whatever it was that took him, their faces fading away and their eyes turning white as a full moon...

Red dripped from Garrow's hand, yet he kept his will.

He counted. Waited.

A bead of sweat snaked from his brow and stung at his swollen eye. He took a shaking breath.

His gaze followed the mouse called Bryce as he moved through the line, the mouse who that worthless Bard saw sneaking around that night.

"Steal from me?" he said. "You steal from *me*?"

Bryce walked with his head down, shuffling along with the others. The mice had broken into a single file line, Gavin walking ahead and Vincent behind. The image of the knife leaving his hand and bouncing away into the dark returned to him again and again. He felt that emptiness. The sinking pit in his stomach.

What if he messed up tonight? What if everything failed because of him?

Richard dropped a mug, spilling water over the ground. He laughed.

Funny. It was funny.

And then Fletcher's arm swung and toppled him to the ground. It didn't hurt, not really.

"Pick it up!" Fletcher screamed again.

Richard blinked. Right, the rat was saying something. Now he felt Fletcher's boot in his side. Richard spun, the world turning end over end. He felt sick now. And the rat still yelled.

Another mouse hurried to the water trolly at the rat's order, and the line shuffled on.

Richard rose to his knees, coughing and hacking at the ground. The mug had come to rest before him. Water leaked from its dented mouth, turning the ground around dark. He plucked it from the mud. Shook it, feeling the pebbles of dirt pepper his face. He wiped his mouth.

Extra flavor, he thought and chuckled again.

Fletcher stood over him, filling his vision like a mountain. Richard met his gaze, feeling a smile begin to play at his face as he thought of a menu of deliciously *horrible* things he might say to the rat.

But in the dark, just past the rat's broad shoulder, Richard's eye spied movement. Something that shouldn't be. His gaze twitched away from the rat and focused on the blur of the walkway stretching over the dig site. Something was up there leaning past the flimsy railing and grabbing for the moving rope of the lift...

The walkway shivered under Garrow's feet as the lift came closer...closer. Just seconds away now. His eye burned with the sweat pouring from his head, but he dared not take his gaze from the mouse.

The mice inched along.

Garrow freed the knife from its sheath. He'd spent that morning sharpening it to a razor's edge.

The mice inched along.

He lifted the knife...

Richard saw the rat up there. He saw the wink of a blade as he brought it up.

His shout was cut short by the Fletchers' boot. Richard doubled over. *That* he felt. He tried to pull his mind from the fog, but this medicine... clouded everything.

"I don't think you're listening to me, Volunteer." Fletcher filled his gaze again. The rat's eyes were globs of fire. "You didn't take too much of Dorgue's sugar water, did you?"

The knife tore through the rope like teeth through bread. The line dashed from Garrow's grip, nearly taking his arm with it. He hissed, smelling blood and hearing a *pop* in his shoulder. He clung to the walkway as the pain twisted under his joint like an iron poker shoved through his armpit...

Richard saw the lift as it fell. A block of sliding earth, plummeting home again. His mouth dried. A chill wrapped its claws in his gut. Dorgue's medicine at last drained away but Richard desperately wished it would return, If only to throw a blanket over this nightmare.

Who's it gonna hit?

Richard forced his gaze to the line.

Bryce stood directly beneath it...

The mice hadn't a clue. No one did. Garrow wanted to keep it that way. He stumbled from the swaying walkway and into the cold packed dirt of one of the upper tunnels. He clutched at his arm.

Had he complained about his eye? That had been nothing. This was like a broken bottle grinding into the joint of his arm. He tasted his stomach bubbling up his throat and bit his lip, sucking air in bursts.

He'd fix it. He'd fix this. All he had to do was get back up top. Get to his room. Get some leverage to pop his arm into place.

But first...Garrow lifted an ear and waited for the bang...

A smell filled the air. A sharp, earthy smell. Bryce frowned. That was odd. The lifts should be well on their way by now. Was the hoist running slow?

Bryce tipped his face up and a pebble bounced from his forehead, breaking apart. He blinked the dirt from his eyes.

Bryce's sudden halt brought the other mice to look up as well. And for a moment, a heartbeat, all was still.

Bryce watched the lift turn over once in the air. So quiet. He could hear the patter of the loose dirt around him, and muffled gasps of the other mice as they climbed over each other to get away.

That thing is gonna kill me, he thought.

One day late, it turned out. If he'd only kept a hold of that knife. If they'd only managed to leave the night they'd planned.

Things could have been different.

He closed his eyes...

Two hands pressed into Bryce's spine and he was in the air. Spinning. Tumbling. He came to rest, scrapping a red path on the ground with his knuckles.

Bryce's eyes snapped open.

Vincent stood where Bryce had only moments before. His hands were still held out before him. His face, muddy from the morning's work, was as calm as Bryce had ever seen it.

He looked his way...

Then the world exploded.

FIFTEEN

Once the entry wound is identified, apply tourniquet above bite (belt from uniform if medical team not handy) and prepare knife to cut away affected flesh. Suck any poison or gall from wound and wrap in ammonia-soaked wrappings. All bites to neck are fatal. Mercy killings left to squad leader's discretion.

— Excerpt from Snake War Medical Pamphlet

"WANNA TRADE?"

The voice speaking was old. It pulsed in his mind like a rumble. Bryce couldn't see. He stood in darkness.

"*Do you?*" the voice asked again. "*A trade?*"

A knife dipped through the shadows, held by a gnarled hand with pebbly knuckles. Coarse hair grew from its pale skin. The fingers shook as if cold, but the knife point held still. Perfect and sharp.

Garrow's knife.

"*A trade?*" the voice asked again, bobbing the knife closer.

He was repulsed.

The voice, the hand, the knife... all of it stunk of decay; of vile bones hiding beneath the earth. He wanted to run—to leave this dream—but Bryce felt his arm reaching out for the blade.

His fingers brushed the knife's edge. He felt the cut, the heat of it. Then the voice,

"*What would you trade?*"

Bryce opened his eyes.

He laid on his back, spine straight and arms crossed over his chest. The dim light of a lantern rattled overhead on a hook, casting knife-sharp shadows. In his skull, a rumble pulsed once...twice...then left. Bryce breathed in shock...and relief. How long had he been so...distracted? That rumble...had it been with him since—

And then the pain. Just a warmth at first, like a dot of blood on cloth, but then it grew. It spread and turned sharp.

His face...

His eye...

What was wrong?

"Keep your hands away from the bandages. You don't want me to start all over again."

Bryce's mouth went dry.

Dorgue.

"That's right. Everything coming back now?" The rat leaned into view. He stared down. His pale, dead eye studied him. Dorgue tilted his head.

"You keep this up, you'll end up looking as pretty as me."

Bryce brushed a hand to his face. He felt the softness of bandages from his jaw to his brow. And there was a special wad of gauze fastened over his left eye.

His eye.

Something was wrong with his eye.

"Had to patch up your neck some as well," Dorgue said nodding to the heavy gauze clinging to the underside of his jaw. "A lot of shrapnel. You got it the worst."

"Well, the worst of those still with us," Dorgue added.

Bryce swallowed and felt a prick. That scared him. His throat felt raw. Felt cut. He struggled past it and worked some life back into his mouth.

"Am I…"

"Alive?" Dorgue lifted a brow. "Last I checked. You're in Hospital, it's been one hour since that rope snapped, and I'm afraid you will have to rest a while before returning to your duties."

The rope, the dig site, the lift… It was all a haze. And what hid just beyond was too horrible to see.

The rat shook his head and his voice rose, turning sour. "*Such* a waste," he said. "Such a *colossal* waste. We're so close. We can't afford to lose any others, let alone an *entire* lift!"

The lift had fallen. Smashed to ruins.

And something else…

Bryce struggled to rise, but Dorgue held him in place with a bony arm.

"Don't get excited. You need *rest.*"

Fire ran up and down Bryce's spine. He was too weak to fight the rat. "Where's Vincent?" he begged. "I need to see Vincent."

Dorgue sighed and pinched the bridge of his snout. His eyes squinted shut. Bryce could see black dots coloring the rat's hand.

Blood. *Bryce's* blood.

Then the rat spoke. Bryce watched the movement of his lips and felt the words land in his ears.

"Vincent was crushed beneath the lift," Dorgue said.

The rat studied him, his good eye roaming his face and his mouth in a thoughtful frown. Dorgue lifted a brow. "Did you hear me, boy?"

Had he?

Bryce remembered looking up. He remembered watching as the lift turned in the air.

Once.

Twice.

"His death was painless as far as I could gather," Dorgue said. "That should be a comfort. That much weight... Death was instant, I would say."

Vincent had pushed him. He remembered the mouse planting his hands on his back, sending him sprawling over the dirt and mud. He remembered looking back. He remembered Vincent closing his eyes.

The wrong mouse died today.

Bryce thumped his head on the bunk and winced at the dull ache between his ears. He brushed his fingertips over his bandaged eye and felt a sharp, *stinging* heat.

"You got hit right in the eye," Dorgue said. "I managed to get everything out. You might not be at twenty-twenty vision, but you won't be blind either. Just be sure to keep the bandage clean. I'll have some medicine mixed up for you, come morning."

Morning. They wouldn't be here in the morning.

Dorgue rose, taking up his tinkling carpet bag and stretching for the lantern. Before he left, he gave Bryce a look, his dead eye finding him as easily as the other.

"You should feel glad," Dorgue said "You're alive. You're breathing. You have been gifted another day. *Your reward awaits you*, child. Say it."

"My reward awaits me."

"Good. Very good."

Then the rat tipped his head in a nod and left him in the dark.

For a long while, Bryce kept still. His mind felt empty, yet it raced a mile a minute. Thoughts like irrational shouts of panic exploded in his mind only to die like sparks. He could have spent hours like that, shaking and reliving the same nightmare over and over.

He should be dead and Vincent shouldn't. Simple as that.

When it became too much to bear he hobbled from his bunk, feeling through the dark. He had to find the others. He had to…

The floor rushed to meet him and Bryce fell to his hands and knees as the room tilted sideways. His skull felt fixed to blow as the pressure behind his eye grew hot. His heart felt like it was screaming. *He* wanted to scream. Alone in this dark place, with only the sound of his ragged breath for company…

That and the ghosts.

He clapped his hands over his ears. Don't even think it! Next, he'd be feeling them pawing at him in the dark. He'd go mad.

But maybe he already was.

"*Oh, Vincent,*" he sobbed. "*I'm sorry, I'm so sorry.*"

He rose to his knees and found the bunk in the dark. He clonked his head against it and bit his lip at the pain behind his eye.

What were they to do?

We still have the knife.

But without Vincent, what hope did they have? Richard didn't know this place. He didn't know the rats! He'd never tasted their anger like the rest of them had. How could he think he could-

We still have the knife, the voice said again. Bryce held his head in his hands and wept.

The voice he heard was Vincent's.

Richard scratched the mud from his arms, but it was quickly turning to glue. A dark, stinking, glue. It was everywhere; on his clothes, his face, in his ears. He spat, tasting it. He'd throw up if he could, plenty of the others had. Ol' Green Tooth Teague holding the prize as the worst offender. Fletcher had yelled at him till veins stood out on his skull.

"*It's just a little blood!*" the rat had said.

Richard looked to Fletcher now, standing over them all from the walkway with his arms crossed resolutely before him. He looked to be speaking to Worth, the lithe rat nodding at this or that in his slow, controlled way.

Creeps.

The drops had finally worn off. His wrist felt sharp, and every smell in the dig site turned his stomach one way or the other. Richard had wandered away from the others and sat on a board—detritus from the lift—and stared down into the dark of the pit. The scaffolds, the mud, the buckets.

This had been Vincent's whole life.

Gavin slunk beside him. The coal-black mouse had worked harder than all the others to dig Vincent out of that wreck. He hadn't bothered to claw the mud from his arms and face and it laid drying in crackly patterns.

He sat next to Richard, and for a time, that was all they did. They just sat. Looking down into the dark. And even if the mouse wanted to talk, Richard didn't know what he would say. What could you say?

Sorry?

Condolences?

He's in a better place?

Folk had said those sorts of things to him when his mother had died. Again once his father followed. Words didn't help. At least they never helped Richard.

"I feel...nothing," Gavin said and looked at his hands. "And I feel...dead. All at once."

"You're in shock. It'll hit you before long."

"Yes."

Gavin looked to what remained of the lift. Bits of wood still littered the area surrounding. A depression was all that remained, like a boot-print in a garden.

He ran through the events again. Fletcher, standing over him. The mice, lined up like good little slaves. And the lift...that rat way up in the walkways...sawing away at the rope...

Then the world turned to noise.

Gavin nudged him. "Richard, you hear me?"

"What?"

"I asked what you think we should do."

Richard frowned and rubbed at his face. "Oh, you did?"

"Yeah," Gavin nodded toward the crater and the mice standing like ghosts around it. "What now?"

Gavin wept then. He threw his hands over his face and doubled over. Very sudden. Very quiet. Gavin's shoulders shook. He twisted his hair in his fists, knuckles turning white.

"*I didn't...*" but grief swallowed the rest of Gavin's words.

Richard couldn't look upon Gavin's pain, so he focused on his own. The tattered bandage around his arm had nearly given up the ghost. The medicine smell had gone, replaced with the odor of sweat and mud and death. The pain grew by the moment. He still had some of Dorgue's drops left, but he dared not take any. At least not yet.

Richard blinked. Shook his head. "Nothing changes," he said. "We have what we need. Vincent wouldn't want us to give up."

Gavin nodded and wiped his face roughly with the back of his hand. He shook the tears from his fingers. And that was it. Gavin's mourning ended.

The sentiment seemed to spread to the rest of the dig site. Like a bruised fighter rousing from the ground, the time of quiet came to an end. The rats whistled for movement and an extra allotment of water was divvied out. A rare thing, Richard judged by the wide eyes around him.

Richard took his mug, it was the same one he had dropped, the one with the dented mouth. Dirt still colored its edge, seeping into the water in an oily streak.

Richard stared.

"Drink it," Gavin said.

"I will."

Gavin shook his head. He'd already drank his and was moving his mouth to catch the grit in his teeth. He spat on the ground.

"How do you folk survive out in the world if you're so fussy about water?"

"Our water isn't brown."

Richard took a sip. It was tepid. Salty. He fought the urge to gag, and to his surprise, actually managed. He set the mug by his feet.

"Do you think Bryce will be alright?" he said.

Gavin studied his toes a moment before saying and gave a brief nod.

"Bryce'll be alright," he said. "He's stronger than he gives himself credit for. He's hidden his busted knee well from the rats. A little wood to the face?" he shrugged. "Stings like hell, but he'll keep on."

Richard nodded.

The other mice of the dig site sat in little groups. A few wept silently, but most held stoic faces staring out at nothing. Richard wondered if this was how they always treated the passing of one of their own.

Richard had looked away when they dug out Vincent's body and loaded it into the lift. No matter how many times death crossed his path, it was always a surprise to him how thin that line was between being something with a voice and dreams, to becoming an *object*. A chore to carry.

"Aren't you going to…" Richard made a face, "Sing over his bones?"

It was like asking if he thought rocks could dance. Gavin's face tensed, as if unsure of Richard was poking fun. "I don't follow," he said.

These mice really didn't know anything, did they? Richard wondered how much was worth explaining. "Everyone knows the Song," he said. "It's…what we do. To remember them. Someone sings."

Gavin's face eased as he mulled that over.

Richard had only sung the Song once before. Kathryn had sung it for mother, so when father died it was decided that it would be Richard's turn. It was only fitting that the Sovereign's son had the honor of singing over his bones.

Gavin nudged him out of his thoughts. "Would you do it?" he asked.

"Do what? Sing for Vincent?"

Gavin's face was heavy, but his eyes were bright. He said, "I think he would have liked that."

Richard glanced at the rats up on the walkways. "This might not be the place for it," he said.

"What kind of song is it?"

Richard twisted his face. "It's kinda long. A dirge. Voices only. No instruments. It's like:

I'll save your name from olden foe,
Be he rust or sword or sling,
For by the stars or ocean's tow,
These bones again shall sing.

Anyway, that's a little of it. It's about promising not to forget someone. Not letting their name fade away, you know?"

Gavin nodded. "I'll never forget him," he said. "No one here will. The whole world will know his name once we all leave this place."

Richard tried not to make a face. Vincent's plan to get them all out would be a death march. Richard couldn't show his face in Green Hill if he had the blood of a few hundred innocents on his hands. That would be too many songs to sing.

"I had an idea," he said. "I was hoping I could get your thoughts on it."

"I thought you said nothing's changed."

"We're still making our break tonight. That hasn't changed."

Gavin frowned. "So tell me," he said.

Richard told him. About the Deep Wood. About Green Hill. About the army waiting for them should they make it back. Richard spoke it all in a harsh whisper, keeping half an eye on the rats as they moved about.

Through it all, Gavin's face remained flat. He listened, dropping an empty stare at the ground. When all was said, he closed his eyes in thought.

Fletcher sounded a whip somewhere above. All around, the rats and mice came to life again, forming their lines and finishing the last of their rations.

Still, Gavin sat.

Would he see reason? Vincent had been so adamant, that he hadn't even given the idea a thought. *'Seeing folk in need'* and all that.

You can't help folk if they're *dead.*

Gavin said, "You spoke to... To Vincent about this?"

Richard plucked his mug from the ground and let the water slosh. "Yeah, I spoke to him."

"What'd he say?"

Richard peered into the water. He saw his own face. His snout was puffy and swollen, the veins in his eyes stood out like red spiderwebs, and his fur was so matted with mud he couldn't see its color anymore.

He brought the mug to his lips and forced a swallow. It was like lapping drink from cobble-stones.

"He thought it was worth talking over."

SIXTEEN

It is unknown how many children were truly stolen from their families—as clear records from the time of the Vanishings do not exist—but the full number couldn't have been sustained on the kidnappings alone. We are still looking into how invasive Dorgue's reach truly was...

— Jonathan Quick, The Sunday Circular

BRYCE DRIFTED THROUGH THE hours like a fog, in and out of wakeful dread and smothering nightmares. He was aware of the other mice drifting into Hospital as the day ended. The smell of sickness and old blood smothered by medicine followed them in. So strange to have so few in a burrow, each of them ignoring the other, alone in their own well of misery.

His eye hurt. His soul hurt. Exhaustion clung to his mind yet refused him rest. He didn't know how long he lay there in that bunk, wrestling with guilt and running from the dark thoughts he knew would destroy him should their creeping fingers get hold of his heart.

He woke to Sampson's hand on his shoulder.

"Can you move?" Sampson asked.

Bryce eased open one eye. The other shivered behind its bandage, but Bryce forced it still. His throat clicked when he swallowed.

"Vincent's dead," Bryce said.

Sampson stood over him. He held a candle in his crushed hand, lighting his pale fur. His tired eyes moved under heavy lids. "Yes," he said.

"He pushed me out of the way of the lift."

"He did."

My fault. Bryce brought his hands to his face. Anger now. It flashed through Bryce's skull like ember sparks. *Why would Vincent do something so stupid?* Nobody needed clumsy Bryce, they needed Vincent! They needed the mouse who could still remember the sound of the wind and the colors of leaves. The one mouse in this terrible, mean world who still knew how to speak *hope*.

Nobody needed a mouse who dropped knives.

Sampson nudged him again, drawing him out of his dark place. "Everyone's meeting," he said. "Folk are already gathered. We need you up there."

Bryce laughed but the sound must have been vile because Sampson startled back, his eyes round and worried.

The sight only made Bryce angrier. He showed his teeth. "*What?* Is there anything else you lot want ruined? I bet if I tried really hard, I could cause a cave-in and squash us all to slime. How's that sound?"

Bryce glared. Daring Sampson to challenge him. In a cruel way, Bryce wanted to tear the strong mouse down. He wanted to hear his condolences and spit in his face. If hope was a cup of cool water, Bryce was ready to snap at the fingers that offered it.

Sampson stared, his face glum and heavy. The pitiful candle he clutched in his ruined hand dribbled wax down his crooked fingers. His voice rumbled in the burrow, no longer whispering. The other mice in Hospital cowered in their bunks.

"My father's name was Dane. Did I ever tell you that? It's the only thing I can remember from before."

Very few mice could remember anything besides Dorgue's Tree. Vincent had been the only one who could recall more than snatches of feelings or smells.

"I can't recall what sort of mouse he was," Sampson said, "But his name is as bright as torchlight in my heart. And that light guides me. It pulls me."

Sampson glanced down, his face turning ugly. Bryce feared for a moment he might grab hold of him and throw him to the ground.

Sampson said, "If you've no light of your own... If you're blind down here with no memory to guide you up, then please trust in ours even if you can't see it. Dorgue's done his best to stamp out any memory of home that might cause us to look up with hope. Today, hope hangs by a thread, Bryce. The slightest breath could kill it."

Sampson's mouth firmed and the candle flame shook in his grip. "And that *bastard*, Volunteer knows it."

The anger in Bryce's heart fled in an instant, replaced by cold dread. He sat up, grabbing hold of Sampson's arm to steady himself.

"Tell me."

Sampson growled. "He's rallied the others. They've gathered in the secret burrow. Richard says he has a new plan to get everyone out of here and it's going to happen *tonight*."

"What is he planning?"

"I don't know, but I think he's already talked Gavin into it. We need you up there."

Bryce pushed his legs off his bunk. His knee grumbled like a toothache, but the pain in his head somehow made it manageable. The pain and the fury. "Help me," Bryce said.

They hurried out from the burrow, the light of the candle leaving with them. The mice hiding in their bunks watched it go with wide eyes, drinking the light until it was long gone from view.

Bryce kept a hand on the wall as he followed the tunnel. His head hurt and his knee was stiff, but he could walk. He could move. Sampson kept at his side to steady him, but Bryce was becoming more sure of his footing with every step. He had to be. Vincent was dead and who knew *what* that Volunteer was planning?

Bryce felt a groove in the wall and stopped. The secret burrow was just above. He found a hold on the wall.

"Give me a boost," he said.

"Alright, slow down, you'll break your neck."

Sampson hefted him up toward the ceiling. With some effort, Bryce found the opening and wriggled through. Dust coated his face and made his hands chalky. In the small space, he climbed faster, kicking pebbles as he went.

He always hated the tight climb into the burrow. The dark closing around him and the sharp, untrustworthy holds in the rock that would be giddy to trip him up and send him rattling down. Bryce spied light above him now. Just a hint of it. It peeked through the blanket they'd draped over the opening. Bryce cleared his throat and threw up the blanket, causing those gathered close to the hole in the floor to startle back.

The burrow was bursting. So many dusty faces looking back at him, so many names springing to mind. There were some Bryce hadn't even known were part of Vincent's group and some he'd only spoken to a handful of times while in Dorgue's Tree.

He saw Richard, standing in the center of them all. His face was drawn and exhausted, dry mud hung from his fur, and the bandage around his wrist had tattered into strings.

Richard raised a brow. "That everyone?"

Bryce's fist connected with Richard's chin and the burrow erupted.

Richard, mostly from shock, swung blindly and missed clocking Bryce's patched eye by inches, instead he knocked Bryce's skull good and made him feel like a rung bell, but that was neither here nor there. Bryce aimed to kill this stuck-up volunteer.

"*Who do you think you are?*" Bryce screamed as the crowd of mice tore him away. Bryce kicked air. "*You come here! You take over? You—*"

Gavin's hand clamped over his mouth. Bryce tried to worm away, but Gavin held fast. The only noise in the burrow was Sampson still struggling to fit through the hole in the floor.

Bryce had never struck anyone before. He'd never been so angry before. They had worried Richard was a spy from Dorgue? No, this mouse was much worse. He was here to lead them into the flames.

Richard spat blood from his mouth and glared. "I'm trying to help, you *idiot.*"

Bryce's ground his teeth. "Help how? By picking fights with the rats? By tossing away Vincent's plan like it was *slop*?" Bryce shrugged from Gavin's grip. "Vincent is gone less than a day, and you think you can lord over us?"

Richard's face stretched in surprise. He blinked. "You need to take a minute, Bryce."

"Vincent had a plan. He was going to get us *all* out of here."

"And we still may. But first, we all need to…" Richard spat again, wiping away the red from his mouth, " *Talk* about it. Okay?"

Hugo spoke up from the crowd, "We might as well get started then. Don't have much time." He nodded to Gavin. "Go ahead and show everyone."

Gavin didn't give Bryce a glance as he moved to the room's end. He reached up into a crack in the wall and pulled forth a folded blanket. Dust wafted from it, and the mice began to murmur amongst themselves. But all hushed at the sight of the blade he pulled into the air.

Garrow's knife was large in Gavin's hands, like a small sword. Its edge held a dull gleam and the nicks in the metal's face looked sharp and wicked in the candlelight. The mice beheld it with wide eyes.

"A pretty thing, isn't it?"

All looked to Richard. He regarded the room with squinted eyes. "Congratulations. You have a pitiful little knife that's hardly sharp enough to cut air, let alone skin."

He pressed into the middle of them, looking at each in the room, eyes blazing. "Getting every mouse out of here at the same time is risky, dangerous, and foolhardy." Richard settled his glare on Bryce.

"But what if you had another choice?" Richard said. "A smarter choice? Before we rush into this and get ourselves *killed*, let's take a breath and consider a moment."

Richard turned to the others holding out a finger to count them. "I see only a fraction of the mice of Dorgue's Tree here. Were you planning on waking all the others below and filling them in on the way? That's a lot of folk to keep calm. A lot of folk who've proven themselves to be…less than trustworthy. And that's before we even *get* outside.

You have no idea what's waiting for you out there. If you go blindly into the Deep Wood, you'll die the same as you would here. Maybe even worse."

Bryce had enough of Richard's doom and gloom. He could see the others' faces beginning to fall into worry. He remembered what Sampson had said about hope hanging by a thread. Bryce moved on Richard again and stuck a finger in his face.

"I guess it's all just too hard, then," Bryce said. "We'll just roll over and *die*, yeah? That's what you want, *Volunteer*? Because I promise you, if we stay here much longer, things are only going to get worse for everyone."

Bryce saw Richard's face grow darker and darker as he spoke. The mouse from the Deep Wood glared, his mouth a hard line.

Gavin, who had shadowed Bryce just in case he tried to throw another punch, shifted his stance and cleared his throat. "I think you should cut to the point, Rich."

"Yeah!," Hugo said, "The point besides reminding everyone that we're all *dead*."

Richard blinked. His eyes shifted between Bryce, Gavin, and the mice beyond. He took a breath and his stormy face cleared into something that was almost calm. He said, "It's just like Bryce tells us. If we stay here it won't end well. And it's just like *I* tell you, if everyone goes out, well…I'll spare you the details."

Bryce was sick of this talk. "So what do you want us to do?"

Richard smiled. "Well, I get Green Hill to march five thousand troops through the Deep Wood, cutting down anything that has the mind to jump out at them, and then they'll hack Dorgue and his rats into little, *little pieces*. How does that sound to everyone?"

Silence in the burrow. Bryce tried to understand. "Five... *Thousand...*"

"And that's not including the Red Cloaks," Richard added. "If they go along that's an extra two hundred."

Bryce's glare lost direction. His eye drifted past Richard, focusing on nothing. "...Red cloaks?" he echoed.

"Yes," Richard clapped Bryce's arm and stepped past, showing his hands to the crowd. "An *army* everybody. You know what an army is? It's a moving cloud of blood and sweat, itching to kill whatever isn't wearing the right uniform. When I get to Green Hill, I'll wind them up and point them at Dorgue. We won't have to worry about outrunning the rats *or* dying in the Deep Wood. We'll be safe. Everyone will be safe."

The mice held perfectly still. Every mouse, save for Bryce, whose eye drifted back and forth in its socket. He closed his mouth. Opened it again.

"An...army?"

"Armed to the teeth and here in a matter of days," Richard said.

Gavin shouldered past Bryce. "How many days?" he asked.

Richard wagged his head back and forth. "No more than ten, I should think."

"Who g-g-goes?" Simon called.

Then Ed clapped his hands to his face and cried, "*Who stays behind?*"

Once the idea was in their heads—that only a select few would go—it was hard to ignore. They started to bustle and murmur, a slow quiet build of panic. Bryce felt it same as anyone. It brought a wobble to his stomach.

Ten days...

Richard raised his hands to calm them and Gavin rose to help.

"We are just talking," Gavin said. "That's all we're doing right now. Talking. If anyone doesn't like this idea, he should be heard. But one at a time. *Quietly*."

Hugo settled back against the wall, the others scurrying to make room. His face was dark and his hands shook on his knees. "Fine. Fine." He took a long, shaky breath. "Who's it gonna be then? How many leave tonight?"

"We'll have to keep the group small," Richard said. "We'll have to move fast. No more than three, I'd say."

Gavin nodded, staring at the blade in his hand with new determination. "And we'll be against whatever is waiting outside..."

"Only if we're heard," Richard said. "I'm not gonna lie, it'll be dangerous. This idea isn't without risk."

"But still..." Sampson said, his voice rumbling the burrow. He moved his gaze up from the ground, his eyes tired, and looked to Bryce. "... safer than all of us trouncing out."

Richard's face broke into a smile that touched his eyes. He nodded. "Much safer. Yes."

"And what about all of us left behind?" Hugo said. "When the rats notice some of us missing..." he showed his hands. "They won't be happy."

Another mouse spoke up. He had a notch in his ear and patchy gray fur. He shivered where he sat pulled at his ears. "What if they *kill us* for it?"

"Or torture us?" another squealed.

The room began to slip again into a panic. But then Gavin spoke. "The rats wouldn't dare," he said. "Tell me, what happened when Richard knocked Bard flat on his tail and then tried to claw Teague's eyes out? Did they hold him under the mud?"

The burrow murmured.

"And today, when poor Vincent was crushed, what did Fletcher say? What did the rats do once everything was cleaned up?"

Simon frowned, his eyes growing wide. "...They g-g-gave us..."

"Water," Gavin said with a nod. "When was the last time we were given extra water?"

Sampson answered.

"Never," he said and brought up his crushed hand. "When this happened, you know what Fletcher told me? *That's why God gave you two*. Then he kicked me walking again. No trip to Hospital and no visit from Dorgue. He didn't care if I wasn't at my fullest. But today?" Sampson almost smiled, the realization dawning, "All of a sudden we're valuable and the loss of one of our own is a great tragedy. Even Bryce was brought back to speed as quickly as Dorgue could manage."

It was true. Bryce couldn't remember a time when Dorgue came down over something as menial as an eye. Even Richard's wrist had been odd.

He thought back to what Dorgue had said, "*Such a waste. We're so close.*" Perhaps close enough to want them healthy instead of limping? After all, the rats were stuck down here too. If the work dragged on for much longer...

"I'll stay behind," Sampson said. He stood, his ears brushing the ceiling. "When the rats notice you're gone, I'll claim to have helped you."

Bryce thought of what the rats might do in that case. "But what if they—"

"Look at me," Sampson said. "I'm as strong as three of you. They wouldn't dare kill me if they're as close to the end as they think. I might get whipped, but I've been whipped before. I'll survive." He nodded to Richard. "Just don't take too long."

The other mice in the burrow whispered to one another. Bryce let his fingers drift to feel the bandage under his chin, the patch over his eye. *Had the rats lost their edge?*

Hugo raised his hand and all became quiet. "So," he said. "Who's it gonna be?"

None spoke up.

If Sampson was staying behind, there was only one choice. Bryce took a breath. "Gavin should go," he said. "Out of all of us, he's the most careful. The safest."

A murmur of agreement rose around them. Gavin lifted his hands.

"Alright," he said, "Then I say Bryce should go. He was with us when we stole the knife, so it's only fair if he's with us when we use it."

He threw an arm over Bryce's shoulder. "I hope I don't offend anybody when I say, there's no one here I'd rather have at my side if things go wrong."

"*When* they go wrong," Hugo was helpful to point out.

Bryce couldn't find words. Yes, he wanted to escape more than anything, but was he truly the one to go? He looked down at his hands, at the calluses covering his fingers.

You dropped the knife, remember?

Richard stepped forward. "I hear you, Gavin," he said, "But Bryce is injured. If this is going to work, all who go need to be at their best."

"Still knocked you on your butt," Hugo said. The mouse grinned. "Besides, you're not looking so hot either."

Simon called out from the candle, "W-we should call a v-vuh-vote!"

"All in favor of Gavin and Bryce?" Hugo said.

Bryce watched Richard's face. The mouse had seemed pleased at the thought of Gavin joining the trek, but his face had turned sour as the hands began to rise. Every hand in the burrow came up. Ed raised two.

Richard sighed. "Alright then," he said. Then he crossed his arms, his face wincing slightly as he touched his bandaged wrist. He smiled at them.

"Who knows how to start a fire?" He asked.

SEVENTEEN

A slo mouz, is a dead mouz. A dead mouz, is a gud mouz. A
gud mouz is bes plantd 3 fut deep.

— A scrap of writing found near Dorgue's Tree, Author Unknown

G ARROW LET THE BOARDS under his arm clatter to the floor. Splinters clung to his fingers. He tried to focus on that pain if only to block the agony in his shoulder.

He'd found biting his tongue helped.

They had spent most of the day ferrying what remained of the lift—up into one of the old storerooms, just a few levels above the dig site. Close enough to still hear the clanging music of the work, but far enough to be a right pain for all those involved. The other rats had quite the time with it, grumbling this or that when they thought Fletcher wasn't listening.

Garrow didn't grumble. He kept his steady pace—not stopping, not slowing—until every scrap of wood had been accounted for. He carried his burden like he might carry a newborn—cradled in one arm. His other, he left motionless at his side.

As the day went on—crossing the swaying walkways and climbing up steep half-circles before crossing to the other side to do it again—Garrow waited for the ruckus that might accompany the discovery of a knife amongst the mud and the blood and the splinters. He could imagine it...

"Wait, this imp's gotta knife?"

"Where'd he get a knife?"

"Not from me*!"*

"Well, he got it from somewhere*! Come on then, who's missing a knife?"*

And if Fletcher investigates which of his rats had misplaced their knife... It would be *Lou* left holding the short straw.

But as more and more detritus got cleared away, the more Garrow began to worry. Had he hit the wrong mouse? That Candle Hall imp had been sure he'd seen the one called *Bryce* sneaking around. Garrow had even caught the whelp glancing up into the walkways on more than one occasion, and that all but confirmed it in his mind. The guilty couldn't help but give themselves away, you see.

But when they at last pulled what was left of the mouse's body out of the wreck. Garrow cursed when he didn't spy a knife clutched in the whelp's ruined hand. Fletcher had the body sent up to Dorgue for the old rat to do whatever it was he did with the dead ones. Maybe he ate them. Garrow didn't care. The knife was still missing.

What if the mouse hadn't kept the knife on his person? *But where else could he be hiding it?*

Garrow was too exhausted to puzzle out where that worthless worm had stashed the prize. He took up scrap. He climbed the walkways. He bit his tongue at every jolt that cut into the secret places beneath his shoulder.

And now, Garrow stood in the dusty store room. The sound of the work below faded into echoes, replaced by a red roar in his ears. He stared as the scraps of wood and timber and mud, all thrown together in an unholy pile. So much trouble from so small a thing: the flash of a knife and the snap of a rope.

But now it was done.

The lift had fallen. The mouse was dead. And Garrow's knife was *still missing*. Now he'd return to his room, shut the door, and pull his arm up...and up...*and up...* He'd pull until—

"I said you look dead," Worth repeated.

Garrow couldn't hide his jump of surprise, but he did his best to keep his mouth flat, and not bite off a chunk of his tongue.

Two rats stood at the doorway, Worth and Lou.

Worth was dusting the dirt from his hands. He'd somehow managed to stay mostly clean. Lou, however, was a trash pile with eyes.

Garrow frowned. "Nothin' wrong with me," he said.

Lou rubbed his cheek onto his filthy arm, painting his face with muck. "*Right*, and I'm a gut fish! You look uglier than a viper sick from rot." A laugh in his throat broke into a savage coughing fit. He doubled, making a noise like he was sucking air through a knitted bag.

Garrow smiled at the little rat. He'd kill him one day. One fine day. He'd do it with Lou's own knife, he decided. But after the work. After the mice. After they were all out of this godforsaken forest of death.

One fine day.

He peered past them. Garrow could see out into the shaft and catch a hint of the Hoist, a square of light out there in the dark.

Things will go slower with only one lift.

Garrow huffed. It was worth it to squash that filthy whelp. How much time could it add, anyway? All Garrow had to do was collect his knife from the filthy vermin downstairs, maybe cut a few of them down to size, and then wait the rest out.

Days now. Only days left. That's what the whispers were upstairs.

"Garrow," Worth appeared behind him. "You got mud in your ears? I said you look ready to chase your ghost."

Garrow couldn't turn his head without earning a spike of pain. He stared ahead. "Nothin' wrong with me."

Garrow left them and stepped out onto the walkway. The slats clattered underfoot and despite the sway that brought a flutter to his stomach, he kept his arms limp at his sides. Far, far below, he heard the noise of the mice as they worked: the cling of shovels and the shouts of the rats guarding over them.

The noise…he could feel it. It shivered inside his shoulder, like a devil stretching under his skin.

He had to fix this. He just needed to get the right angle…to twist just so, and, POP! Everything would be better. The relief would be as sweet as drinking gold from a sunrise. He focused on how wonderful a thing relief would be as he climbed the crisscrossing walkways up and up until here he was at the heavy oaken door of the Hoist. He nudged it open with a boot.

The rat working the Hoist was a snappy fellow named Tack. At least that was everyone's best guess at his name. His teeth were long and hung low from his lips. He smelled like spit, blinked a lot, and was missing half of his tongue. He showed his teeth in a grin as Garrow toed his way in, stiff as a board.

"*Arrow*," he mewed, smiling wide and letting what was left of his tongue lull over his teeth. Garrow tried not to look at it. None had managed to get the story of what had happened to the rat, and what the others had imagined hadn't been pretty.

"Arrow, Arrow," Tack laughed.

He'd kick the lunatic if he could.

A shrill whistle came from far below, and Tack set himself to bring the lift back to the Hoist, cooing to himself as he reached for levers and eased ropes into wooden coils.

The Hoist shook. Garrow's shoulder sparked.

Worth eased through the oaken door after Garrow. The lithe rat peered down the shaft at the dim glow of the work far below. He shook his head. "That should be the last load for the day," Worth said. "I really thought that one was gonna make it."

Garrow couldn't care less. He stomped past the little rat working the controls. "You know who's on watch tonight?" he asked.

"Ferris," Worth said and turned an eye to Garrow. "You've had two nights in a row, yeah?"

Garrow's skin squirmed under Worth's gaze.

"Tonight, I'm sleeping," he said and left the shaking room. His boots touching the solid ground once again quieted the ache in his shoulder, but only slightly. Garrow bared his teeth as he walked alone. At his side, he wrapped his fingers around the hilt of Lou's dagger.

He'd have to put off sleep for another night. Tonight he'd be paying a little visit to Ferris.

Then he'd be hunting.

EIGHTEEN

The Long Walk are good at guarding the Deep Wood from
fire. Almost as good as they are at gouging out eyes and
wearing them as necklaces. True, squirrels don't make the
best of friends, but they're far, far worse as Enemies.

— Hamish Geralt, Captain of Green Hill's Malitia

I T WAS AGREED SAMPSON would go with them as far as the dig site to light the fire and help if the rat on guard proved to be a problem. The others met them just beyond the mouth of the Burrow. They'd brought their blankets.

"For the fire," Ed said and pressed the scratchy bundle into Richard's arms.

Richard couldn't see the other mice in the dark, but he could hear them. Feel them. Richard couldn't be sure of the number, only that it was sizable. Possibly even more than had been in the secret burrow.

So much for secrecy.

He felt Gavin place a hand on his shoulder. "In the coming days," he said to all gathered there, "be careful to stay calm. Even with Sampson shouldering the blame...things could get difficult once the rats notice us missing."

Richard heard a chuckle, and Hugo said, "Things have always been difficult."

Facing rats with whips, living in mud up to your chin, eating gruel and moldy crusts... Honestly, Richard couldn't imagine things being much worse for them. "Ten days," he said. "Ten days and it's over."

Nothing more was said. One by one, the mice came and placed their hands on their shoulders. A last goodbye.

Richard recoiled at first. This many pressing in to say their farewells was just the sort of thing he'd sneak off early to avoid. He'd done the same the night he left Green Hill. He knew Kathryn had planned one final dinner to be eaten together in vapid silence while she pretended nothing was wrong.

Richard had packed his rucksack and left in the quiet of the morning.

His rucksack. It was still in that bush, wasn't it? His change of clothes, his flint and starter, his wineskin (oh! his poor wineskin!), and the thing he had wrapped up and hidden away in the deepest folds of the pack—the one thing Kathryn had urged him not to take.

Father's knife.

A final mouse took Richard's hand in his own. The fingers were shaking, and his grip faltered. "All our prayers go with you," he whispered.

Richard didn't recognize the voice.

And then they were gone, slipping away just as quiet as they had come. Richard, Gavin, Bryce, and Sampson stood alone in the tunnel. Four, soon to be three.

"We should go," Gavin said.

Garrow's arm went back in its place with a crack. The scrap of wood he held between his teeth snapped like a brittle bone. He stood by the wall, trembling, breathing.

He spat the wood from his mouth. The relief should come, right? His hand hovered over his arm, shaking. After a deep breath, he tried to lift it, and Garrow could have wept in relief. He could move his arm again. While he couldn't bring his hand much higher than his waist, it was a start. He'd get better.

He reached for the door with his good arm and eased it open. He brought his eye to the crack.

The hall was dark. Empty.

Everyone was no doubt asleep in their quarters. Who was it that Worth said was on duty tonight? Ferris? A skinny runt with warts peeking out from his ears. Garrow could bully him into relinquishing his responsibilities easily enough.

He found him in the Hoist prepping a lift to go down. Garrow's heavy step startled the other rat.

"Gore!" he said with a jump. Ferris had to grab hold of the lift's ropes to keep from tumbling over. "What in the blue heck's got in your head, coming up on a body like that? Fit ta' give me the starts!"

Garrow smiled at the rat. "You got watch tonight?"

The look he gave Garrow said he did indeed have the watch tonight! Ferris spat on the slatted floor.

"Whadaya want, fatso?"

Garrow clomped closer, boards creaking beneath him. "I been thinking," he said. "Awful strange what happened to that mouse today. Awful strange."

Farris squinted. "Not so much, if you asks me. You drop a brick on a body's head... well, they blink once 'er twice and fall over dead. Now, You drop a *wagon* on 'em," he shrugged. "Dead minus the blink'n, *I say*. What's so strange about that?"

"It's just funny is all, that a lift should snap so close to the end of things."

"Don't hear *me* laugh'n, fatso." He picked at his ear. "Speak your say, I've gotta spot 'ta sit, down yonder."

"I'm saying I wanna take a closer look. You worked your hands to nubs, today. Let me take the watch. I'm rested plenty."

Ferris's frown turned into a wily grin. "You know... I *am* a bit sore after a full day of whipping those sorry cusses down in the Pit. Lookit' my legs. Mud's dried the hairs all twisted."

"You should see after that before it sets too long."

Ferris nodded. "Just what I said," and was already moving from the lift hiding a smile, lest Garrow get wise and change his mind. "You're a true saint, fatso. With statues and everything!"

He slipped away into the dark. Garrow could hear the idiot's choked laughter as he went.

Good so far. He stepped up on the lift and began his descent, grunting as he pulled the release over his head. His shoulder still had plenty to complain about, but at least he could move it again.

The lift dropped with a jolt. Garrow kept a firm grip at the rail with one hand, and the other he kept in a vice around the hilt of Lou's knife. He wet his lips and watched the shrinking light of the Hoist as he drifted farther and farther down.

There would be a guard at the dig site. The hope was they'd be lucky and get someone like Garrow, who'd be drunk and dead to the world in the small hours of the morning.

Richard paused at the turn and lifted his nose to sniff the air, but all he could smell was the dust in his nose. He clapped a hand to his mouth to kill a sneeze. It buckled in his throat like a punch, but he'd kept silent.

Unlike Gavin, who was shuffling in place behind him. At least…he thought it was Gavin. He reached an arm back and patted at the snout he found in the dark.

"You're sure there's only one standing at watch?" Richard said.

Gavin pushed him away. "The rats all take turns. Tonight, it should be Ferris at duty. He doesn't drink like Garrow, but he's usually asleep by now."

"He'd better be asleep," Sampson said.

Richard jumped at the rumble of the mouse's voice. "Just… Everybody keep quiet, yeah?"

"You're the one talking," Bryce said.

Richard took a breath. Held it.

He didn't need to be picking a fight just now. At least not yet. They rounded the turn.

The blankets under Richard's arm started to slip again. He bounced them lightly on his hip, renewing his hold. He asked, "How close do you think we are to the dig site?"

"You have a hand on the wall?"

"Yeah."

"Feel for two bumps as you go. That'll mean—"

Something sharp cut into the sole of Richard's boot. He jumped, throwing his arms back, and landed in a confused tangle atop Gavin, dropping his share of the blankets. The other mouse crumpled beneath him, his final word stretching long.

"What in blazes?" Gavin hissed, shoving Richard to the ground.

With no light to see, Richard imagined a parade of horrors... An ugly nail shoved up through the meat of his foot and poking out like a flag at the top. The head of a shovel, left rusty and hungry on the tunnel floor, slicing a deep ribbon in the ball of his heel. A shard of wild glass, worming its way through bone just as easily as it would wet newspaper.

Richard sucked his breath at the sting. "*What is it? What is it?*"

Gavin grabbed hold of his foot. "Hold on, let me see it."

"No! Don't touch it. I need a doctor!"

"Will someone hold his arms, please?"

Sampson took hold of his wrists and crushed him in a hug. "Just keep still," he said.

Richard's blood rumbled in his ears. Gavin had his foot pinned under his arm, and Sampson was overstepping every boundary. "Unhand me *this moment*, or I will—"

"I got it, relax."

Richard slumped to the ground as either mouse loosed their grip. As he did, another sharp needle of something slipped into his hip and Richard sucked in a breath. He searched for it with his fingers, wincing when his thumb grazed the bur. After a short mental count, he pulled it free.

"Saint Sansa," Richard said, rolling the thing between his thumb and finger. "Is this a thorn?"

"It's a shard," Bryce said. "Candle Hall isn't far from here. They must have laid them out."

So there would be more. Richard took a breath. These shards were vicious little things if they could get through his boots. "How big of an issue we thinking here?" he asked. "This gonna be a problem?"

Gavin sucked his teeth. "We can shuffle through alright," he said. "Noisy though. And slow."

"Couldn't we… use the blankets to sweep our way through?" Richard said. He padded the dark for the ones he'd dropped and earned a prick in the meat of his hand. He hissed and shook the thing away, sending it tinkling down the tunnel.

Gavin said, "*Noise*, remember? If we send them scattering the sound will echo straight to the dig site."

Sampson rumbled. "And if Bard's folk are waiting…"

"They'd have the same trouble as us with the shards," Bryce said. "They won't show themselves."

Richard pulled himself up. "That a promise?"

"I don't make promises."

Richard laughed. That simplified things.

Ever since the meeting, Bryce had been withdrawn. His anger over all that had happened today, Richard could understand it. Losing a friend so sudden… It had taken some time for Richard to come to terms with what had happened to his mother. To his father.

But, he'd had Kathryn to talk to.

They collected the fallen blankets and shuffled along. Richard felt the little pings of the stone shards as they scattered from their wake, sounding like the wind-chimes that warded the markets in Green Hill come spring.

Richard pictured it. The smell of baking bread on the wind and the noise of warring street vendors lulling the drunks to sleep as children stole crumbs from their tables.

Life.

So different from this eternal dark he'd found himself in.

His hand found two gouges on the wall as his fingers went tap, tap. Gavin had said something about that…

"This tunnel is about to meet another," he whispered. "We're about to pass Candle Hall."

The shards were thicker here, it was like wading through acorns. And though they kept a mourner's pace, he still felt the occasional prick and sting as they moved along. And Richard was wearing shoes! The others had to make do with just their bare feet.

Light ahead.

Richard felt his heart warm despite himself. He knew the light meant trouble…but it was light. He peered over his shoulder at the others.

Gavin was stone-faced and steady.

Bryce had his brow knitted tight over his eyes. He looked worried. The patch over his left eye was bright compared to his dirty fur.

And Sampson was a tank keeping the rear. The hulking mouse dipped his chin ahead. They had arrived at Candle Hall.

The sudden silence of their halt was embarrassing, as the jingle of the shuffled shards came to a sharp stop. In what little light they had, Richard saw the glint of thousands more. They shone like starlight. How on earth had Bard managed this? It would have taken years to get all this from the dig site.

Then again…all they had down here were years. He motioned to the others.

"We just…walk past them?"

Gavin gave him a shove. "You have any other ideas?"

Richard didn't. And besides, Bryce was right: no way was Bard or any of his cronies going to march out and stop them. He looked down at the sharp glint surrounding them. Bard had painted himself into a corner.

The mice kept close to the wall, their feet dragging and the sharp noise of the stone shards fanning before them.

Richard could see into the burrow now. The lone candle, gone to nearly a stub, looked out at them like a lighthouse. He couldn't make out any detail beyond the glow.

He strained to see.

And the first ball of mud hit his face.

It exploded over his eyes, spreading into his mouth. Everything went stinging black and Richard yelped in surprise.

His boot came crunching down on a nest of shards.

More mud came flying their way. Richard could hear Gavin and Bryce grunting in pain as they stumbled. Sampson filled the tunnel with a stomach-grabbing growl as the mud rained around them.

Another glob connected with Richard's shoulder. He brought his other boot down and felt the spurs dig into the meat of his foot. Gavin grabbed a hold of his arm before he could tip into the mess of shards. He spoke through his teeth.

"Don't. Fall."

Another spur slid into Richard's foot. "NO KIDDING?" he snapped and was rewarded with a mouthful of grime.

They scrambled as Candle Hall continued their onslaught. Sampson, dripping with the dark mud, gritted his teeth and swiped a blanket across the floor, sending a swathe of shards into the burrow. A shriek came from the dark and the mud stopped for a moment.

Just a moment.

So much for secrecy. Richard scratched the mud from his face. "You're all crazy!" he said.

The mud started again, and a hand clasped onto Richard's wrist and pulled him away from the others. His feet scrambled, earning scores more cuts. Richard cried out and fell—

Onto smooth ground.

His palms scuffed on the worn path of the tunnel, but it was better than the knives he had been expecting. The patch of shards ended just past Candle Hall, it would seem. Richard smiled, tasting the mud on his lips.

"Guys, keep coming this way! We—"

But there was someone else here with him...a scuttle in the dark. Richard jerked to attention, working to dig the mud from his eyes, but he was too late. Bard was on him before he could flail away.

Bard took fistfuls of Richard's fur and twisted him around, forcing him to lay prone on his side. Richard tried to work his fingers into Bard's grip, but his wrist...He bared his teeth and sucked breath like a tea kettle.

"Let...*GO*..."

Bard gave his scalp another yank and leaned to whisper. He could smell...ale on his breath. "Naughty, naughty, Volunteer. What would Fletcher say?"

Richard reared his skull back and connected with Bard's face with a crack.

Bard's grip slipped as he howled and Richard scrambled away. He could see the shapes of the Candle Hall mice as they flung mud. Gavin, Bryce, and Sampson all hung to one another as they strained to stay upright.

The mud drizzled in clumps over their bodies, painting them dark in the candlelight and growing into a slippery pool around their feet.

Richard rubbed the mud from his face. *Too much noise, too much noise!*

He could hear Bard somewhere in the near dark. The mouse breathed with a ragged fury.

"You...are NOTHING to the Void..." he said.

Richard could see him in what little light the candle allowed. Bard had pressed his shoulder to the far wall, clutching at his face as blood trailed down his arm. His eyes snapped to meet Richard's and his lips spread in a hiss.

"You can hear it," he said and stumbled from the wall. "The Void. It can speak to you if you *listen*. Dorgue taught me how."

Bard let his hand fall from his face. His eyes glowed murder and his pattern of scars shone gold in the candlelight. In one hand, he carried a stone.

"Our reward awaits us, you FOOL!" he said.

Richard pulled himself to his knees and raised what he hoped were reasoning hands. He smiled his very best smile.

"Great," Richard said. "That. Is. Great. Dorgue will be so very pleased with you. I'm sure he'll be just giddy, yeah? Let's just take a little breath here—"

Richard ducked under Bard's swing. The stone in his fist sparked the ground, scattering embers as Richard grappled with him. The two fell to the ground, snapping and biting and rolling.

Bard scratched at his neck.

Richard got him by the ear.

They tumbled into the stone barbs as they writhed like serpents.

Mason's voice came to Richard then. He remembered the dusty training fields beyond the city walls and the golden rat shining in the spring sun as he took hold of Richard's jacket and slammed him into the dirt.

"What do you do, pup?"

Richard had struggled for breath. "I...fight?"

"No. You get away," Mason said. "You have those clean teeth, use 'em."

Then Mason crunched Richard's face into the dirt until he did just that.

And now here, so far from those wonderful walls, he found himself in the same spot as dirty hands gripped either side of his skull. Bard's mad eyes burned in the candlelight, glaring out from dark sockets as he puffed stale air into Richard's face.

Richard lashed out blindly, snapping whatever he could get his teeth around. Then Bard's hands were gone. Richard brought up his knee and kicked until the mouse vanished into the dark.

Richard's blood was still buzzing when he felt a pair of muddy hands tear him from the ground and toss him over a broad shoulder.

"Stop! Stop! He's biting me!"

"Richard, please calm down. You—"

He flailed his arm and connected with someone's nose. Another muddy hand clamped down on his elbow, pinning him. Electric agony awoke in Richard's fracture.

"We're through, alright?" Gavin's voice. "You can calm down now. Calm. Down."

Sampson had him in a bundle over his shoulder, Gavin and Bryce padded along at either side, and Richard's wrist felt like a fiddle string pulled wrong.

"I'm so tired," Richard said.

Sampson rumbled a laugh. "Is that all?"

NINETEEN

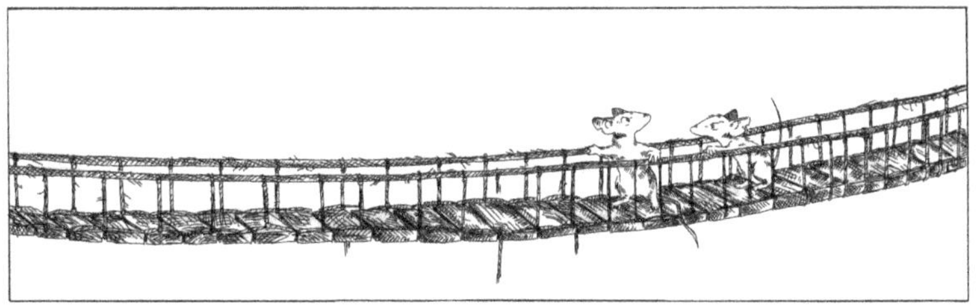

There's nothing an Aterox touched that hasn't *turned
'ta river slime. The Snake War. The Hurricane. The
gore, filthy,* Vanishings—*them's a cursed lot, mark my
words.*

— Dane McCay, cab-driver in Green Hill

GARROW WAITED IN THE dark, knife laid naked on his lap. The dig site was silent, like a body without breath. He'd come down on the remaining lift, stomped onto the pact earth, and sent the contraption into the upper darkness once more. All of this in silence. All of this with hardly a puff of breath.

Now he waited.

Garrow drew his thumb over the crust of his swollen eye. He didn't think it was infected. He *prayed* it wasn't infected. The pain had lessened, so that was fine, yes? He tried to open it, but the lids had fused shut like a clam. So Garrow left it alone.

He felt along the edge of Lou's knife with his thumbnail. Interesting that all the knives down here were stolen. Interesting.

What if he took their eyes? That was a chummy thought. *And why not?* After crushing that fool Bryce under the lift, blinding one or two of the offenders might go a long way in...encouraging loyalty. What was one eye to a mouse?

Hadn't Dorgue cut out the tongues of that first group? Garrow was only following his example. Why, Dorgue might even be proud of him when all this was over. Garrow smiled at the thought.

"Well done Garrow," he'd say. "I've been looking for a resourceful sort like yourself. I'll need a few Governors when all this is over. I hear the Salt Cliffs are beautiful this time of year."

Yes. After all is said and done, Garrow might just find himself lord of one or two sparkly cities. And who knows? Maybe someday, Garrow could slip something special into the old rat's cabbage and take the rest.

Garrow Nogmire, Sovereign of the Middle Kingdom. A reward indeed.

But what was this? Garrow perked an ear.

Commotion...shouts... A fight?

He padded to a stop at the tunnel leading to those filthy burrows. He grimaced at the ache in his shoulder and let his nose drift ahead.

Garrow could smell them: fear and sweat. In his fist, Lou's knife seemed to sing.

Don't kill 'em, he told himself. Just a poke here and there—a cut or two—then he'd take what was his and kick their sorry hides back to the hole they crawled from.

Garrow could hear them inching along. Smell their worry and stress as clear as if they'd rolled in dung. Garrow smiled.

Before this pitch-black hell, Richard had only ever been in one *real* fight. It had been late, the gates of the city were closed and the moon had vanished behind the stormy clouds of winter. The only light had been the shadowy flicker of lanterns set between shops on the road. The wind cutting through the tall, stone buildings above rattled his teeth and the stolen necklace he clutched to his chest was colder than ice between his fingers.

He had plucked it from a shopkeep's table near the Spire. A worthless little trinket, yes, but taking it from under the old beaver's nose had been a thrill. He still held a flutter in his stomach as he slipped into an alley. He'd spied the Red Cloaks patrolling the street ahead and thought it best to take a darker path.

He didn't see the vole rush him until it was too late.

A jab to the gut, a knee to the groin, and Richard crumbled into the garbage with a crunch. The vole was on him, his thin hands working through his jacket. Detached, the ordeal reminded Richard of watching one of the kitchen maids scaling a fish in deft, practiced motions. The vole had mugging perfected to seconds.

He found the necklace in his fist and scratched.

"Gimme that bit a shine!" he said and took a fistful of Richard's hair, pulling his face up into the shadows of the alley.

The vole dropped him as if a plague danced in Richard's eyes. The Vole's little, tooth-filled mouth opened in a silent squeak and he was gone. The *patpatpatpat* of his feet over frozen patches of ice chased after him like a ghost.

Richard lay there a moment. Breathing. Shaking. The Red Cloaks passed the mouth of the alley, giving the briefest glance to the mouse lying in the filthy heap before moving on.

They hadn't recognized him. But the vole had.

Richard wasn't sure how long he'd laid there. Too scared to move. Still clutching that stupid necklace in his fist like a child. He didn't leave home for weeks after that. He'd have nightmares where he was chased through the narrow alleys of Green Hill by unseen monsters and woke up tangled in his blanket.

Now he'd had three fights in two days. Richard hoped what came next would be more of a game of wits, rather than muscle. He rubbed at his face in the dark, feeling the mud smear and crumble in his fur, and strained to hear over the beat of his own heart.

"How far out?" he whispered.

Bryce answered, mere inches away. "Not far," he said. "Very close."

Richard took a breath, closed his eyes, and imagined a wide-open space around him. He breathed the smell of mud and banished the hints of ginger and figs leaking into his psyche.

Almost out. Nearly there.

Then Bryce and Gavin came to an abrupt halt.

Sampson eased Richard back to the tunnel floor.

Richard stared into all that blackness. "What do you—"

Gavin's hand shot back and clamped his mouth shut with a click. Richard froze, eyes wide, straining to see. *One of the Candle Hall mice? One of Dorgue's rats?*

They held their breath in the silence of the tunnel.

Waited…

Finger by finger, Gavin released Richard's snout. In the dark, he heard the other mouse say, "Thought I smelled something. If Vincent were here—"

The rat came at them like a spider in the dark.

Richard jumped back, blind and panicked as he felt the zing of a blade sing through the air. He scrambled away. Whoever this was, he was huge. Richard prayed it wasn't Fletcher. Or that psychotic Worth that had caught him outside. If so, this would all be over before it started.

He heard the rat growl and swipe out with his knife. One of the others, Sampson it sounded like, let out a shout of pain.

A rock exploded against the wall, raining dust and crumbs over them, and Gavin swore before chucking another. Richard guessed this one struck the rat, by the roar he let out.

Richard felt his own throat open in a yell. They had a weapon, didn't they? "GET HIM!" he screamed. "WHO'S GOT THE KNIFE? WHO—"

The rat plucked him from the wall like he was nothing more than a child, his fingers raking Richard's shoulder before finding a grip on his collar. The rat's arm dug beneath Richard's chin in a chokehold. His fur felt bristly and sharp. Richard struggled, kicking out, but the rat only squeezed tighter.

He felt the cold prick of a knife.

Garrow's breath was rank and hot in his ear. His voice cracked as he spoke. "Everybody keep your place," Garrow said, "or I'll cut him a new stomach."

All became quiet. The puff, puff, puff of the rat's breath tickled his ear.

Garrow spat blood. Gavin must have gotten him right in the jaw. "Who's all here?" he said. "Speak up or I make a mess."

Richard ground his teeth and tried to squeal, but Garrow's arm was tight on his neck...

He wanted to scream. *Rush him! Get behind the rat!* Instead, he heard Bryce's voice stammer from the darkness.

"It's...just me...master," he said.

Richard felt the rat shudder. The hold around his neck loosed but for only a moment. It returned with fury. Richard felt his eyes bulge.

"*Bryce*," Garrow said, almost a gasp.

"It's just me," Bryce said again, his voice very small. "I'm right in front of you. We didn't want—"

Richard's stomach lurched as the rat swung out. "*I killed you! you're dead!*" Garrow screamed.

The world turned end over end. Richard's legs swung high and he felt his boots scrape the tunnel ceiling. He tried to swallow, but his throat clicked against Garrow's arm.

He's swinging me like a rain bucket, Richard thought. How long until his head just...popped off? He bared his teeth as Garrow swung blindly, the knife zinging through the air.

The rat caught nothing.

"COME CLOSER, YOU DEVIL!" Garrow cursed.

Richard clawed at the rat's arm. Couldn't breathe. *Couldn't breathe.*

The pitch-black around him faded to purple, and the roaring in his ears became rolling waves. A strange numbness washed over him.

This is death. I'm dying.

Richard's vision turned odd. He saw shapes and hues drifting across his eyes like color oozing through a river. Beautiful and horrible nonsense.

But then swirls of madness... noticed him. They *smiled* at him. moving together, they formed a new form and drifted close.

Richard saw the shape of his Father. His golden eyes cut through the chaos. He regarded Richard.

What a mess you are.

Richard struggled. He stretched his mouth to breathe, but Garrow's arm had his throat pinned.

The colors became millions and Father leaned close, turning solid. Richard spied the glint of glass in Father's fur, flecks of shards.

Still though... you're alive and I'm dead.

His hand drifted out from the mist. It was older than Richard remembered. His father opened his mouth and showed ancient teeth in a gapped grin.

Wanna trade?

Then Garrow hit the ground.

Richard rolled to the cold of the tunnel floor. He opened his mouth wide and wheezed air. Sweet, *sweet* air.

"Hold him!" Gavin shouted.

Sampson and Gavin had leaped atop Garrow's back and had the rat by the neck. They sounded like they were rolling in a fit on the ground. Richard inched away, back toward the wall. The rumble of Garrow's growl shook Richard's very heart. He could hear the rat choking, hear him wheeze, and then the panicked scuff of the heels on the tunnel floor.

Then all was still.

Richard leaned heavily against the wall. He pressed his fingers against his neck. Swallowed. Swallowed again. "Is he...Is he dead?"

He heard the crack of flint in the dark, and Bryce's face shimmered into view. He held a candle in his fist.

"I found it on the ground," Bryce said. "He didn't light it. He was...waiting for us."

Richard turned to see his attacker in the new light. Garrow laid belly down, one arm twisted awkwardly to his side. Sampson had both arms wrapped around the rat's neck, dangling Garrow's head an inch from the floor. The rat's face had gone to color, his eyes twitching but seeing nothing as his breath whistled through an empty grimace.

Sampson unwound his arms and Garrow's head dropped to the ground with a clap.

Gavin had been caught beneath one of the rat's legs in the fall. Sampson helped him wriggle out. "Well, he's still breathing," Gavin said.

"Yeah," Sampson said. "The old tic was on duty after all."

Richard could have almost laughed. Almost. "I thought you said the *other guy would* be."

Gavin shrugged. "He must have replaced Ferris and camped out for us."

Bryce's face looked hollow behind the light of the candle. He turned his wide eyes to the dark beyond. "How did he know we were escaping tonight?"

"I doubt he knew anything," Richard said. "If he did, he would have told someone, yeah? Do you see any other rats coming to his rescue? No. Now help me find his knife."

That got them moving. What a help Garrow was proving to be, providing not just one but *two* knives.

They spread out to search for it, edging around the rat's unconscious body like it was a poisonous mushroom overflowing from the passage's center. Bryce held the candle high, dripping wax as they looked.

A minute passed. Richard crossed his arms, then winced as he bumped his wrist. "How do knives always end up skipping away down here?" he said. "It can't have gone far!"

Gavin shook his head. "We can keep tracking back...but..."

"We don't have the time to spare," Sampson finished.

Richard bit his lip. Closed his eyes. True, they didn't need another knife. The plan only needed one. Still...be nice to have.

Tick-tock, Kathryn might say.

"Let's get to the dig-sit," he said. "Maybe Sampson can find it on his way back after he lights the fire."

Richard blinked. The light was fading and he found himself standing alone. He spun to see the others already marching for the dig site. Sampson and Gavin hauling blankets and Bryce lighting the way.

They were eager to leave.

Bryce held the candle overhead, sending wild shadows over the dig site.

He saw the scaffolds, where he'd spent so many days imagining their collapse. He saw the walkways high above, vanishing into black. Utterly empty and void.

And he saw the crater center of the room, a messy imprint of mud and wood. Most of the mess had been cleaned up, but Bryce spied a muddy splinter of wood, angling from the ground like a finger. He knelt to pull it free, and it crumbled in his hand.

Gavin set a hand on his shoulder. "He'd be proud of us," he said.

Bryce nodded but didn't have words.

"Where should we light the fire?" Sampson asked.

Richard stumbled to a stop at their side, bowing to catch his breath. "I say we light it right here," he said, dipping his chin to where Vincent had met his end. "The rats might think the fire is a retaliation, rather than an escape attempt. Might buy us an hour head start in the Deep Wood."

Vincent's last act had been to protect his friends. His entire life was spent looking for ways to get back at the rats. Using the place where he gave his all against Dorgue?

"I think he'd like that," Bryce said. And it was settled.

Sampson built a little fort of blankets as Gavin stared up into the walkways, his eyes darting back and forth. "We cut there," he said, "Three bridges up. You see it?"

Sampson looked up from his work and followed Gavin's finger. The mouse squinted. "I see," he said, "but barely. This candle don't show much."

"Well once the rats come running we'll need all the distance we can get," Gavin said.

Richard looked up into the dark. Crossed his arms. "And there's a passage that leads up from here?" he asked.

Bryce nodded. "Other side of the dig site." He pointed the way. "I remember carving it out last year. The way is steep."

Bryce passed the candle to Sampson. The mouse loomed over them and gave them a nod. "You best be quick about it," he said.

Richard smiled. "When this is all over, I'll invite you all for cake," he said. "That's a promise."

Sampson's voice was stern when he answered. "Don't make promises."

They left Sampson there and walked into darkness.

The path had been cut into the wall and twisted like a corkscrew all the way to the Hoist. Well, not *all* the way. As they climbed, the ground would level out before reaching the walkway. Then they crossed to the other side, and the next path leading up.

In the dark, Bryce's feet chronicled the journey. The wooden slats were old and splintery, set with little space between them—not enough to fall through or get your foot caught, but they'd pinch if you stepped wrong. Bryce was careful not to get a toe caught. And when he sensed granite under his toes, he walked hugging the wall, fearing the drop inches away at his side.

Behind him, Richard huffed and puffed.

"Is it this steep the whole way?" Richard asked.

Gavin shushed him in the dark. But then he couldn't resist himself and said, "That's why the rats mostly use the lift, you see."

Once or twice after crossing the walkway, the path would fork, leading either further up or deep into the dark of tunnels long abandoned. Bryce would catch the smell of them and memories would flood.

"The old burrows are that way," he said, pointing into the dark. "I'd forgotten how they smelled."

"Never mind that," Richard shuffled past and pointed down into the dig site. "You reckon we're high enough?"

Bryce looked over the edge and spied Sampson below. The candle in his fist was the smallest light, but it bathed the dig site in a dim glow. He lifted a hand to them. Bryce lifted a hand back.

"That'll do," Gavin said. "Now, Sampson lights the fire. When the rats come, we need to be ready to hide."

"Right. In those dead tunnels, I imagine?" Richard said. "I can't see anything. Didn't you say these had been mostly filled in?"

"We'll have a few nooks and crannies to use."

Bryce took a step deeper into the dark passage and sniffed. This far up... the smells were waking some of his earliest memories.

Fletcher tossing him into a bunk, snapping at him to quit squalling.

Eating crusts and hiding little bits under his chin for later.

Begging the rats for a candle. Bryce frowned and tried to remember... There *had* been a rat who'd given them a candle once. He hadn't been around for long.

What had his name been?

"*Bryce*," Gavin said. "Come on, we gotta find a place to duck into."

They found a space just as they sensed the first tendrils of smoke. Gavin called them over and they squeezed in, packing tight. Bryce twisted his head to see out. Then twisted the other way when he realized he was spying out with his eye patch.

"I can see firelight on the wall," he said.

Bryce felt Richard straining to turn, but they were so pressed in Richard couldn't even twist his neck to see out.

"Oh, wonderful," Richard said.

Bryce shushed him. "*Listen.*"

"I hear something," Gavin said.

The mice tensed. This was it. The rats were coming.

They held their breath as commotion echoed dimly through the tunnels. Bryce could hear shouts, lost in the distance. But then a roar blasted from above like the voice of vengeance.

"*WHAT IS THIS?*" Fletcher's voice gripped Bryce's heart and set his legs shaking. Suddenly, the thought of the horrible rat finding them and dragging them out seemed to be not only likely but the cold, hard truth. Bryce pressed deeper into the crack in the wall. Richard grunted but tried to make room and poor Gavin—crushed against the wall—remained completely silent.

They waited.

Rats dashed by, soaring down the passage as their torches lapped at the air to keep up. Fletcher's tirade got closer and closer.

"STOP! STOP!" the rat screamed. "We're right over the flames! Pull the lift up! *PULL THE LIFT UP!* Jump to the walkway, and,

GET

DOWN

THERE!"

Bryce frowned. *Over the flames?* Sampson had set the fire in the ruins of the old lift… Hadn't he?

Richard squirmed. "You're crushing my wrist."

"The rats aren't taking the lift all the way down," Bryce said.

Gavin spoke up, his voice muffled, "*What?*"

More rats ran past. Many more. Last of all Fletcher, still screaming curses. His eyes were fire and Bryce swore he saw steam billowing from the rat's shoulders.

He held his breath as he passed.

Once the thunder of footsteps died away, changing to the rattle of boots over the walkway, Bryce found himself sprawled flat as Richard angled to pry himself out from the tiny space.

Richard clutched his arm to his chest, face tight.

The air had become unbearably hot and smoke drifted through the air, scratching Bryce's throat. Bryce scrambled for the bridge. Above them, just one level up, he saw the lift as the rats had left it, hanging in a lazy sway, not far from the next walkway.

Then he risked a peek down and gasped.

The dig site was engulfed in flames as if the dirt itself had caught fire. The rats scrambled around a growing bonfire. Some tried to beat it back with shovels, but the fire had grown too hot to approach. Even Fletcher himself couldn't stand near it for long. He held a muscled arm over his face, rushing into the heat with a shovel before darting away again, roaring in a fury. The smell of burning hair wafted up the shaft.

Gavin stumbled to Bryce's side, struggling to free Garrow's oversized knife from his belt. He looked on in horror. "What in blue heck did Sampson *do*?" he said. "We wanted the fire to draw the rats out, not kill everybody we left behind!"

Bryce shook his head. The heat rising to meet them tussled the fur on his face, blowing smoke into his eye. He blinked, digging in a knuckle.

"They'll put it out," he said. "They have to put it out."

Gavin could only shake his head as he worked the knife into the rope bridge. He gripped it with both hands. "Lend me a hand with this?"

Richard coughed behind them.

"Guys," he said, voice strained. "I think the fracture opened back up, or something…" He doubled over, hugging his arm. "I think…should probably take…more medicine…"

Bryce and Gavin sawed with the knife, its jagged edge doing little at first—then more as the fibers began to pop one by one. "Just hang on," Gavin called back. "Let's take this one step at a time."

The walkway shook as they worked, making the knife buzz in their hands. Bryce was certain the rats would notice. Certain they'd look up and drag them back down into the dark. He risked a peek down.

The fire had almost reached the scaffolds around the pit.

"I'll just…take a little," Richard said.

"Just hold off a SECOND," Gavin hissed. "We don't need you loopy right now."

Fletcher was still screaming orders, pushing rats forward as they screeched at the heat, batting away at the flames with shovels or burlap sacks they'd fetched from the kitchen.

Bryce spied a pair of rats hauling a sloshing barrel of water. They ran for the flames, grinning through the burning heat, the air surrounding them all shivery.

The knife was nearly through the rope, strands cracking like knuckles.

The rats lugged the barrel into the flames.

Bryce had heard the hiss of a torch doused by water and he'd heard a candle spit when pinched dead. But this… It was like the earth itself screamed in agony. So loud, Bryce jumped and bit his tongue in surprise. Gavin reacted much the same, nearly losing hold of the knife from the shock of it.

Had the rats killed the fire? They still needed more time!

Bryce and Gavin looked down.

And the steam rose up.

Heat met their faces and clung like a burning hand. Bryce reared back, yelping in surprise. Gavin tried to stay as he was, throwing an arm over his face, but then he cried out in pain and dashed away.

Smoke and steam enveloped them like a stinging, burning blanket.

"Move," Gavin said, his voice a gasp. "We need to move!"

Bryce waved his arm toward the bridge. "But we haven't—"

He froze. A chill flashed through the pit of his stomach. A quiver started in Bryce's limbs as he looked into his empty hands… into *Gavin's* empty hands. He spun, scanning the ground near the walkway… looking for…

A noise cut the air.

Not as loud as the blast of steam, but sharper, like the ting of a bell. The echoing strike of metal on stone.

It pinged again.

And again.

Then silence. Silence like Bryce had never known. And the first rat cried out.

"Eh, some idiot dropped their knife!"

"Nearly clocked me on my noggin, that."

"Where'd the devil did it fall from? Up *there?*"

In the smoke, as they coughed as quietly as they could, Gavin gripped Bryce's shoulder. "Get a hold of Richard!" he hissed. "We're gonna run."

Bryce's head went light as a soap bubble. *The knife...the walkway...*

And then Fletcher's voice, rising like the guttural roar of Hell itself.

"WHO'S UP THERE?"

Bryce grabbed Richard by the scruff of his neck and they ran. Richard made a keening noise deep in his throat, clutching his arm in private agony, but he followed with little fuss.

"I'll just...take a little bit," he choked out. "A little...just a swallow."

Bryce could feel him struggling to dig the vial from his jacket as they ran the sloping turn, their footfalls scattering pebbles over the edge. Shouts followed from below.

So much for their head-start.

The path leveled, and Gavin pulled for the walkway almost dragging Bryce behind him.

Bryce's mind raced. The plan's the same. Run the way up, get to the hoist... Now they just had to outrun the rats. Easy.

Bryce was thinking up the next lie to tell himself when Gavin came to a skidding stop before him. Bryce slammed into him, wooden slats thumping under their heels.

White-hot panic raged in Bryce's heart. He found his hands reaching for Gavin's neck, to push him out of the way. To scramble past in a frenzy. In his mind, forty-foot letters flashed, MOVE, MOVE, *MOVE!*

Then his eye drifted past Gavin.

A dark shape stood center of the walkway, cleaning his thumbnail with the point of a knife. Angry red light lit him from below. He looked up from grooming his nails and raised a single brow.

Bryce felt his insides turn to water.

The lithe rat called Worth let out an exasperated breath and shook his head.

That's that, Bryce thought. Even if they had managed to drop the bridge with their stolen knife, Worth would have been here. Waiting for them.

The rat peered down the shaft. His knife flashed red in the dark.

"Good work there. With the fire," he said.

Worth took a step.

The mice shuffled back.

"Pity you didn't think much beyond that," Worth said. He spun the knife in his hand like a magic trick. So sharp it sang. His stride was long and the mice stumbling back were too shocked to run as the rat gained ground.

Worth leaned close, his eyes blazing.

Then Richard ripped past Bryce and Gavin, nearly pushing them over the side as he forced his way through. His cheeks bulged with Dorgue's medicine and he spewed it in a wide spray. The reddish liquid hit Worth's face and he reared back in surprise. He blinked rapidly and a growl grew in his throat.

Bryce watched as the red crept into the rat's eyes. They seized shut as if someone had strung a wire over his features, stretching them into a violent, trembling line.

The rat screamed in agony.

Gavin pulled them moving again, ducking under Worth's arm as he swung blind. Bryce felt the zing of the blade as it brushed the fur of his ears.

Worth raged as he fell to his knees, unable to follow. Every muscle in his neck stood out like cords and he hissed through clenched teeth, dragging at the wooden slats of the walkway with his nails.

Richard's breath came ragged in Bryce's ear. "My throat is burning," he said, tears running down his face. "That stuff's like fire!"

Bryce dared not look back. Dared not look down. He focused on the *slap, slap, slap* of his feet as he raced across the walkway.

Just keep running. Don't stop running.

Then, at last, the rats doused the last of the fire and darkness fell like a hammer.

TWENTY

— A notice, posted by The Council of Green Hill

RICHARD WAS GOING TO die.

As if his heart gasping for blood and his lungs filling with burning fire weren't enough, these bridges were getting *longer*. At least, Richard was pretty sure they were. He wished he hadn't wasted so much medicine on that sea rat. He could use a little numbness right now.

The sound of pursuit below them was a great motivator though. Grade *A* stuff.

After the fire had gone out, the rats had wasted no time in sending a merry bunch to chase them up the walkways, while the rest of them worked on reclaiming the lift they'd left swinging over the first bridge.

Richard could hear them down there. The mice were still ahead, but not by much. That first walkway they'd almost cut free had given the rats *some* trouble. They hadn't been able to run across it and maybe a few of them fell. Richard couldn't be for sure in the dark.

"*You're better off JUMPING!*" Fletcher roared from below.

They must have gotten on the lift again. And now Richard had a stitch in his side. That was lovely. Very helpful. He felt the bouncing clatter of the walkway vanish underfoot as Gavin steered them up another chest-crushing slope.

Rats zigzagging up the bridges behind them.

Rats acceding with the one good lift.

Oh, and look. Fletcher had lit a lantern. The darkness began to shrink away as the rats in the lift rose closer and closer. As Richard ran after Bryce's heels, he could begin to see the steep path underfoot, if only faintly.

The rats were getting closer.

Richard dared not look.

Just like running the streets behind the market, he kept telling himself. *You've been doing that since you were five.*

Yes, but in Green Hill, he didn't have to worry about marauding rats, eager to throw him from high places. The vision of his father came to him, beckoning him into the dark.

Richard was going to die.

"Look!" Gavin shouted—more of a noise, hardly a word—but Richard caught his meaning. Richard risked taking his eyes from the path and glanced upward.

The Hoist was just above. A square of light in the dark. He could hear the racket of ticking gears like rain clacking at windows. He could smell oil too, the heavy, *sour-smelling* kind they used on the city gates in the winter.

Nearly there.

"I'LL CATCH YOU! I'LL GUT YOU!" Fletcher yelled up.

Now, Richard *did* dare to look down. He saw rats crossing a walkway just beneath them. That green tooth creep was at the lead, stumbling on like a panicked drunkard. A *fast* stumble. If his heart didn't pop like a soap bubble, he'd catch up sooner than Richard cared to think. But it was the rats on the lift that worried him.

They were raising themselves by hand, drawing rope through their little pulley system as the hoist above clicked to pick up the slack. Richard wasn't sure how it all worked, but *apparently*, there was no one above to pull whatever lever needed pulling to bring up the lift. A stroke of luck for the mice. Unfortunately, the rats were making good time.

Fletcher's eyes dripped with hate. His teeth clamped like a vise and stretched the cords of his neck. He strong-armed the coiled rope, thrusting the lift higher and higher with every pull. Richard met his eyes and saw murder waiting there.

"I WARNED YOU, VOLUNTEER," the rat said.

That you did, Richard thought. *The thing is, you never gave me a chance to warn* you.

The rats on the lift threatened them with raised fists and blades.

The rats running the lower path hissed curses with what little breath they had.

And the mice crossed the final bridge and turned the corner.

They stopped at the Door.

If Bryce and Gavin's lax expressions were anything to go on, neither one had ever seen a door, let alone thought of the concept of one. They stood like they had stumbled across a dark omen. Richard shouldered past them.

"Move it! They wanna murder me, remember? *Move!*"

Richard threw all his weight at the door, praying that whatever had it latched was more for stopping the thing from creaking in a draft, rather than keeping unwanted visitors out. He barreled through.

It crashed open, vibrating on its hinges, and Richard landed in the room beyond, lit by a lonely lantern that clattered by the door.

That hurt. He could have just opened that, couldn't he? Richard gritted his teeth and tried to rise. "*Quick! Bar the door! Bar the door before—*"

Richard's words were lost among shouts rising from below and the noise of the walkway bouncing under so many boots.

They were coming. They were almost here. And that idiot Bryce just *stood there*, frozen like a ghost in the doorway! Gavin, at least, had managed to scuttle inside, squinting in the dirty lantern light with his head on a swivel. He threw up his arms.

"*What do we do?*" Gavin said.

Richard was back up on shaking legs. Sweat poured down his face. "*Get the door!*"

Gavin got Bryce by the collar and dragged him in as the eyes of the first rat rounded the bend, mad with rage and dripping with foam.

Gavin slammed the door as the rat met it head-on with a blast of teeth and flesh. Had Bryce not come to his senses by then and tossed his body against the oaken door as well, it would have tossed Gavin aside with all the grace of a hammer bashing a skull to splinters.

Still, the rat managed to force the door open a crack. Richard spied the rat's soft green teeth and swollen nose. Teague's hand slithered past the slim opening to rake the wood. His fingers worked like spiders as he tried to snatch at Gavin's arm.

The door groaned in agony. Bryce's and Gavin's feet began to slide out from under them, inch by inch. Bryce had sweat dribbling from his face with his one good eye twisted shut. "*Richard,*" he gasped. "We need to close this."

No kidding.

Richard spun. If this was meant to be a secure room, then there had to be a way to seal it shut. And if there was a way to seal it shut…there had to be an easy way to do it. He hadn't seen a keyhole, so there must be…

And there, resting on the wall near the door, a heavy brace. Richard ignored the shiver in his arm as he heaved it over his shoulder, turned, and brought it down on Teague's scrambling hand. The rat screeched and pulled his arm from the door nearly losing the tips of his fingers as it slammed home.

Richard dropped the brace into the door's iron bars and stumbled away. He heard Teague screaming and bashing like a troll on the other side. Richard took several steps back, watching the door shake and buckle.

"I don't know how long that will hold," Richard said and turned to give the room a better look.

The room was much as Richard remembered: a big wooden box with a doozy of a drop cut into the floor. Except this time the lifts were missing from the room and the *clack clack clack* of the gears overhead repeated every few breaths like a metronome, giving the mice a cruel reminder that while one door may be blocked, another was very much still open.

Richard peeked over into the void. Fletcher and his rats were just below. Maybe a minute away.

"Okay." Richard spun, straining to make sense of all the pulleys and bits of machinery in the ceiling.

There. A mess of leavers on the wall attached to a dented mechanical box. Ropes and pulleys spidered out of its head and connected to the metal maw of gears on the ceiling.

Gavin stared at the quivering ropes stretching down to the lift and growled. "I can't believe I dropped that knife!"

They jumped as the barred door buckled. More rats had become available to throw themselves against it. Richard snatched the lantern from the wall and crossed to the mess of levers. He didn't have time for this!

"One of these has *got* to stop it," he said.

"Or bring them up faster," Gavin moaned. "How do you—"

Richard wrapped his arms around a heavy iron bar and arched his back to bend it down. The bar went *CHUH-CHUNK*, and Richard stumbled back, throwing out his arm for balance.

The room seemed to shiver and the noise of Fletcher's assent paused as the rat tugged in vain on the rope. The rat shouted up, "*You filthy, dirty—*"

The spool overhead burst into motion, spinning with a sound like a roar as it spit a spool of rope. Screams echoed from below as the lift plummeted.

The Hoist rumbled and the mice ducked in fear. And then, with the violence of a breaking limb, the gears in the ceiling seized and the room shook as the rope snapped taut. The machinery groaned in agony and the racket of panicked rats changed from screaming to curses. Richard, his legs suddenly shaky, crept to look down into the dark.

The lift had dropped a fair bit and was now swinging in a clumsy arc. The rats that had managed to keep from flying off clung on for dear life. The only rat who wasn't a shivering mess was Fletcher, who gazed up at Richard with such a sneer. "*I'm gonna skin your EYES!*" he roared.

Bryce rose shaking to his feet, his lips pale. "Slack," he said.

Richard backed from the drop. "What?"

"Slack," he said again. "Sometimes, the rats call for slack when they're working on the lift. Drops it. Loosens the rope. But, I think it's supposed to be on the *ground* before you—"

"*SLAAAAAACK!*" Richard screamed and pulled the lever again.

With a rumble like a storm at sea, the spool vomited another length of rope and the mice ran from the room before it could slap taunt again, grabbing the little lantern on the floor as they went

Bryce's knee hurt like hell, but each step seemed somehow easier than the last. As they ran up the turning tunnel, following the light of Richard's lantern, Bryce found himself actually laughing. Laughing!

"Oh, I'm gonna breathe so much air!" Richard called back. "I can't believe how light I feel right now, this feels like a dream."

Gavin grinned. "It's all that medicine you took," he said. "You'd feel like floating regardless of where you were."

"I don't care," Richard said. "I'll take what I can get!"

Bryce had to agree. They had gotten this much good all their lives.

They were getting *out*.

They'd left the Hoist far behind and passed through the rat's quarters without so much of a glance left or right. He had a moment of panic when he saw all the rat-sized passages, but Richard seemed to know where he was going. Bryce felt another ping of hope in his chest.

Richard's our guide now, he realized.

He led them up a crumbly passage—sometimes narrow, sometimes wide—and steep. *Plenty steep.* Even so, Bryce raced it. They all did. The aches and pains he'd felt in the mad scramble up from the dig site were all but forgotten as they followed after Richard's light.

They were going to do it. This was going to work!

"Wait, wait!" Richard said, skidding to a halt. They gathered around the lantern, shivering in their excitement and panting for breath. Bryce looked to his feet and saw pebbles mixed in with the dirt. And above—just catching the warm light of the lantern—were thin, stringy tendrils twisting down like bony fingers. He reached to touch one.

"Roots," Richard said, clapping Bryce on the back. "We're nearly to the top!"

The thought brought a lump to Bryce's throat as he plucked a root from the ceiling. Bits of dirt came down with it, sparkling them with dust.

"Feel this," Richard said, pressing a hand to the wall. "Wet to the touch. Rains must have started."

Bryce felt the wall. The dirt here was soft, a deep earthy black that smelled...sweet.

"Rain?"

"Yeah, the wet stuff that falls from the sky? Makes your clothes stick to your fur. There's buckets of it, I bet." Richard took up the lantern and gazed up the passage. "This next part," he said biting his lip, "might be tricky..."

Gavin looked from his place on the wall, where he was giving one of the roots an exploratory nibble. "What does that mean?" he asked.

"Well, Worth and that other guy had me blindfolded on the way in," he said. "So I haven't technically *seen* the exit to this place."

He got moving, climbing the pebbly slope with a skip. "Come on," Richard said. "I can't hear the rats, but that doesn't mean they're not on the way. Let's keep that head-start, yeah?"

So Bryce and Gavin followed.

The farther up they went, the easier it became. The slope turned friendlier and eventually evolved into stairs—something of a wonder to the mice of Dorgue's Tree.

And then, like someone had spoken a magic word, the dirt path became wood, but not like the wood from the scaffolds or the walk-ways, this wood was a crisp gray. It shined. The walls and ceiling changed as well, and Bryce let his fingers drift over its face. It felt polished, like stone.

Richard grinned back at them. "We're in the tree now," he said.

"What if Dorgue is up here?" Gavin whispered.

Richard raised a brow. "The old, shaky guy with the cane? I hope he is! Then I'll get to sock him right in his creepy face."

Bryce said, "We're just trying to leave, remember? Does any of this feel familiar to you?"

Richard frowned. "It's an empty stairway leading up, so yeah. So far so good."

That stairway led up a good way. Every so often Richard would stop and study the walls with his lantern. He kept shaking his head and muttering.

"I don't...get it," he said. "We're surely above ground now."

"What do you mean?" Gavin asked.

"I mean we should have stumbled across a way out by now!" He stared into the dark behind them, biting his lip. " And we can't go back and check to be sure. What if we—"

"Hush!" Gavin hissed. He snapped his gaze ahead, farther up the path.

"Don't hush me."

"No, really! Do you smell that?"

They sniffed the air. Bryce could smell the mud drying on their bodies, the smell of smoke and sweat, and the smell of the passage they found themselves in, cold and bare and...

Then Bryce caught it. The aroma of herbs.

Rosemary and Jasmine.

"Dorgue," he said.

And then they came to the door.

The door they'd come across in the Hoist had been a rough and scratchy thing with large, messy rivets and sloppy iron bars. This door was carved, like the wooden passage around them, and utterly black. Unknowable patterns covered its face and its handle was a simple knob of dark iron. The stairway continued, turning into darkness a few dozen steps ahead.

For a moment, the mice could only stare.

"I don't want to go in there," Bryce said, taking a careful step away. "This...is Dorgue's place."

"But it's also," Richard set his ear on the door and put a steady hand on the handle, "our way out."

It was a simple latch and opened with a soft click as if age had worn the bolt to nothing. The door drifted with a sigh, and the mice peeked in.

The room wasn't large. Less than half the size of the kitchen, Bryce guessed. Looming bookcases had been carved from the walls and stretched from ceiling to floor. They filled the entire circle of the room, save for a round window opposite the door and a low, wide fireplace casting the space with a dim, shivering light. Desks were overflowing with notes and projects and jars and pitchers...Bryce didn't know where to rest his eye.

The smell of herbs was strong and the fire was warm.

"Richard," Bryce said. "We need to leave. We need to leave right now."

But Richard only patted Bryce's shoulder and stepped in. "Mr. Scary isn't even here," he said. "There could be something in here we could use. Something to take back to Green Hill with us!"

Richard made for one of the bookcases but froze in his step. His eyes blinked in shock, then again in wonder. A dreaminess came over his face and his shoulders fell in a slow droop.

"*Carpet*," Richard sighed. "Almost makes me want to take my boots off! Oooh, we're gonna make this child-napping creep eat *dirt* when we come back here."

He shuffled to the bookcase.

There were books, tools, hundreds upon hundreds of glass jars, and mugs of every shape and color. Bryce also spied a twisted family of knives hanging in a cubby in the wall, nasty things built with sharp metal and springs.

"Must be his study," Richard said. "This is where the rat does all his thinking. Look, here's a writing desk."

He crossed the room to a wide desk with legs so delicate they looked to be made from spider silk. It was stacked with journals and loose papers. In the dim light, Richard squinted down at them. He snatched a page and brought it closer to the fire, holding it at an awkward angle under his nose. His shadow stretched to fill the room as Bryce eased the door closed. He winced at the click of the bolt. It sounded like snapping teeth.

"Richard, I'm not kidding. We can't stay here."

Richard waved him away, grabbing another loose page from the desk and comparing it with the other.

"We're not *staying*," he said, a frown fixed on his face. "Go and...see if you can find an exit other than the window...a secret door or...something..."

"A secret door?"

"I'd rather not climb out a window."

Bryce shook his head but did what he asked. He angled around the desk and crossed to the window. Gavin was already there with his face pressed against the glass. His eyes were closed and he was grinning.

"It's cold," Gavin said. "Here, feel it."

Gavin stepped to the side and Bryce brought his palm to the window. He sucked through his teeth in surprise at first—pulling away—but then stretched out a single finger. He could feel the rain on the other side; its rolling rhythm.

Bryce couldn't help it, he smiled as well.

The rain streaming down blocked the view of anything they might see beyond, but it moved in such patterns and strokes—almost like it was alive—waving to them from the other side.

"I didn't know you could have so much water," Gavin said.

"Be careful not to drink it when we get out there," Richard muttered under his breath. "The Deep Wood likes its water a *tad* poisonous."

Bryce mulled over that word in his mind. *Poisonous.* Could the outside be as bad as Richard let on? With Vincent's stories of home so large in his imagination, he wasn't sure what to believe. But he knew which one he preferred.

Then light erupted and a *rumble* shook the windowpane. Bryce and Gavin jumped back with a yelp from the shock of it. Richard stared at them from his place by the fire, hand pressed to his chest from the surprise.

"What is *wrong* with you two? My nerves are ruined enough with you screaming at a little storm."

Bryce had thought... Well, Bryce didn't know what to think. Such a loud noise without even a warning, how did anyone up here ever get any sleep? Bryce steadied his shaky hands as another flash and boom broke the air.

Gavin crept to the window once more, eyeing out into the night with a healthier dose of suspicion. "What's making that noise?" he said.

Richard shook his head and pulled another handful of papers from the desk. He shuffled through them. "I told you, it's just a storm," he said. "Storms mean lightning, and lightning means thunder. It's perfectly normal, so will you both be *quiet*? I can't focus with all your..."

He turned a page over.

"...With all your... Wait a minute. *This*... What is *this*?"

The mice gathered. Richard tilted the page so all could see, the glow of the fire showing his fingers through the other side. Bryce squinted at what he saw.

It was a drawing. A strange drawing. Richard turned it end over end, talking under his breath, "What is this?"

Gavin shrugged. "It looks like...a hand? A coat?"

Bryce shook his head. Was this what Dorgue did all day? Sit around, drawing silly pictures of...

Bryce jerked straight when he saw it.

He looked at his arm, placed it next to the drawing, and opened his hand to match the one on the paper.

Richard shuddered violently and dropped the page. It drifted to the floor and curled into a polite little roll. So small a thing, resting on the carpet as the firelight stretched its shadow long across the floor. For a long moment, the mice kept very still. Bryce wondered if he had imagined it; the thing on the paper. He wondered if such a thing could be real.

"That...was a medical drawing," Richard said.

"Yeah?" Gavin dug his hands in his hair like he was crawling with mites. He paced the floor. "Pretty good drawing. Pretty *darn* good."

Bryce stared down at the page, grateful it was turned away. He looked to the desk...all those stacks of paper... He felt as if the room had begun to tip to one side.

Bryce said, "The rats always used to say 'be good' or Dorgue..."

"Would cut us up," Gavin finished.

Richard crossed to Dorgue's desk and shuffled through the rat's other loose pages. Richard opened his mouth. Closed it again. His lips had gone white.

"It looked like he was...diagramming the... The muscle and...skin."

"Peeling us apart like potatoes, more like!" Gavin shouted. He kicked the drawing and sent it fluttering across the room. It came to rest by the door.

So the stories were true. Those horrible stories. *Had Vincent...* The thought turned Bryce's stomach like a punch. "We need to leave here."

Richard nodded. "Yeah. Yeah, I think you're right."

He left the desk as it was and the mice crossed back to the door. The sooner they left this place, the better. Bryce glanced at the knives on the wall. Their curved edges seemed to smile down at him.

Then a click at the door.

Like teeth snapping.

The mice froze. Richard's fingers were hovering just above the handle as the door began to drift open.

They scrambled.

Bryce threw himself into the dark space under the desk. He turned in time to see Richard flatten himself against the wall. The poor fool had nowhere else to go but behind the door, as it eased open.

He didn't see where Gavin went.

Bryce held his breath, closed his eyes, and heard the tap of a cane as the rat entered the study. The dry hiss of his tail as it dragged lifelessly behind him was more frightening than any threat from Fletcher.

The rat's creaking step came to the carpet. And stopped.

The study was silent but for the snap of the fire, the rain peppering the window, and the rumble of another bolt of lightning. Bryce saw the flash even through his closed eyelids.

Then he heard a rasping sound. A crinkling sound.

Paper picked from the carpet.

Bryce bit his lip.

"Did you know that a mouse, drowned in a bucket of water, can be revived a full *hour* later? Such resilient, and yet, fragile creatures."

Bryce shivered. He dare not open his eyes. Dorgue couldn't know where they were. He couldn't.

"I see you've tracked mud in as well," the rat said. "Do you know how old this carpet is? Nearly as old as you are I'd imagine. Think of *that.*"

Bryce couldn't help himself. He opened his eye.

From his hiding place beneath the desk, Bryce could see the rat's long, heavy robes and his gnarled hand clutching the head of his cane. In the other, he held the drawing.

"I hope you didn't think this was poor Vincent," Dorgue said, waving the drawing. "His arms had been turned to jelly, for the most part, I'm afraid. Every bone shattered and splintered in so many ways. No, this was a mouse from back when. Pip I think it was. Yes, I label them here at the top. *Pip.* You remember Pip, don't you?"

Bryce tried to still himself but he was shaking terribly. *He was going to cut them up. He was going to—*

Bryce saw Richard step out from behind the door. In his hands, he held one of the knives from Dorgue's wall. He must have grabbed it before ducking to hide.

Dorgue wasn't facing him.

Richard took step after careful step.

"I usually start with the chest cavity," Dorgue said as if conversing over dinner. He turned the page over in his hand. "Bodies are like puzzle boxes: they must be taken apart *just so* or they're ruined. I'm afraid Vincent was most certainly ruined."

Richard took careful, crouched steps. Bryce had never seen him so focused, his face so strained. He gripped the knife with both hands.

Dorgue spun with his cane.

Richard was too surprised to even think to duck. The cane cracked over the side of his head and Richard jolted—dropping the knife—and fell past the rat, landing like a sack of grain on the ground just inches away from Bryce's face.

Dorgue leered over him, folding away his hands like he hadn't a worry in the world. His eyes snapped to Bryce's. The rat smiled.

"So nice to see you. How is your eye?"

Bryce grabbed hold of Richard's arm, pulling him as he wormed out from the other side of the desk. The carpet burned his knees.

Dorgue followed, moving around the wide desk. "Had a little trouble finding the door out, did you?"

Bryce tried to pull Richard standing, but the other mouse had gone limp and Bryce tripped under his own efforts. His head struck the wall. Just above, the window rattled with another blast of light that lit Dorgue like a skeleton.

"Would you like me to give it a look over?" Dorgue stretched his face in a smile. "Your *eye*, I mean. Imagine if it started to fester. Could go septic, you know. That would be an unfortunate thing."

Bryce hooked his arms under Richard's armpits and forced himself at last to stand. He pressed his back to the window. Once again, the chill surprised him. "Keep away!" He cried.

Dorgue sighed, shaking his head. "Bryce, Bryce, Bryce. You're only making this harder. We can have an agreement. Come quietly. You can go back down to your burrow, curl up in your bunk, and we can all pretend this never happened."

Dorgue unfolded a long finger and gestured down to Richard. "Just let me have *him*. He and I had an understanding, too."

Dorgue propped his cane against the desk and showed his palms. "I won't hurt you. We're nearly finished here Bryce, and your reward shall be—"

A jar exploded across the rat's face, sending amber-colored gel, and who knew what else spraying through the air. Dorgue toppled over the desk, sending papers and journals sprawling to the floor. The rat brought a crooked hand to his face and howled.

Bryce saw Gavin unfold himself from one of the high shelves, holding another heavy jar in his hand that he immediately put to good use. Dorgue, his face dripping and twisted, lunged to the ground as glass and sour-smelling liquid burst across the desk. He reached for his cane and made to impale the mouse, but Gavin was quicker. With a kick, he shot the cane from the rat's hand and barreled past.

Dorgue snatched at Gavin's ankles but caught only air. Gavin never slowed.

"Keep hold of Richard!" he yelled.

Bryce did.

Gavin leaped, hooking Bryce with one arm, and shattered the window.

And so they fell.

Into the night.

Into the rain.

Into the Deep Wood.

Acknowledgements

An army of good people deserved to be thanked here at the end. I'd like to thank my family for being patient with me through this process and for their advice and support. Big round of applause for my brother Josh for his wonderful cover, and to my sisters Chloe and Abby for their charming illustrations. I'd like to thank my early readers, Dylan & Jordan Frostad, my brother Tim, as well as Tim McKay (double Tims!) who had many helpful critiques. Thanks to E.L. Montague for his invaluable input and the only one (thus far) to pick up on the fact that there are no... well, I guess I won't spoil it.

And special thanks to **YOU**, whoever and whenever you are.

I wish you the best.
-Isaac Anderson
08/04/2024

Review This Book!

Reviews keep books alive (or kill them dead if you so choose). So please take the time to drop a handful of stars or whatever new-fangled rating system they may have come up with at the time you're reading this.

Maybe it's *quarks* now.

Yes, rate this book *10/10 quarks!*

About the author

Isaac Anderson is a writer living in sunny (rainy) Miami. He is the author of *A Song of Bones*, *The Garden Maze*, and is currently working on sequels for both.

You can follow him on **X** at @zoofries and probably even follow him in real life if you happened to walk down the right street at the right time (though that would be pretty weird).

www.ingramcontent.com/pod-product-compliance
Lightning Source LLC
Chambersburg PA
CBHW051121300726

48981CB00021B/493/J